# THE SECRET AND CODE

## A Susan Dax Adventures

STEVENSON MUKORO

WORKBOOK PRESS LLC
187 E Warm Springs Rd,
Suite B285, Las Vegas, NV 89119, USA

Website:        https://workbookpress.com/
Hotline:        1-888-818-4856
Email:          admin@workbookpress.com

Ordering Information:
Quantity sales. Special discounts are available on quantity purchases by corporations, associations, and others.
For details, contact the publisher at the address above.

Library of Congress Control Number:
ISBN-13:        978-1-956876-14-7 (Paperback Version)
                978-1-956017-64-9 (Digital Version)

REV. DATE: 09/11/2021

# BOOKS FROM THE SUSAN DAX SERIES

Cold Heat

Susan Dax

Dying Hard

My Name Is Susan

The Lighthouse Guards

Assault On Westminster

The Doomsday Organism

Guns, Death and Mr. Krakauer

# THE SECRET AND CODE

*A Susan Dax Adventure*

Stevenson Mukoro

*"From you let my vindication come,*
*your eyes see what is right"*

**Psalm 17**

# PRELUDE

Agent Alice Foster had just opened the front door when the first shot hit her in the chest, exploding it in a gaudy explosion of Kevlar and flesh. She whirled, turning her face away, her hand instinctively reaching for the sidearm on her hip. The second shot blasted the back of her head apart. The man behind her caught some of the flesh and felt the small rivulets of blood erupt onto his face. Next, it seemed as though the whole damn house exploded in a hail of automatic weapons fire from the rear, combined with the shotgun blasts of the man next to the fellow who shot the female agent. The bodyguard behind Agent Foster caught her falling body but could do nothing as a hail of bullets struck him in the mid-section. He died within a mid-step.

In the living room, Agent Tyler Shaw sitting opposite the man he had come to see rose up, with a carbine Smith & Wesson weapon in his hand. A hail of shotgun pellets from across him hit him in the tummy. He shuddered and fell, landing behind a centre table. He caught a glimpse of one man shooting from the side of the building and two figures coming towards him, all carrying automatic weapons. A quick assessment of the situation and he knew he was caught in a perfect crossfire ambush.

'Fuck!' Agent Shaw swore.

Injured and bleeding, he grabbed the hand of the aged potbellied man across from him and pulled him down. Agent Shaw was a little surprised at how unruffled his host was. He shouldn't have, considering who the man was. He grabbed his hosts arm and dragged him towards the nearest exit. The door to the next room. As they darted for the next room, slugs from a pistol tore up the floor, tracing along their footfalls. Without looking at what he was aiming at, he fired backwards at one or two of their assailants.

They avoided a couple of shots but the second hail of fire from the automatic weapon was more of a spray of bullets than a volley of shots. Blistering slugs blasted Shaw's left tibia apart, while three seared through his back. He went down with a thump and was already dead when the second blast from the shotgun hit him. The shotgun blast also hit the aged man in the back of his torso. As he lurched forward, he grabbed hold of his side. His calm demeanour was instantly replaced with that of trepidation. He scrambled to his knees and he started yelling in a pleading voice.

'Noooo, nooo ...'

He crawled maybe two paces before a ringing shot caught him in his back and he went down.

Two figures dressed in black robes walked calmly up to him. If his mind were working, he would have speculated as to why they were wearing soft plaid sandals on their feet. As it was, he was thinking of mercy, wishing he would not die.

The two figures stood over him, and then the third gunman joined his counterparts. They all stood silently staring at his haemorrhaging bulk with impassive expressions and bland faces. 'P-please, p-p-please, I-I will not say a … will not … p-please …' he begged with one hand raised hoping to shield his face from any bullet.

Without saying a word, they raised the arms and squeezed the triggers of the weapons in their hands. The old man's body reverberated hard against the cream coloured carpeted floor, body fluids, blood, and flesh splattering ubiquitously.

When the three men were done, they knelt over each of the bullet-ridden bodies, removed a flask from their pockets, and applied some of the contents from the flask on each of the cadaver's foreheads and hands. Standing up, they each fired one bullet each into the foreheads of the carcasses at their feet. The most prominent of the men knelt over the aged man, performed the same ritual before producing an athame. He carved something onto his bloodstained chest with the double-edged steel knife before rising and calmly walking out the door with the rest of his sandal-wearing cohorts. They closed the door gently behind them.

\* \* \* \* \* \* \*

Every year Michael Ornithar had promised to take his whole family for a trip. He had been promising his wife each and every year since the kids Sarah and Mickey Jnr had reached that age when they can appreciate such a vacation. Each year he had to break his promise because of work or inconvenience sake.

'We'll go next year' he'd promise his wife Cynthia.

Cynthia Ornithar would huff and give him a resigned remark. 'Promise' Michael would pledge.

This year he finally kept his promise. If only for an instant of time.

The kids were all packed and excited and so where their parents. The family SUV's trunk was bursting with equipment. Camping gear, clothes both casual and eveningwear, snacks and everything else they could think of.

Mikey and his sister were competing heavily against each other in the Astro Bot Game of the PlayStation 4 console attached to the monitor of the child seats in the rear, Cynthia was working hard to solve a particular Sudoku problem while Michael was driving swiftly and carefully, following the digital navigator device on the dashboard.

Passing through I-40 in Palmdale, a short cut towards the San Francisco/Sacramento interstate, Michael turned west with a red Datsun turning right behind him. It was a mistake he will forever curse himself for.

They never heard the slugs shredding through the vehicle but they felt the impacts. The red Datsun behind him almost skidded into his rear but in less than 3 seconds, the impact of Michael Ornithar's promise tore his family apart.

Several bullets from an automatic weapon tore through the cottage's windows and found themselves ricocheting through the family car of the Ornithars.

A slug tore through Cynthia's shoulder and buried itself in little Mikey's temple. His brain took the brunt of the slug, dead but not dead in an instant. One slug nicked Michael by his left hand ripping off his pinkie finger. Miraculously, Sarah escaped with barely a scratch as the SUV slammed into a thicket of bushes and as the red Datsun occupant stunned with what he had just witnessed climbed out of his vehicle and darted into a nearby brush.

Later in the hospital, Cynthia looking down at her brain dead son wishing her loving husband had once again broken his vacation promise. What she wouldn't give for one more broken promise? She would have hated him for doing that but then her family would be intact. Little did she know.

* * * * * * *

I could not make it to Shaw's funeral. News of his death and funeral didn't reach me until I was 93 metres from the 5895 metres summit of *Mt. Kilimanjaro*. A burst transmission to me from Seymour to my sat-phone was the unfortunate way I heard of it. My ascent via the northern Lemosho trail was my subjective incentive for foiling a covert corporate data-pilfering ring. When Shaw was brutally murdered, I was in *Pangkalansusu*, Indonesia at the time. Undercover, wearing a wig that itched and heavy prosthetics to pose as an intermediary for a corrupt data broker willing to part with some rather sensitive company secrets. I had played my role well to the American banker who represented the conglomerate anxious to get their hands on the fake corporate data I was willing to part with. So well did we track the information pipeline from the banker to the Kailuan Group out of China and all the links in the chain, that breaking it altogether was not going to be a problem.

Several months ago, it had come to Seymour's attention that one of my most prodigious companies, Petronas Corp based in Japan and number 52 on the Global 500 corporation list was having its proprietary Intel, leaked or stolen. And it was not just happening to us. We also learned that not only my company was suffering from this slippery espionage ring but five other conglomerates had also been hit. All our in-house security and even the authorities had no idea how to deal with it, at least within the law.

Seymour and I came up with a plan of sorts and I volunteered to follow it up with months of undercover work. With the resources I had, even with a couple of bullets thrown my way, it wasn't long before I had reached the end of my investigation.

When Shaw was being murdered, I had just narrowly escaped an ambush and was heading for a rendezvous with one of my contacts. The news of his death ruined my mood for the remaining climb to the summit.

Shaw had been, in my opinion, one of the FBI's more better agents. He was astute and steadfast in his appointed responsibilities. His blueish slate dark eyes and plump lips were a worthy memory to remember. We had shared some sticky situations in Texas and North Africa. Situations that try a person's soul. I hadn't forgotten how cool he could be under pressure or the help he provided when I was once up a creek without a paddle.

Now someone had murdered him and the FBI had no clue whom his killer or killers were. Finding them was going to be a pleasurable experience.

# *ONE*

I landed my Hawker Siddeley 126 with its mid-range tri-engine on one of the two landing strips at the Gray Butte airstrip just east of Palmdale outside of the scorching, smug filled city oflos Angeles. In the cockpit, I had been pondering on a riddle someone had mentioned to me, but I put it aside as I taxied down the runaway.

Seymour had arranged for a hotel courtesy car to pick me up and true to his duties, parked in front of the furthest hanger of the field was a dark green suburban with a hotel insignia on its side door. I wasn't surprised to see when I stepped off the plane with my travel case in tow, a plain black SUV with official US government vehicle complete with tags and a man standing next to it. The driver of the Suburban vehicle saw me and climbed out of his vehicle.

The man beside the SUV, a tall, expressionless man in an ill-fitting ready-to-wear black suit was leaning against the hood of the government vehicle but quickly straightened himself and his tie when he saw me approaching. I recognised him instantly as a bureau man.

Walking up to me, he pulled out his credentials, which

were issued by the FBI. 'Miss Dax?' he inquired.

'Yes'

'I am Agent David Mills. Would you come with me please?' 'May I ask why?'

'Deputy Director Prideaux would like to see you'

I've never heard of this Deputy Director and I was inclined to refuse this request. However, I guess if I refused, this agent would definitely insist. I nodded at him, handed the hotel's courtesy driver my travel case and asked him to follow us.

The city shimmered in the distance like a towering glass hammered by the sun. The city of Angels, - what a very ill- chosen name for a city that has inhabitants with low moral code and even lower fidelity -, was larger than forty of the individually incorporated US cities combined. Boasting of a very ethnical diverse population, a Mediterranean ambiance and expansive metropolis, the city is the most populous city in America, save probably New York and Washington. I didn't hate Los Angeles neither did I love it. During my earlier visits, I had accepted that Los Angeles was going to be an acquired taste. It still was.

The SUV raced along a less than inhabited state road with the digital speedometer alternating between sixty-eight and seventy. We headed away from the LAX area, away from the Howard Hughes Promenade, which I really wanted to see and headed east towards Palmdale and Littlerock.

I had come to this city to answer four prevalent questions relating to Agent Shaw's death and the FBI was about to answer two of them.

Where and when! Where, was somewhere we were

headed and when, I'll have it answered at my journey's end. The two other questions, "why" and "what", were the other questions I will personally find the answers to. The city's traffic was less than convenient but the flashing amber light of the truck made a less than conducive journey a bit bearable. With the courtesy driver following close behind, the truck swept around a curve and onto Pearblossom state highway and then the Sierra Highway. An hour later, we were skirting Lake Hughes before coming up on a town called Castaic. We drove at length towards one of the many single and dual family and holiday unit homes that bordered the town until the vehicle stopped at one that was neither a holiday or family unit but a cottage. It was ideal for that second home that you need to go to for relaxation and recuperation. Mills climbed out and opened the door for me, just as the hotel driver parked right behind. He remained inside the vehicle and watched us walking up the driveway towards the wooden cottage.

Mills's carbon copy with straight-faced features was outside, standing by the door. Mills escorted me into the cottage that once upon a time had a lot to offer despite the obvious recent renovations it had undergone.

I winced inwardly from the smell and the macabre feeling I received when I stepped inside. The place might have been sealed up for weeks but it still seemed to hold the grim smell of death. Mills led me through the cottage with large open windows on the ground level for light and bright spaces. I was betting that this cottage had more than two bedrooms and bathrooms. The eat-in kitchen was an island and so was the formal living room.

Proceeding from the living room was a primed closed wooden glass door that led through to an enclosed sunroom. Mills winked at me before tapping twice on the door.

'Enter'

Mills gestured for me to advance.

Two burly men were behind the door when I entered. They stood aside to let me enter.

I entered a shimmering open sunroom decked with a natural- fibre wall that covered the iridescent quality of orange kravets with Mills following me closely behind. I could smell the stain of fresh paint and sawdust. Most surprising was the amount of fixtures and living accruements. The accruements were a number of Pharaonic, Roman and Greek artefacts that littered the place. I noticed there were one or two pieces from the Renaissance or more precisely the *Da Vinci* era and a cracked prehistoric Roman vessel encased in a glass jar. It wouldn't be a surprise to me if each of those particular pieces cost more than a couple of hundred thousand dollars. I began to think that the owner of this place had the semblance of taste. Strangely, though the paintings on the wall were cheap murals from perhaps a local artisan.

Several of the windows were open tousling the dark hair of a man whose back was towards me. He was staring out at the exciting view of a pond that stretched on.

'Good morning Miss Dax' a youthful but derisive voice greeted me 'How was your flight?'

'As well as it could be' I answered.

The owner of the voice turned towards me. I was a bit taken aback by the appearance of a boyish face on the head a young man, probably in his thirties. He was wearing a *Da Ville* top coat over a grey three-piece tailored suit and tie and had the appearance of a yuppie from Wall Street.

I knew better.

He gave me the once over with his pale green eyes, then said 'It's strange, but when I receive a request from an NSA Director to accommodate the requests of a British civilian, I tend to be inquisitive but in your case I wasn't'

I wonder what he would have said if he knew that my influence extended past his White House or the Pentagon. Or that the last quarterly statement from a two-desk office address located in Brenner, Liechtenstein detailed my current net worth as over thirty-five billion six hundred and thirty million dollars and increasing. What would this deputy director do if he knew that my wealth could bankrupt his agency or starve the resources of a nation?

With a wealth that comes from a clandestine global empire of companies, industries and subsidiaries, all in various fields of enterprises including communications, biotechnology and biomedical, transport, real estate, group holdings, co-ops that I myself have barely heard of and that even includes aerospace, I could do almost anything.

Many of my companies are governed by a board of directors and operate over or under a rubix cube of holdings, firms, and affiliates that rarely, if ever, interact with one another. Most of them have no chairperson or CEO. That position is reserved for a mysterious recluse sometimes referred to as *Director One Nine Eight Four*, which just happens to be Seymour or in some rare instances, me.

My empire consists of more than 300 proprietary patents and thirty-four percent of the Bancroft family group. Meaning, I own the controlling interest over the family group that owns the Dow Jones & Co and its other major corporations and affiliates the world over. This also means that, I possess at least twenty percent of trading that happens on any given day on the NASDAQ, or the London and New York Stock exchange.

To the world, I am Seymour's personal assistant or executive assistant, whatever the occasion calls for. An aide-de-camp who aids her boss to manage an anonymous multi-billion organisation. Off the record, I am an enigma, a nobody, an ordinary person with no business profile or portfolio and especially no society column. Additionally, thanks to some strategically placed friends and resources, I barely have an electronic footprint. Meaning, there is barely a mention of me on the web.

'I take it you're Deputy Prideaux?'

'Deputy Director Benedict Prideaux' he corrected 'Ok then Director, I'm here, let's get on with it'

'Straight to business? I like that. They told me you do not waste time, you don't, do you?'

'Who said that?'

'Hmm … let's say your reputation has preceded you'

I had a good mind to ask him for the answer to the riddle I had been pondering on the plane. However, this was not the time or place.

I glanced at Prideaux's burly escorts then back at him. From their expression, could it be that they were fascinated by the thought that I had come all the way from England to investigate a murder and doubtlessly thought that I was more than a little crazy? I would have thought so myself even if these guys were too puffed-up and conceited to mention it.

'I came a long way Director; please enlighten me, on why I am here?'

'I've been asked to brief you and equip you with all necessary information needed for this investigation. As for your question, this is where the killing of our agents occurred' he revealed, gesturing with an angry chop of his hand at the room we were in.

'Ah'

He made his way over to a magazine rack, took out a folder, and tossed it in front of me. I picked it up and went through the dossier the FBI had made concerning Agent Tyler Shaw and Agent Alice Foster's murder. It wasn't much, it only gave the last case they worked on and final reports of the two agents who were killed, the circumstances of their deaths and the autopsy reports of five individuals who all died the same way. Severe lead poisoning. No details of what they were investigating, if they were indeed investigating a case. I had no doubt they were, but the bureaucracy of the FBI had the question flagging in the air. On the other hand, it could that the FBI were censoring me.

'I understand you knew one of our agents'

'Hu huh' I answered still reading from the file folder. 'Tell me about the vacationers'

'Oh the Ornithar's. They were unfortunate bystanders' he gestured with his chin towards the road 'They were on their way to see the sights … the er … Walt Disney Hall and the Griffith Observatory in LA, that kind of thing, I think. First vacation for them in a while if I understand it right'

'There was a casualty?'

'Their son, age 7. Braindead. They will be pulling the plug on him day after tomorrow'

'Can you try to delay it for a while?' 'Why?'

'Just do try please, while I think of what to do'

'So you intend to search out the culprits huh?' he asked with curious inquisitiveness in his voice.

'You got it in one' I replied absentmindedly as I continued to familiarised myself with the contents of his confidential case file. 'You know we've got this situation under control. We aren't

totally incompetent, you know'

'It's been three months, how under control are you?'

'Look, I'm not in favour of letting you loose on some sort of vendetta' Prideaux said, gesturing with a quick chop of his hand. 'I'm only allowing this because we have gotten nowhere in the months since, and we just might need fresh eyes on this'

He gave me a levelled look, as he handed me a leather wallet with a three-year-old photograph of me and credentials from the FBI offices, he then added. 'The details of their murder are practically non-existent. We know there were two to four individuals and they were professionals'

'What makes you say that?'

'One of the gunmen circled the house and approached it from the rear, catching Shaw in a crossfire. Also they arrived in a stolen small truck which was abandoned, scrubbed and burnt five miles down the road' he pointed 'And they used an electronic jammer'

'Hmm'

'We are assuming they approached the house, two

talked their way in and took our guys completely by surprise. They also killed the man Shaw had come to meet and two others who were in here at the time' There was a trace of bitterness in his voice as he added 'We can only guess at their motives'

'It says here slugs came from automatic weapons and a shotgun?'

The wind buffeted our faces as we made our way to another room in the cottage. Mills followed silently behind 'Yes'

'Quite the hard-core use of weapons'

'Yeah, someone definitely had a bug up their arse' 'Any idea what Shaw was doing here?'

'From his field report he came to meet the lessee of this cottage, Ritchie Francesco'

The way Prideaux uttered the name implied that he expected me to know who he was.

'Ritchie Francesco?' I inquired 'Am I supposed to know who that is?'

'You don't know him?'

I scanned my inner rolodex 'Sorry but no'

'He's a retired Cosa Nostra don, known as "Peacemaker"' I halted in mid-paragraph 'Cosa Nostra?'

'Yeah'

I sighed inwardly.

The Cosa Nostra! The mafia! That meant the five families of the New York Cosa Nostra or as more commonly known, the Mafia or Mafioso. The Bonanno's, the Lucchese's, the Colombo's, the Gambino's and the Genovese's.

The Cosa Nostra is an organisation I wished I didn't have to be mixed up with. Despite the media boasting that the mafia was down, they were definitely not OUT. Granted, the five families are not a force they once were, they still weld a compelling force in America. The Mafia in America is known for their particular nastiness and with their stock in trade being anything from loan sharking, blackmailing, extortion, labour racketeering, political power, corruption, drugs, controlling influences over labour unions. They also have a good grasp of power to influence almost any construction, the justice system and most of the ports in and around most major ports in the United States.

They make tons of money depending on the rackets or the rank. For the moment, though they've been operating underground, staying out of the spotlight, consolidating their holdings, and pouring it into legitimate businesses, which is damn smart. It can aid them in rebuilding and recovering their territories from repeated attacks from the authorities and their competitions. With ties to the Bravta, the Ndrangheta, and other drug cartels, they are slowly regaining their once powerful reputation when they finally come out to play.

The powerful of the five Brugad families, the Genovese's, for example is probably worth $370,000,000 with "made" men and associates numbering approximately 280.

When dealing with the mafia it is not only wise to have your bases covered but you must also have nerves of steel. To deal with them I would have to be something close to a lion tamer, because most of the people I would have to get involved with will be just Vermin. Whenever possible, I always try to stay well away from them because their obnoxious and cold-hearted methods just might turn me obnoxious and cold-hearted.

'Francesco's a legend in his own right, a big earner, who retired here after a heart attack or if you believe the rumours after a long and loyal service' Prideaux permitted himself a thin smile. I looked about the house. The large windows, the easy bake kitchen, the openness of corners. This was not a place I would expect a mafia don to stay. Retired or not.

'How old was he?'

'Sixty-nine. Yes I know' he replied 'What bull' Prideaux continued 'Shaw learned Francesco was leaving the country with a million dollar pension to retire in the home country and he wanted to establish a contact itinerary or system with him'

'What on God's earth would they have to talk about?'

'We think travel plans' Prideaux's unusual durable voice held a ring of untruth.

'Travel plans?' I inquired 'Hmm'

'You going to tell me the real reason?'

Prideaux sniffed hard, then relaxed his shoulders. 'Francesco was an associate of ours'

I should have known 'I see. He was an informant'

'No, no' Prideaux protested 'More of a convenient collaborator.

I wouldn't even go that far because he only collaborated when it suited him'

'What exactly did you have on him?'

Prideaux glanced at me and remained silent for a while 'He had a particular vice for a specific sort of company that would be frowned upon in the family'

I thought for a moment and realised what the Deputy Director was hinting at. 'I see'

Francesco was a man who had a taste for cowboys. A chap in chaps kind of guy. I pondered if he was into branding or lashing. 'Yeah. Which as you know in his particular field of engagement is very detrimental and could be damaging if the wrong ear gets wind of it'

'To say the least. I take it you have photos, maybe videos of his unusual dalliances?'

Prideaux silence was enough to inform me that the FBI had less than they thought they had.

'Look … he was a man who was trusted and respected by many. Not only by the conflicting factions of the Brugad but also by some of their enemies with … let's say objectionable vices that can be detrimental to the intentions of the United States and her allies'

'What brought him to your attention?'

'Oh he once had a touchy errand abroad that was rather messy.

His conduct on the matter brought him to our attention' 'What errand? And please be specific'

'You must understand. Francesco …' he paused 'He was a captivating and complex individual. Most people respected him because of his ability to calm tensions, maybe due to his once bloody reputation when he was young. He was a genius at smuggling and contributed effectively to the family's collective effort to curtail not only a Venezuelan smuggling ring but also several Albanian human trafficking operations. Both here and abroad and he vigorously fought against drugs sold to children. He was a stickler for that'

I noticed he didn't answer my question.

I looked about the room 'I see he has an expensive antiques hobby'

'Yeah, he did have quite the collection'

'For a don that seems an odd hobby, don't you think?'
'Yeah, I know'

'Good for him'

'Yeah well, he got wise to an opium deal in Afghanistan that blew sky-high which caused a bit of dissention with his people back here'

'This was before his heart attack I'm guessing' 'Huh huh'

'But something about that operation made him valuable to you somehow'

'According to his last report, Shaw thought he somehow gained knowledge of a particular illusive terrorist cell that has been getting a bit of attention here in the States. Something to do with several artefacts'

'And your agents where here to what … persuade him to give up what he knew?'

'Francesco's virtues were lacking … but like most Americans we all fear the recurrence of 9/11, and there were strong reasons to believe he would cooperate with us. Shaw believed that'

'How sure was Tyler of his Intel? Or that Francesco even had Intel to begin with?'

'Oh yeah yeah' he nodded his head 'We had verification of his Intel. Evidence he delivered on two occasions. No, we had all the confirmation we needed to prove his Intel was on the level and substantial'

'You could have just forced him to reveal his Intel'

'The top brass didn't believe that would be appropriate, besides Shaw had a suspicion that Francesco was holding back and that he had more than Intel to share'

'What more could he share?'

'Shaw didn't know. Francesco only hinted at it'

I stopped reading. Something in the case file caught my attention, the mention of a nurse.

'Hey what's this? A … nurse … Anna Feldman?'

'Oh yeah … there's that too. It's a twofer' he teased indignantly 'Apparently, two weeks ago, that Nurse Kirov was gunned down in a drive by together with her boyfriend outside her studio flat in Palm Springs. Guess what happened when the locals fed the ballistic report of the slugs in her body into AFIS?'

I had no need to guess. 'Matching slugs fragments with the ones here?'

'Got it in one'

'What connects that shooting with this one?' I asked

'We haven't got a clue? We fed all we knew about her into all our profiling models, even the computer ones. She was twenty-four, a junior night nurse at the local general hospital, going to night classes for a degree in veterinary medicine, which also explained her volunteer work on the weekends at veterinarian pet store. Had a thing for dolphin figurines and was in the process of figuring out if she wanted kids. Mother lives in Florida, father deceased, had two other siblings. Sister, Rachel a kindergarten teacher, married with two kids in Ottawa and a brother somewhere in Africa volunteering with the "Doctors without borders" organisation. So apart from the matching cartridges found in her, there was nothing about her that connects in the remotest way to our dead mafia Don'

I wondered for a moment. That couldn't be just that. There

must be a reason Shaw's killers went after her, a link, somehow, somewhere 'Boyfriend?' I whispered almost to myself. 'What about the boyfriend?' I glimpsed the file notation for his name 'Er … Bruce Windemill …'

'He was even less noteworthy. This could be just coincidence' The silence from my end informed him otherwise 'Ok! Well the kid … er Bruce was a carnie who had just turned twenty, had a misdemeanour beef regarding graffiti when he was thirteen but that's just about it. He was doing a part time stint at a tattoo parlour and was training to be an Engineer or Electrician. One … of the two I think. Our killers either made a mistake or just felt like killing two harmless kids to make their bones … prove they could do it, what the fuck!' he cussed exasperatedly. For a yuppie style manner of dress, he was not what I expected. Unlike his other counterparts, Deputy Director Benedict Prideaux seemed to care for the little people.

'Calm down sir' I urged unsolicited.

Prideaux led me into a room that smelt heavily of sawdust. He gestured angrily. 'You should have seen this place before the remodel. They sprayed enough lead around here to sink the USS Eisenhower' Prideaux said handing me a folder of photographs.

I skimmed through them but suddenly paused and gulped over the pictures of Ritchie Francesco's dead body. It made me weak at the knees and sickly as I stared at them. Taking in a deep breath, I closely examined the photo and his bloody chest. There was something off about it. Apart from the bullet-holes there seemed to be an enormous amount of blood on his chest that had not been caused by the slug holes.

'Did they do something to his chest?' I asked Prideaux showing him the photo.

'Oh that! Yes. They carved something on his chest'

he replied, taking the photos from me and thumbing through the set. He produced a couple of shots and handed it to me. They were close-up but clean autopsy photo of the late Francesco's chest. The carvings were bare, methodical and callous.

I could not quite make it out but my Arts History degree kicked in and to me it seemed to me that they were Runes. A calligraphy known to certain Germanic tribes in the 1st and 2nd centuries.

ᛋᛜᛗᛖᛋᛖᚲᚱᛖᛏᛋᛗᚢᛋᛏᚱᛖᛗᛜᚠᛁᚾᛋᛖᚲᚱᛖᛏ

'Are those runic letters?'

'Excellent' he complimented me 'It took our cryptologist several hours to match and decipher it'

'What does it say?'

'It says "*Some Secrets Must Remain Secret*"'

'Whose secret?' I enquired 'The mobs? An unknown extremist group?'

'Beats me'

I shook my head as I made my way into the next room.

Examining the room and comparing the corpses with their positions in the photographs, I made a quick assessment 'These guys were quick, efficient and coldblooded. This Francesco was a tough character from what you've told me. Heart attack or not, the murderers wouldn't want to take any chances'

'You can say that again'

I went over to one of the open windows and took a deep gulp of cool air that streamed across my face. 'The two men who were with …'

'His personal bodyguards'

'Well … all this to me seems like a hit' 'Yes it does' Prideaux countered

'Or it was made to look like a hit for our benefit' 'We did consider that'

'Have you explored it?'

'We did, but it didn't pan out'

'Yeah? And what did the mafia have to say?'

'They profess to be appalled by the death of one their esteemed and trusted dons, even if he did make some enemies in his reign'

'I bet'

I thought for a moment and asked 'This new terrorist cell you suspect, what's it called?'

'We have no idea. Look I don't care. It's been more than three months and the most significant thing to us is that two of our top guys were killed under circumstances we can't yet rationalize, more than anything we want these killers found'

'Not to mention the political or in-house fall-out you face, concerning the slaughter of a female agent'

'You have no idea'

'Of course I do. I'm a woman, aren't I?' I paused and began to think. I was still thinking when I began to surmise the odds of the why the killers did this heinous crime. 'There can only be three probabilities. Francesco's connection to this new cell of yours, maybe they found out and …. The other possibility is someone from his past came calling for payback or the Mob just wasn't willing to part with an annual million dollar pension and silenced him'

'Four possibilities'

'Four?' I enquired staring him in the face. 'Robbery. His pension plan'

'What about it?'

'His first year stipend was here'

'A million dollars … here … in cash … don't tell me, it's missing'

'Yeah'

'Killing and ripping off one of the Mob's respected dons, even a retired one is not only madness but it would take balls of steel' 'You think whoever did this was sane?' he rhetorically asked

'C'mon'

Prideaux had a point. An excellent one. No one is stupid or crazy enough to steal from the Mob.

'It still could mean that this was a larceny'

'I believe I covered that assumption' he replied solemnly I swore 'Christ'

I followed the Deputy Director outside. There was something else he seemed to be holding on to or holding back. I satisfied my curiosity by asking him what it was.

'Are you a mind reader Ms Dax?'

'Don't be daft. You wouldn't be telling me all this if you didn't know more than you're telling'

He was silent for a while then as if making up his mind he straightened his tie and said 'There was a witness'

'A witness?'

'Yeah, someone who escaped this massacre'

'A survivor?'

'Yes and we just found him'

* * * * * * *

The witness was a boy. Let me rephrase, he was a manling. A male, probably in his very early twenties. He was brunette, young and well-developed. Although he wore a coat with the collar turned up, I caught a glimpse of his face as he turned the corner from the restaurant he was in. His cheekbones where above average, protuberant and wide. His eyes were soft, with a fragile set of features unblemished with the scepticism and resilience I had half expected. With one hand in the pocket of his leather coat, he walked to a parked car. I wasn't sure, but I could just make out the butt of a silver gun in his pocket and the enormous package between his legs.

'Hold it' Prideaux said to the man operating the laptop.

We were seated in one of FBI's low-keyed surveillance van studying the shaky motionless image on the screen, which must have been taken by someone using a mobile phone. 'His name is Marion R. Steiner' Prideaux said

"Marion" was a girl's name. 'Marion?' I asked

'Yeah, I know. I think one of his parents was a John Wayne fan or something. Anyway, I think he goes by "Steiner". Let me tell you, he wasn't easy to find. All we have on him is that he entered the country about a month before the massacre, from a London connecting flight and apart from a brief stay in LA he has been in Francesco's company since'

I was having a little trouble believing what Prideaux was telling me about Marion. His activities didn't exactly go with the fine boned face and soft eyes.

'You sure he's Francesco's lover?' 'Yep. No question about it'

I let out a disappointed sigh.

'The bastard had good taste'

'Probably' Prideaux said, in a sardonic tone. 'We have no clue as to who this Marion … Marion Steiner was before he crossed path with Francesco'

'Good for him. When was this filmed?' 'Four days ago'

'And that was a gun in his pocket?' 'We think so'

'Did your man make contact?' 'No'

'But you do need to, don't you? You need to know what he knows don't you?'

Prideaux ignored my questions 'His phone GPS puts him around the cottage when it was attacked. It wasn't until a few days ago that we realised that he wasn't one of the victims. We thought it was a mistake because we assumed he was one of the bodies at the cottage. So we got to tracking, but he covered his track too well for us to pinpoint his location, until one of our agents spotted him on a Facebook page and went exploring'

'He looks frightened. Who's he running from?'

'Your guess is as good as mine' Prideaux said dryly 'The Mob, the authorities, us?'

'Probably all three'

'Or conceivably someone else. You'd be glad to know, I'm letting you ask that question'

'Why me?'

'Because we need a civilian to approach him, we think he'll make us easy'

I glanced down at the luminous dial of my Breitling neon vivid, black stainless steel wristwatch. I've been patient, now I was eager to get on the road and get on the trail of Shaw's killer. Since the trail was a tad cold to suit me, Marion Steiner was at least a place to start but first I needed to know if the one of our three theories was applicable.

'Could I have a phone?' I asked Prideaux's man sitting next to us.

'Why?' Prideaux asked

'I need to confirm if the Mob is behind this'

As with most of the organisations, the mafia have set ranks, rules and structure. Some are rigid and opportunist methods, while others are erratic, irresponsible, and damn right nasty. They are known for their particular nastiness and with their stock in trade being trafficking of arms, prostitution, gambling and drugs they provide a most significant problem for any police authority. Fortunately, I knew whom to call to find out.

I dialled a number with a New York prefix. 'Elena Shalamov please'

Elena Shalamov aka Miss Golighty was a stripper whom a Russian Mob boss Ivan Doversky took quite a fancy to. In under a year he never made a move without consulting his stripper *goomah* or "mistress" in more polite circles. When one of his many rivals killed him, she quickly stepped into a position of influence, eliminating all rivals, including the one that killed her lover and took over most of his operation.

'Yes who dis?' she answered in her heavily accented English. 'Hallo Elena, it is I Susan'

'Susan … I not know any … ah wait … Dax? Dat you?' 'Yes Elena'

'Susan! How you are? You no call, no write … what how things?'

'Things are splendid Elena … I'm just caught up in something right now concerning an associate of yours, probably'

There was a pause 'Ah Dax … you know how we work … we no see, no talk, no hear'

'I'm afraid I do know' I acknowledged, rubbing the side of my face.

'I never think of day come, you call me' 'Well Elena, that day has come'

'Do not tell me you in my city'

'Oh Elena you are hurting my feelings … would that be so terrible?'

'We still have trouble from last time you here'

'Relax Elena, I just need some info from the reigning five mob families'

'The Borgata dons? About what?' 'Ritchie Francesco'

I glanced at Prideaux whose face flaunted the fact that he didn't approve of my call 'Ritchie Francesco? "Peacemaker?" He's dead' Elena stated.

'Yep. I know'

'That east side problem, not our concern'

'Perhaps but I'm sure you have fingers in all sorts of pies' 'Why I tell you?'

'That's a good question … oh maybe because you owe me' 'You think so?'

'How's your hearing, Elena?' I asked

There was another pause. A long one. 'Ok maybe I agree, but why call me?'

'You are the only daughter of a bitch in your kind of business that I can stomach. Even if it's the Russian

Brand'

'That not so bad a thing?'

'I wasn't going say anything. Now are you going to fill me in?' 'No, I do one better. I call you'

She informed me she'd call at a specific hour, and then hung up.

For some reason, I found my conversation with Elena kind of unrewarding.

'Missy Golightly?' Prideaux asked me hesitatingly 'The Jezebel of Queens. Couldn't you think of someone else to call?'

'Four others, but they wouldn't be as cooperative as her' I confessed 'So where was this taken?' I asked pointing at the laptop with the shaky image.

'In a small town in Oregon called Prine' Prideaux said handing me another file folder 'He's been living there for the past two months under an assumed name, a … um … Larry Steinberg'

I glanced at the file folder the FBI had of Marion Steiner before asking to have another look at the video.

'Of course' he nodded to his man in front of the laptop. The video started up again. I listened to the gruff voice of the agent behind the camera reporting the activity of the man we were watching. We watched the twenty something year old walk hurriedly to a parked car. He glanced over his shoulder twice in as many steps, his hands reaching into his pockets every time. His movements though mannish-like, had moments of hesitation. He got into a red Datsun and drove away, the camera phone followed him until he turned a corner.

After asking the technician to blow up and refine the images, I noticed his hands creeping towards the gun butt. Yes, they were smooth and clean but on his palms I could just make out newly formed callouses. That could only mean he had done some hard work in a rough muddy earth. I wondered if it was of significance. 'We've arrange a cover story to explain your appearance, after all, we don't want to scare the poor guy' 'I won't need it'

'But …?!'

I opened up the trucks rear door 'Don't worry, I will contact you when the time is right but I'd like to go get some rest now'

'How will we …?'

I forestalled his enquiry 'Oh I bet you have your ways of keeping track of me'

# TWO

Most of my previous visits to *El Pueblo Nuestra Senora la Reinda de Los Angeles de Prociuncula*, the official name oflos Angeles, were always froth with hullabaloos and complications, this I had no doubt, was shaping up to be no different.

My courtesy driver took me to the InterContinental Hotel where Seymour and I had rooms on standby for whenever we needed to stay in LA.

With mafia involvement, I did not intend to compromise any of my three residences in Los Angeles. As we journeyed on the freeway towards LA and my hotel, I stared out of the tinted glass of the suburban watching the sunlight wink off every available glass surface, gleaming at me from every smug infested hilltop nearby.

After about two hours of driving, we arrived at the hotel, where I alighted, however, not before I tipped the driver heavily and buying a copy of the LA Times at a nearby Newsstand.

When I checked in, I was handed an overnight package

from Seymour, which I guess had something to do with business. I didn't care for the package at that moment, instead I leafed idly through the LA Times as the private elevator glided up to my room.

During the journey here, I had gone through every conceivable scenario I could think of concerning Shaw's death. For a trail so cold, I hated that the only lead was this Marion Steiner. I knew I shouldn't complain, there might just as well be no lead at all. Nevertheless, considering the scenarios, I knew I was going to need some help. Maybe more help than the FBI would be willing or even able to give. I was going to need Brice Darlow.

Brice Darlow was a junior professor of Advance Mechanics at UCLA but he was not like most academicians. Some fourteen years ago, he was primarily known as the greatest sniper and gunsmith in Canada. A genius with a gun that he was recruited by a munitions R&D workshop in Los Alamos. He had a motto he always relied on *"Money and weapons belonged to those who earn it"*. He definitely put his shooting skills to use, competing in several archery tournaments and finally the Olympics where he won gold in two archery contests. After his success and too much partying, he developed an atypical fetish and a taste for expensive wines before falling on hard times. Once upon a time, I was at a party where I happen to overhear his Belgian opponent - the silver medallist at the Olympic games - ridiculing him and his chances of recuperation or surviving the bad patch he was undergoing. It turned out that, with a particular set of skills that were useful to the right sort of nefarious people, he had become a target. I didn't like the way he, an Olympian, a champion, was being mocked but couldn't do anything about it. At the time, I was doing some zero-G training in Noordwijk, Netherlands

Neutral Buoyancy Laboratory centre, at the European Space Agency's leisure and I couldn't arrange the time for a protracted search. I enlisted Seymour to locate him and put him on ice. After Seymour found him, I used one of my liberty weekend passes, to pay him a visit and made him an offer. Luckily, for him, and me he accepted my offer.

It became known later in our relations that he had a family, which meant he had something to lose or hold onto. A daughter and an ex-wife,. A bitch of a woman who was about to marry a Tele-evangelist conman and was denying him any sort of visitation rights. I went to have a little chat with the ex-wife and her fiancée in the company of a $1,000 an hour lawyer and Jeremiah Crow, a paid struggling contemporary actor dressed as a cop at my side. I gave them the choice of having a lawsuit slapped on them so fast for child endangerment it would take their whole married life to reimburse the expense of appealing or give Brice as much visitation rights as he desired. It was a no brainer, the ex-wife tearfully explained that she was only denying him visitation for more alimony and that she would be glad to give him longer visitations as long as she wasn't taken to court. Her fiancée who was miserably drunk had nothing to say. I settled Brice somewhere comfortable near his daughter, which was Los Angeles and gave him the means to do whatever he liked, hoping he'd return to some form of research. Instead of choosing guns mitting, which I hoped, he chose mechanical design R&D and a chance to get to know his daughter again. Brice was a quick study, he took to engineering like a fish to water and extended his skills to almost anything mechanical. He did very well because he had an almost truly mystical quality when it came to mechanical engineering and in

LA, stars and the eccentric were always convulsing over the items he made. However, his gun-smiting hobbies were what interested me. Over the years, we came to know each other fairly well. He knew I was wealthy, through Seymour who he assumed was my benefactor. That part of me was secret to Seymour and only a trusted few. That part of my life he didn't need to know. Since I finance some of his little inventive firearm projects in return for improving my shooting skills and furnishing me with little gadgets of interest to my capers, he had no need to know.

Yes, I would need Brice's help and one or two of his exceptional items.

The elevator doors on the InterContinental slid open to my preferred rooms, the Presidential suite.

The Presidential suite of the InterContinental Hotel was designed in a light airy manner. It had lalique fixtures, silk woven rugs and an entire floor that faced east to catch as much sunshine as it possibly could. The cosy enclave comprised of a front marble foyer, a tiffany skylight, three fireplaces, a circular balcony, two billiards room and two black counter tops. Below my feet was a thick burgundy carpet. Some of the features of the first front room included a wet bar, a large holographic screen relaying the news, pool table, stereo equipment, glass table tops and a two of three comfortable L-shaped rosemary coloured couches. Yes, the suite had a very inviting feel.

Before calling room service, I mixed myself my special blend of a Sparkling Sunset drink containing an ounce of dry gin, dry Vermouth and 3 teaspoons of Kirsh. While I sipped on it, I made a buy on the dark net for a special requested item to be delivered to the hotel's gift shop. I ordered some lunch before making my way over to one of the bedrooms to strip off my clothes. After undressing, I loosened the pins in my hair and stood in front of one of the wall mirrors next to a dresser.

For a long minute, I examined my body. My torso, my breasts, and the faded little scars on my tight smooth cherry-coloured skin. My legs and arms still felt stiff from my mountaineering jaunt, so I performed a few calisthenics to see how flexible they were. I began with some handstands, some sit-ups, a Sugar Ray footwalk, a couple of Ali jabs and ended it with a De La Hoya finish.

Next, was to get my mind right. I sat naked, cross-legged on the carpet, my hair down and loose. I shut my eyes, blocked all necessary senses of my surroundings, and deliberately slowed my breathing as the evening twilight filtered through the fibreglass windows.

I had no idea if there was grief for Shaw within me, until I could literally feel it ooze out of me gradually, until I was numb enough to settle into a conscious trance.

My mind became bare and as motionless as my body. I engaged my mind and body to the art of meditative breathing as done the *jiujutsu* way, the adept Japanese ability or more accurately the ancient Egyptian art of focusing ones mind to one single purpose. In my case, I was trying to bring forth the essence of my chi, which is an intuitive mind trick to starve the imagination of unnecessary thoughts.

It was something I had picked up, on one of my imposed sometimes, useless travels. When Seymour found me, he immediately sent me to every karate sensei he could find and those rarely known for my training. Every three to six months during school holidays, I was under the tutelage of a master in the finer arts of martial arts self-defence. His excuse was that he wanted me prepared for anything and everything. Given my young virulent childhood, my wealth and cavalier nature he sure knew I had to be tough enough to combat any crisis imaginable. Be it business wise or physical combat. He even, for eight months, had me under the tutelage of the famous former Ballet dancer Svetlana Alexandrov, because he thought a little grace in my walk would be beneficial. It must have worked because my plié according to Ms Alexandrov was "above subpar".

I cleansed my mind of any tension regarding Shaw's death and all the hundreds of small things that could happen. I was preparing my body and mind for a battle of wills. Mine against whom ever had killed Shaw. In the seconds of me finding out about Shaw's murder, I had already decided that I was going to avenge his murder. When at last I felt I was relaxed enough, my mind and body purged, I rose and got under the shower. So much grime had accumulated on me from the journey to Castaic not to mention my long flight from Tanzania, that it felt in lieu or as long as I remained under the shower, I would begin to feel energised and refreshed.

After about thirty minutes, I returned to the bedroom, sweat dripping down the whole length of me. I glanced down at my legs.

Whoa! They needed a shave. I was about to climb back under the shower again when someone knocked on my door.

I wrapped a towel around my chest, walked over to the door, unlocked, and opened it.

It was a maître de with my lunch order.

As the maître de set my order down, I tore open the parcel Seymour had sent me. Inside was a proprietary I-Pad for my eyes only. I tossed it onto the couch, handed the maître de a tip, then picked up my new flip phone, and first called Seymour with instructions concerning the boy Michael Ornithar Jnr. When we were done, I then called Brice.

After a salacious greeting and a welcome to LA, he gave me an address of his newest enterprise.

I informed him that I would call on him after I've had some rest. Five hours later, I picked up my special requested item from  the hotel's gift shop and hailed a cab. We drove for more than an hour, until we got to the destination of Brice's address. The cab pulled into a car park in front of a medium-sized modern building with whitewashed glass walls, their glaring transparency relieved by an alluring abundance of chrysanthemums in the borders, rock gardens and window flower boxes.

Brice's new endeavour was aptly called *"Shandra's Mechanical Trails"* in reference to his daughter's name.

I made my way into an anteroom that doubled as a display sukkah and asked for Brice Darlow. It seemed that I was expected. The forty something odd years of a sandy haired figure otherwise known as Brice approached me. His clothing looked neither new nor old but they were tailored, and it suited him perfectly.

I counted three other people in the background apart for the receptionist, which I presumed were his employees.

Brice greeted me at the doorway of his new cavernous laboratory of mechanical effects with a soft expression and a big smile across his face. Grabbing me round the waist, he lifted and then twirled me.

'Hello my little gem' he whelped happily.

'Hallo Brice'

'My gem, so what have you've been up to?' I grinned

'Me?'

'Yeah, what nifty little troubles have you been up to lately?' he teased

'You've got that backwards mate, precisely what have you been up to?'

His staff chattered perplexing among themselves. They naturally had no idea who the strange woman making their boss embarrass himself with, but they were surprised by his obvious affections for me.

'Oh this and that. Jesus girl, you still look marvellously good looking'

'Thanks, and so do you Olympiad'

After a long pause he turned to me 'What's that?' he asked glancing at the gift shop bag in my hand and giving me a sparkly smile.

'As if you didn't know' I sassed, handing him the gift bag.

He opened it, revealing the old wine bottle

' No way ... a *Montrachet 1968*... sublime' He whelped opening up the carrier bag 'Did you know that there are only six bottles of this left in the world? Hell, do you know how much this is?'

'If you have to ask then you can't afford it' 'Hell Susan, you do spoil me'

'Yeah, I'm do hopelessly try'

He grabbed me again and twirled me.

He set me down and glanced at my feet as he guided me towards the interior. I had taken special care to wear Nikita type open-toe shoebox court heels for his benefit. Brice had a thing about people's feet, especially mine. He was a foot fetish enthusiast but a harmless one. He considered my toes and feet as the right shape and size for a woman of my statue. For some reason he had a hypothetical sexual focus for how any woman's feet were shaped. He even gave feet and toes names. He named mine the first and only time he ever got glimpse of them.

'Madeline looks great, how are Josephine and Anita?' he asked as he handed the bottle to one of his subordinates.

Looking down at my feet, I replied 'Oh much better since last time you saw them. So are Gabriella, Gina and her sisters. Beatrice is a bit worse for wear'

Beatrice was the intermediate toe of my left foot that had suffered a little touch of frostbite during my latest climb.

I indulged his fetish but kept him in check of his unusual fixation.

'What happened?' he pondered 'I slipped'

He winced 'How far?'

I relayed my recent stint ascending Mt. Kilimanjaro and how during my ascension, I had one or two missteps.

'Is she in pain?'

'More or less. Much better than Joe and Anita'

He grinned capriciously, remembering 'Ah poor dear Josephine and Anita'

Josephina and Anita were the two left toes of my left foot that suffered frostbite some three odd years ago. To the naked eye, they look normal and salubrious but I have little or no feeling in both of them.

'Easy on mate' I cautioned him light-heartedly.

'Geeze, Susan' he said in his usual mischievous Canadian monotone. 'I once suffered a fall climbing, breaking my ankle and one of my ribs'

'Was it painful?' I asked indulging his parallel.

'I wouldn't recommend it. It was worse than a hangover in June'

'Oh I bet it was' I remarked smiling.

He ignored my jibe and asked 'So how the devil are you, babe? You look thin, my dear … ah that will not do. I think I should fatten you up'

'What a horrid thing to say to a lady, Brice'

'Come on now Susan … your old man would not approve if I didn't at least sit you down and make you relax enjoy yourself in some useless activity'

'Later, for now, I've got problems'

'You always have problems my dear' he corrected me 'Is that why you are here?' he inquired, his face registrating one of the many hundred unnamed emotions he was capable of. The one he displayed, I recognised was that of amusement.

'I'm on a hunt, and I don't have a clue what kind of hunt it is.

Man or beast' I replied

He should have looked taken aback or shocked at my explanation, but there was no reaction. He simply stared at me still smiling. I stared blankly at him for a few seconds.

There was every need for Brice to see me as irreverent. For some reason he always acted like Seymour. A mother hen when it came to me. Protectively fussing over me and the highly specialised products he concocts for me.

Like Johnny Boyd his London counterpart, I could never really deprecate his fantastically clever concoctions. Hell, they've saved my life more than once.

Brice guided me into what looked like a showroom but in fact was a white room of glossy design. We halted at one of the white-topped tables. On it were several items, hard box clutch handbags, jewelled two part sandals and bangles, belts, ring, necklaces, and even clothing. They seem to be sorted in male and female accessories.

'How about something new in the women's department?' he asked with a flourish and smile.

'You're not thinking of patenting chastity zip-up pants and steel rimmed Wonderbra's?' I joked with a fleeting smile admiring the items on the tabletop.

'Try one of the bangs' Brice insisted

The bangle I chose was a black oversized stretched one with a white stripped thick etching in the middle.

As I slipped it on Brice said 'Press the stripe'

I did as I was told. The bottom of the bang slid sideways and I found myself holding an empty square panel.

'You could fit anything small in there' Brice said 'Any micro circuit like a GPS transmitter or bug, for example'

'Convenient' I commended

As I admired the bangle, Brice picked up a necklace 'This goes with anything' he explained 'but I doubt this would do you any good'

'What do you mean?'

'You don't like flashy things do you, my dear?' 'Oh you know me so well, Brice'

'Besides, Seymour has a gift ready made for you' 'Excuse me?'

'Joel' he called out to one of the males in the background who nearly jumped out of his skin.

'Yeah boss?'

'Tell Sam to get that caballero we've been working on ready, will you, lad'

'Ok boss'

Joel scurried away.

'Seymour got you to make me something huh?' I asked 'Yeah' he said with a grin. 'He called about a week ago informing me that if you did come my way, I should provide you with something with a little oomph'

'A little oomph?'

He handed me a note from Seymour.

*Handle With Care,*
*Contents, "Priceless"*

Damn it. I was getting a little too predictable, at least to Seymour. Gesturing for me to follow him, we made our way to the other side of the showroom where it led to a garage-like egress and a short stretch of obstacle-littered lane extended out towards a block of racing lanes.

'Seymour wanted you to have a recycled car that wasn't great looking but had more than a little scat under its hood'

A blue stripped white coloured *1969 Shelby GT350 Mustang* came roaring through the garage opening, weaving and zig- zagging its way through an obstacle lane and then braking hard, screeching hard to the right of us.

Seymour had got me a car. That is so just like him.

Brice standing there, next to me grinned proudly and

so did

I. 'It could do 160 miles per hour in a pinch, has some authentic offensive and not so acceptable defensive refinements and she's so perfectly fine-tuned it will give a *Stradivarius* a run for its money' Brice announced smugly, like a proud father.

I personally owned more than forty vehicles, not counting those owned by my companies. All of them were of different shapes, sizes and makes but this car was from Seymour, I immediately fell in love with it.

'I've redesigned everything within' Brice said as we both leaned in to look at the interior 'The Traction-lok axle, the dashboard … notice the rim-blow power steering and the Polyglas GT five spoke dueller tires'

'So it's immune to spikes'

'Yep and the engine is not bad to look at either'

I knew about the Shelby cars. They are the most unique, desirable vehicle of the Ford and Shelby convertibles. The most coveted of American muscle cars. 'Well, whatdoyou think?' Brice asked as Joel got out of the still purring car.

I couldn't think of anything that interested me more than getting behind the wheel and possibly manhandle this tempestuous beast.

I stepped up to open door and glanced at Brice with an expression that said, *"Would you mind if I took this tempestuous beasty for a ride"*

Brice grinned and said 'You need not ask'

I got behind the wheel and for a moment, I could still smell the new leather fragrance of new interior. The leather styled dashboard had been equipped with a digital TV box and settings. I tapped the accelerator gently, the car snarled, responding nicely to my touch. I stepped on the clutch, engaged its gears, and slammed on the accelerator. The mustang roared in response to my manoeuvring of the steering wheel and the accelerator pedal. I roared off towards the obstacle lane. For a moment, I fought the steering wheel but got it under control as I bore down on the first cone barrier. Using the handbrake in conjuncture with the clutch, I cut the mustang at the last minute, screeched round it and skidded the car into a deliberate spin, whipping it around back to where I had come from and stopped. My body was vibrating when I stepped out of the vehicle.

'Show off' Brice snickered, commenting on my driving skills 'Well?' he asked

'I love it'

Brice's face beamed contentedly. I wasn't sure it was me or the car he was pleased for. 'I hoped you would'

After an hour going over the operations of the Shelby and picking up a couple of items, I got in the car to drive off.

One of his workers walked up to him and asked in a whisper but within my lip-reading capacity. 'Who the hell is this woman you bend over for boss? You never do that for anybody, why her?'

Brice chuckled and said in a matter-of-factly way 'She's the woman who put the Range in Range Rover, my boy'

I grinned as I gunned the Shelby, leaving Brice not only in high spirits but also in a happy place as I drove back to my hotel. Relaxing on the king-sized bed with the I-Pad Seymour had forwarded to the hotel from Seattle for my assessment. I went through the detailed résumé's of several potential Chief Operations Office for the new Petronas Corp division that Seymour had insisted I go over. A factory, that despite not knowing where we were going to build it in America was in need of an operations officer. He had consulted Sandra Loc, one of our directors who headed a solar powered station in Sokoto, Nigeria but they had not made great strides.

Chief on their headhunting list was Jeff Sandberg, nicknamed the "The Shark" because of his relentless undercutting of brick and mortar standbys. A ruthless executive who bet on Kobo's online retailer's low prices and unbeatable customer service. Second on his favourites list was Rebecca Day, a fluent technologist who knows how to converse with business leaders. There were five others on Seymour's list but I didn't jell with any of them, not even my preferred choice. A Patrick Ward, a Strategist for Intuit Group, known for his unconventional but deft extemporaneous moves. Their resume's where not all statistic's. Due to Seymour's due diligence, he had included details of their social lives and hobbies. Despite all the minutiae, it was all avant-garde to me. No, I could not make up my mind, so I tossed the I-Pad aside and took hold of the folder Prideaux had given me. I flipped back the cover and settled down to read over the file on Ritchie "*Peacemaker*" Francesco.

Born Richard Bracero just after the Second World War, he had an impressive and colourful career to say the least. His parents immigrated from Sicily to the U.S. in the early 60's and settled in Brooklyn. He grew up within the established Sicilian and Italian community, which included the criminal underworld. His criminal record as a Cugine was non-existent except for a charge of aggravated assault and theft, which were just misdemeanours. Both incidents were summarily dismissed. This meant from an early age he was either smart or chose his associations within the criminal community with care. I tend to believe it was both. That or he simply did not exactly exist.

He grew up as close friends and most importantly as a good earner with the once powerful mob boss, now jailed *"One-Eyed Pete"* or as he is famously known as Gianni Gambino the cousin oflegendary mobster Carlo Gambino. Not only him but also Peter *"Petey Red "* Caparelli, of the Genovese crime family and Matthew *"Marty"* Zambrano, of the Lucchese crime family. Both men who would eventually become the leaders of their respected families.

Ritchie Francesco's closeness with Gianni Gambino was a very rewarding and fruitful alliance. In the 70's and most of the 80's as a lieutenant, his association and friendship with Caparelli and Zambrano became so productive and rewarding for them that their criminal and business opportunities flourished everywhere in the five boroughs of New York and beyond. Unfortunately, good days do come to an end.

On July the 8th 1989, the brutal murder of Bartolomeo *"Bartee C "* Cammarano, the mob boss of the Bonanno crime family and Baron *"The Baron"* Grifoni, a high-ranking member of the Castlelammarese Clan in Detroit over a minor dispute of truck spare parts plunged not only New York but also the East/West coast into an undeclared mob war. A war that was unceremoniously acknowledged by the FBI and other law enforcement agencies as the "Castlela-Nostra "Nuts" feud". A wave of violence spread, unleashing a trail of blood that spread across half the country. Within a year, 58 alleged Cosa Nostra members were decimated, hundreds more were indicted and jailed or placed in witness protection. Though some FBI officials argue that the number of deaths were in the hundreds.

Somehow, a year later the negotiations initiated by Ritchie

Francesco because of his numerous associations within the five families brought the feud to a screeching end. It is said that despite keeping a low profile he had earned the nickname "Il Pacificatore". Or as it's known in English "The Peacemaker" from that point on, he was confidentially confirmed and designated as the unofficial *Consigliere* for the five families.

However, it was noted, by one of the FBI's analyst that, that one incident including the bloody Colombo crime family war that began the next year which lasted three years, excluding the several violent disputes involving the Russian Bratva and other European street gangs over the years, definitely weakened the mobs power and influence.

At the time of his death, "Il Pacificatore" Francesco had served a total of five alternating years in jail for his efforts in intra-family violence, he had no children but had been married thrice. He had had many sexual exploits over the years and his female counterparts varied from the prominent and to the imperceptible. Ritchie Francesco was politically connected, had top priced lawyers on speed dial, was known, and respected by many, including Frank Sinatra jnr, Zoey Basile, Rupert Murdoch, Moretti Junior, John Franzese the underboss of the Colombo crime family and others.

In a nutshell, he was an untouchable and an untouchable was never, ever be touched. It was an unspoken rule and code of the mafia. And yet he was touched and not just touched he was murdered and murdered brutally. No, the mob wouldn't do this but that was just my opinion. They had too much respect to go over the unprincipled lines.

Though, I had to wonder, what in heaven's name connected this brass man of criminality with the subtle tones of youngsters just starting out in life like Anna Feldman and Bruce Windemill. A junior nurse and a Carnie. What in heaven could have connected them both that the only result of that connection was to be murdered brutality? Of course, this could all be coincidence like Prideaux mentioned or it just might be the key that puts all these pieces together to form a very macabre puzzle piece.

It was only when I got to the last pages of the folder that the FBI noted Ritchie Francesco's connection to Marion Steiner. As Prideaux had mentioned, there were no details on his past. From what the FBI could drum up, he sprouted fully-grown several months ago when he met Francesco until his disappearance and reappearance in the town of Prine. The data was meticulously complete, they had the hours he worked as a hairdresser, the floor plans of his apartment, even when he usually went to bed. He didn't really seem to have a social life, friends or family. As near as the FBI can tell, helping the old woman in the next long-stay motel apartment take her rubbish out was as much a social life as he ever had.

On a separate page, there where details of the Deputy Director's man in Prine and how to contact him. After memorising the anchoring key facts of the case file and changing my attire, I delved into my travel case. It was time to get going.

Like a chromatic scale for music, I laid out my ordinances before me in black, white and steel. Together with my own thingamajigs and megadoodads from Brice, I collected them and stuck them in their proper places upon my person. Chief among my armaments were my Chinese Makarov pistol and a stiletto.

The polymer designed Makarov with palm recognition scanner had custom-made compensators with bored chambers and a customised trigger. It was by far the most reliable handgun for me and was my favourite firearm I love to have with me whenever I get myself into dire situations because when she fires, she shoots flat out. There is hardly any need for correction and there are no doubts as to what weapon did the firing. I fitted the Makarov's Bruckheimer soft semi-shoulder holster that retained two 10-round cartridges over my shoulders, adjusting for suitability and stability.

With the Makarov in hand, I retrieved *Saint Peko*, my pencil-thin stiletto named after the Finnish *Karelian* saint that provides rain to fields. Peko had two personally designed leather sheaths. My preferred one could be attached to my thigh, which could be easily detected. Men are very grabby when it comes to frisking women's legs. The other sheath was for my forearm. I obviously chose the forearm chamois sheath because I was most effective with it.

With Peko snug in his sheath on my forearm and the Makarov secure in her holster, I had an assured feeling of being indestructible. Oh what a powerful feeling it gave me.

# THREE

The small town called Prine named after a merchant in the 1870's lay out to the east of the well-known city of Salem, where the Rockies subsided onto the plains on which the town was built. I drove into Prine after about fourteen hours of driving at about eight o'clock in the early evening. From the sign outside the town's limits, the town boasted 8,780 inhabitants and it appeared that save for one tenth of the inhabitants they had all decided to be indoors watching TV, eating TV dinners or something else, even fucking, than be on the streets.

There was a pretty bridge across a river, a scattering of trinket shops and rickshaw pick-up points. As tourist traps go, it was mightily effective way of clogging the pavements.

I wondered was it always like this.

On my way towards Prine, while on the San Francisco/ Sacramento interstate my cell phone started buzzing. It was hardly a surprise to me that it was Deputy Director Prideaux calling.

'We might have a problem' 'And that would be?'

'We might have been compromised' he replied. Doubt filled the pitch of his response.

'Compromised? What sort?' 'We've been hacked'

'Hacked …? The FBI … hacked? I thought you guys had subroutines upon subroutines upon firewalls and heuristic data crawlers and big daddy algorithms to prevent such a breach of occurrence'

'What can I say? Some crooks are just much smarter than we believe'

'So exactly what did they hack?' I asked 'Except for our cases files, not much' 'Let me guess, your current case files?'

'It would seem someone is onto us and perhaps onto Marion Steiner' he said

'Does your man … my contact know?' 'No, not yet. I will inform him …'

'Do it on the QT. The less anyone knows about this operation from now on is better kept between us, don't you agree?'

'Something else, just received the toxicology report on the massacre, it …'

'After all this time you're just getting that now?'

'What can I say, it didn't seem relevant at the time, and I'm not sure how relevant it is now'

'Then let's hear it'

'It seems they each had some organic stains on their persons. Some organic substances, Oleic, linoleic acids and scented balsam. On their forehead and hands'

I considered the chemical composition of both chemical acids. 'Oil …olive oil?'

'Yes'

'Could be they all shared a snack together'

'Perhaps. But cause of death was violent blood trauma for all of them, besides the lab techs tell me it was applied post-mortem'

'Right … no need to alert the food industry'

'I don't fully understand what you're on about but if you're thinking what I'm guessing you're thinking then you better …'

'I know and get it. I should work fast huh?' I griped before hanging up.

I mulled over the significance of both acids and olive oil and their application. It did not really factor in any of my thought processes.

Just after I got into town, I turned into a Valero supermarket Vis a Vis gas station that advertised not only instant but also self-service.

While I was filling up the tank, I took in the lethargic street brightened up by the red gaudy sunset that had disappeared in the distant. The traffic and neon lights in the distant looked like a *Bijay Biswaal* watercolour painting of a small town. I instantly felt out of place with the deadly assorted weapons strapped to my body.

Prine looked nothing like the spot a Gambino or a Mafia don's lover would hide out. That was probably the reason Marion Steiner had chosen it. I should give him credit for brains.

I flexed my tired shoulders. I had been driving fast, ever since I left LA.

'Hey babe, what you up to?' said a cowboyish voice from behind me.

I turned to see a man wearing a face cap over his brunette hair with dirty nails and worn-out boots. He gave me a look that would make a construction worker blush.

I pointed to my Shelby 'Gas'

'Oh' he said as though the possibility that a woman filling her gas tank hadn't occurred to him in the slightest. 'Looks like you've been drivin' all day and night' he said pointing to the insect splatters on the car's windshield.

'Indeed' I observed. He was perceptive. 'You a Tourist?' 'Nope'

'You look like one'

I glanced at my attire, wondering how my plain blue Tempus Fugues T-shirt, tan leather jacket, and blue demin Levi Jeans signified me as a tourist. 'Do I?' I asked

'Yep'

'Since you've been travellin' a ways, I gotta ask why you here?' 'Oh I'm passing through, maybe if I'm lucky, I'll find a job' 'Here?' he inquired with a touch of curiosity.

'I like quiet towns'

'There be other quiet towns'

Blimey, whoever this stranger was, he was damn curious. Too curious.

'I like the looks of this one'

He scoffed 'This one ain't sure gonna like the look of a limey babe like you'

Not that his tone was condescending, his words were just not that kind to my ears. I wanted to walk over to him and knock his front teeth out. Instead, I yanked out the pump nozzle, secured the hose onto the tank. After swiping my credit card through the payment reader and closing my tank cover, I got back into my car and without giving him another look, sped away.

I passed a railroad stop that at one time might have been a large more prosperous one. Driving down the main street of the town, I noticed the two-story building housing the police station and the oldest building in the town, namely the town hall. Tucked between two large buildings was a cubbyhole bar with a neon sign reading "BUD Light" over one of its windows, with a diner next to it. Adjacent to it was a hairdresser. I recognised it immediately from the video phone I had watched earlier as the same one Marion Steiner works in.

Seven blocks down, I found one of the two hotels in town with a three star rating. It was a three-story building that was not only in dire need of a new paint job but a comprehensive renovation. With window screens that were so tattered and torn, I questioned the validity of what made this particular hotel rate a three star. I wouldn't give it one.

As I got out of my car, I took a good look at my surroundings. There was a restaurant across the street from the hotel and a barbershop next to it. At this time of the day, the Bowman restaurant should at least be crowded but from the sounds emanating from it, I was thinking that it was barely in business.

I entered the dimly lit lobby of Econo Crooked River Hotel where the furniture had at least an inch of dust on them and those that didn't were worn and frayed from advance age and use. There was no elevator, only a worn flight of stars. The potted plants were surprising clean until I noticed they were not fresh flowers but replicated plastic. Prine and especially the hotel needed a breath of new energy.

The desk clerk greeted me as if I was the Pope and he was the last Catholic waiting to be blessed before entering the gates of heaven. He informed me that my reservation was all ready for me and that if I wanted a meal he could arrange it for me. If that didn't appeal to me then the restaurant across the road made a mean meatloaf.

'If I'm lying, I'm dying' he applauded as he opened up room 108. In my room, I peeled off my clothing and gear and stepped in  the shower and thought about Shaw, his partner Alice Foster, Don Francesco, Marian Steiner, Anna Feldman and Bruce Windemill and what my purpose of being here at this very moment. With time against me, I would have less time to debate the merits of my presence.

After getting dressed, I thought it was about time to make my presence known to Prideaux's man in town. An agent whom I presumed was a few doors down the hall away from me.

Deputy Director Benedict Prideaux had given me details of how to contact his man, including his hotel and room number. I walked down the corridor softly to room 105. Prideaux's man appeared to be the genuine article even if I hadn't yet made his acquaintance. Nevertheless being the suspicious type, I was going to approach him with caution and check him out.

From the absence of light beneath the door, I took it as a sign that there was no one in the room. After a great deal of training and practical experience provided by the cold streets of Russia, Seymour and the navy I had become an expert at picking locks. The door to the hotel room proved no challenge to my deft handling. An eight-year old kid could have sprung it with a penknife.

Turning the knob, I stepped quietly inside room 105.

A table lamp switched on, surprising me. I whirled, my right hand going for my gun. I stopped just in time to see a bald round-faced man who was beginning to show his middle-aged years in a wrinkled brown coat seated in a straight-backed chair next to a window with a broad smile on his face.

The room was similar to mine, a standard I believe for the hotel. It was devised with a door leading to a bathroom, a *Jakobi* style dual-sized bed, bedside drawer, a single mirrored wardrobe, and drawer chest. Three lamp shades, a mini-fridge, a couple of landscape paintings to brighten up the cream coloured walls and wildlife dyed curtains.

'This is a damn surprise' I managed to say. I couldn't think of a clever opening line or anything better to say.

'Not to me. I was expecting it.' observed the bald man 'But much sooner'

I instantly disliked this man. Ever since I was little, I have had an aversion to bald men. I have no idea why but I just instantly abhorred the man.

'Sorry to disappoint' I expressed, closing the door behind me. 'May I ask, who might you be?'

'Agent Bandler, of course. And you must be the fabled Susan Dax?'

This was Lionel Bandler? His voice on the camera phone when he was giving his report was much gravellier than the voice of the man sitting calmly in the chair before me. Granted that audio recordings do add or take voices up or down octave, even maybe add a decibel or two, still this was not the man I heard. If he was saying he was Lionel, then he is a liar and a good one, if he can sit there calmly without breaking a sweat. Of course, I could be wrong, agents come in all shapes and sizes. There was one way to find out.

'Fabled?' I enquired

'I've been waiting for you for a while' he commented with a relaxed smile, ignoring my idealised enquiry. 'Have you made contact yet?'

'Not yet' If he was determined to find out what I knew, it would be best if I let him try or at least make him feel more at ease with me and find out what I could from him. First though was to figure out if I was right about him not being the agent I came to meet.

I reached into my pocket and bummed a cigarette from my gold cigarette case. 'Got a light?'

'Certainly'

He reached for a book of matches on the table and tossed them to me.

I lit my cigarette and tossed the matchbox back at him. He crossed his legs and leaned back in the chair, cupping his hands on his knees. His eyes never left me once.

'Did you sanitise my room?' 'What do you mean?'

'If I could pick a lock, I'm betting you could also' 'I only got in a few minutes ago, there wasn't time' 'Shame'

'Perhaps' he said 'Now to business. You know how to contact the kid?'

'Yes'

'Good. You do understand it won't be easy making her feel at ease?'

'I'll try not to fuck it up'

With his relaxed smile still in place, he said 'We hope so, thank god. Chicks can always relate to each other'

'We surely can, Lionel' I emphasized his name and his

looked changed slightly.

He cocked an eyebrow 'When did you know?' he asked realising he had been busted, regarding his deception.

'When you opened your gob to speak'

'My voice. Ah we were worried about that but that couldn't be the only thing to set off the suspicion in you?'

'No. "She" is in fact a he' I growled, flexing my right forearm to let Peko fall silently into my palm 'Also, you handed me a matchbox'

'Ah … I see' He picked up the matchbox 'There was an arranged coded contact response, wasn't there?' he asked still relaxed in his chair.

'Let's cut the shit, who are you and who is "we"?' 'I'm the guy who's delivering your death warrant'

The first thing about killing is preparing the mind for the deed. Turning on a lever that will enable someone to carry out the act and then flipping it off with little repercussions to any mental state. I have a disinclination to killing or having to kill. I detest having to do it. Human life is so immutably complete, flawed but precious. For those unprepared or unwilling to kill, it always eats away at the very core of their being. For me, the magnitude of objectively taking a person's life is something I could do without blinking an eyelid. However, I try my best to give choices to whomever I intend to kill. Either directly or indirectly. If I give the choice and it was rejected or unrequited then my motive and more importantly my heart remains unblemished. And so, as dangerous as it seemed, I still wanted to give any of my proposed killers the choice of renouncing their intention for my death and if rejected, let him or her have the death they so prodigiously planned for me.

I was about to respond when with a deft move he pulled up his left trouser leg with one hand and pulled out a revolver with his other hand. A revolver fitted with a silencer. I didn't wait for him to aim. I dropped to one knee and let Peko fly. Peko thudded into his throat, quivering like a dart, his one and only triggered shot smacked into the wooden doorpost just above my left ear. Fake Lionel Bandler's eyes bugged out of his face as he dropped his revolver and reached up with his hands, he leaned forward as though he intended to look under the table.

I caught him as he sagged towards the floor. Damn! He was heavy. I propped him back on the chair, pulled Peko out before using the table cloth to stem the bleeding from his neck and began searching him.

His wallet contained a thousand dollars and a driver's license from San Diego that identified him as Rodney Shahe. They didn't mean much. His papers could be as phoney as a three-dollar note. There were no cell phone, household or car keys. Stuffing his ID into my pocket, I stood up. Things were starting off badly. I had been in town in less than an hour and I was responsible for a death. Not only did some known or unknown entity know I was going to be here, they were unquestionably after the same thing I was.

Prideaux was right in assuming the FBI had been seriously breached.

A killing always stirs things up. Sometimes it is much like playing a roulette wheel and I really hated doing that. People will gather round to study, speculate about the miscellaneous items and digesting every scrap of information available to pass on. In a town this small, it would be a certainty that if Mr Shahe's body were found, this was undoubtedly going to be like that.

After bracing him against the chair, I wondered whether I should do something about the body. I ended up hauling the stiff to the bathroom and stuffing him in the tub. Maybe when the real Agent Lionel Bandler showed up he could arrange for a disposal team to take care of it.

I went downstairs and struck up a friendly conversation with the desk clerk who welcomed the opportunity to chat up a babe. I told him, I had met a man in the hallway while I was taking the stairs down, a round-faced man with a brown coat.

'Ah yes Mr. Morgan, he's a travelling writer. Checked in today room 103'

'I bet his magazine is a great read'

'I wouldna know, he never told me which one he writes for.

Probably some weblog' he joked 'Probably'

After three minutes, I disentangled myself from the tête-à-tête and ascended the stairs again. I performed another larceny on a different door. This time on room 103. There was no toothbrush out, no sign of use on either of the bathroom faucets or any sign he even sat on the bed. The room was spick and span. It would seem he had barely gotten here before he took up his wait for me. It wasn't until I glanced under the bed did I find something of interest. It was a black tungsten briefcase. Slapping the case on the bed, I snapped it open. I whistled with a sound of wonder. There were no writing materials inside but a stripped down *Colt AR-15* Semi-Automatic Rifle with silencer and scope. Boy! It was beautiful, sitting there all oiled up and looking ready for action. In two pouches was a pair of zip-ties, an ampoule of chloroform and a blindfold. Next to it, in a small cubbyhole was flip-phone burner phone. I took it out and checked its history. There were no calls to or from the cell phone, just two messages in the Snapchat messaging inbox. The first one at 13:02 read:

*Prine, Econo Crooked River, 105.*

The second text sent three hours later was an eclectic list of names:

*Agent Lionel Bandler. Susan Dax.* MARION STEINER.

There seemed to be no acknowledgement or outgoing text to either message.

Place and list of target names. Jesus! The only thing missing were timetables. Whoever was behind Mr Morgan or Mr Rodney Shahe, whatever he chose to call himself, knew almost everything and they meant business when he was sent here. Any killer who had the balls to swap jokes with his intended target before the deed was definitely a professional and worth his damn salt.

From the bold highlighting of text in Marion Steiner's name, I was presuming he was the main target. I bet Mr Rodney Shahe's plan was to intercept the real Agent Bandler or myself, find out all he could about his target, especially when he would be most vulnerable. Kill Agent Bandler and me, and then pick off the man- boy from the hotel or somewhere close that had a vantage view of the Mayflower hair salon. One thing I guess he did not count on was me or he had an incomplete picture of his objective, apart from his target, of course. That was why he tried quizzing me without letting his intentions known. He, impersonating Lionel was a very clever ruse to put me off guard and to find out if I had been in contact with his target. Of course, I could be wrong about my whole assumption.

With Marion Steiner's name boldly marked, I knew he was Rodney Shahe's prize. If he missed us but got him, all would still have been forgiven to whoever employed him. What I did not know was if he was to be captured alive or killed. The zip- ties and chloroform in his case would seem to provide a positive commission to capturing one of us alive. I had reservations whether Agent Bandler or I were that lucky.

It was after eleven p.m. when I slipped out of room 103 and re-entered my room.

A voice startled me and for the second time in as many minutes, my hand darted towards my gun. 'You're a very crafty lady, Miss Dax' insisted the man braced on the bed in my room.

The voice was familiar, I had heard it very recently.

When I flipped on the light, I immediately recognised him as the man from Valero gas station whom I exchanged words with. His face cap was nowhere to be seen, his brunette hair, dirty nails and worn-out boots were still a feature of his.

'Lionel?'

'At your pleasure'

I pulled my gun and pointed it at him 'Got a light?'

He opened his hand revealing a silver lighter 'Got a cigarette?' 'Of course I do' I said catching the tossed lighter.

I turned the lighter over. On the bottom, stencilled in

small- engraved words were the Bureau number and name of a Special Agent Lionel Bandler.

Smiling and pocketing the Makarov, I gushed with relief in my voice. 'Thank goodness for that. I've already killed you once today, I would hate to kill you again'

'What?' he demanded, rising from the bed as I tossed back his lighter. His relaxed demeanour was suddenly active and sharp as a tack.

'Don't walk into any dark alleys my friend, you're bound to bump into the opposition'

He knew exactly what I was talking about.

'Damn! Damn! Damn motherfuckers' he cursed 'How the fuck did that happen?'

'Hey language my good sir' I scolded him playfully.

He apologised then queried 'Do you think they made me?'

'I wouldn't take the chance they haven't. If they knew enough to waylay me … here, my guess is that you are like me, top of that inconvenient list'

Agent Bandler rubbed both his hands down his face in annoyance.

'Have you got a fix on them, I mean who the fuck are these wing-nuts?'

I handed him Mr Shahe driver's license 'Maybe you can find out. He was not an amateur'

He glanced at the license and sighed. I chose not to tell him about the burner phone for my own reasons.

'It's not going to be easy'

'I don't care. What have you got for me?'

He took out his mobile phone and tapped a couple of

icons then tossed it to me. Displayed, was a FBI notepad report app, which detailed Marion Steiner's movement from the moment he found him, and Lionel's details of his activities from then up until 6 hours ago. The notepad showed his home and work address, those he interacted with and where he spent his free time. As with the previous report from his superior stated, Marion Steiner was not a sociable bugger, nor did he interact much with others.

How then did the FBI find the fellow on a social media platform if he didn't socialise? That was one of the questions that bothered me on the way here.

'The town had one of those cherry festivals a few days ago and his Datsun was accidentally photographed and posted on the town's Facebook page, otherwise we'd be none the wiser. He's still here, playing it cool, unaware that he's been made. He takes long walks into the woods but I've kept my distance as instructed but not too much. I'm staying two blocks from him but reserved a hotel room just in case'

'Well keep an eye on him tonight. I'll be making myself known in the morning'

Agent Lionel Bandler nodded in agreement 'Oh by the way' he said, eyes widening as he stared solemnly at me 'The boss wants me to be a backstop for you. Is that right?'

'Yes, that is so'

'You don't know me and vice versa. Why would you want me to watch your back?'

'Just a feeling'

'Do you trust me?' he inquired 'Do I have a choice?'

'I suppose not'

There was something that had been bothering me since Prideaux briefed me and wondered if Agent Lionel Bandler will be forthcoming with the truth 'Tell me how you guys knew he was at the cottage in Castaic?'

'It was no big deal really. See we got a report that a red Datsun was in the vicinity. It gave us a starting point to track him using traffic cams and social media'

I stuck my fingers into my hair and tousled it roughly, releasing the weeds within them. I should have known.

Before Agent Lionel left, I informed him about the present in his bathtub and that he was going to have to take of it.

'It'll be a damn pleasure Miss Dax'

I bade him farewell and to be careful. He grinned, flippantly telling me that "Mr. Careful" is his middle name.

The events of the evening had changed the situation drastically. As I ran a brush through my long thick black hair, I thought about the dead man in Agent Lionel's bathtub and hoped Agent Lionel Bandler was good an agent as Prideaux made him out to be.

In the meantime, tactics had to change in confronting Marion Steiner.

# FOUR

Iwas early in getting up. I had been restless for some reason. A jog that early, I believed would clear my head, did nothing of the kind.

In the open air, the smell of the day at the edge of dawn smelt like one of those temporary spring mornings or as the Americans call it *"an Indian Summer's day"*. It filled my nose with a nostalgic feeling. As if it was reminding me of something. Something important that had not exactly happened yet. It also reminded me of an early morning Muslim *Imsak* call in Morocco.

A three-mile jog was enough to dampen that melancholy feeling but to my surprise when I took my unannounced stroll towards the Mayflower salon, I noticed three cars parked outside the three-story bungalow where the salon was housed. Apart from Marion's red Datsun, parked just off the alley, there was a black Volvo and a big black Chevrolet. The Chevrolet was thick with travel-dust and not the usual vintage of the vicinity. I wondered a great many things as I strolled towards the salon. Maybe they had customers that early in the morning, maybe it was a special guest, perhaps just someone looking for directions. Of the many scenarios, I could come up with, only one logic conclusion came to mind. Someone had caught up to Marion and I had failed. When I was only about a quarter of paces from the entrance, I heard a wheezing gasp of agony. I was not the only one to hear. There were a couple of pedestrians who had heard, stopped and were listening to what was going on inside. Not one of them ventured to inquire as to the nature of the sounds or walk in and put a stop to whatever was causing the cry of pain.

I could just hear a cool cultured voice ask '… here is it? Do try to remember'

'*S' il vous plaît je vous en prie… No … Je ne sais pas..* I-I don't know w-wher ….' The familiar voice from the camera phone was saying. From the intonation and pleading, I surmised French was Marion Steiner's first language.

'Stop with the gabble gabble arsehole … just tell us where the fuck it is' grunted an angry voice.

My pace did not change, but my nerves and muscles adjusted as if a switch had been turned on. Part of my mind that was a fighting computer assessed a score of factors. Those good and bad, known or unknown, between one stride and the next.

How many men were in there with Marion Steiner? No way of telling, but definitely more than two. The Chevrolet could comfortably accommodate eight men, but at most, those that will feel secure and cautious to drive in, would be four to six. Peering through the side window would give me an advantage but lose a great one in comparison. If I were seen, I would be at a disadvantage as far as helping Steiner was concerned. Surprise was the one thing going for me and I wanted to take full advantage of it.

I instantly notice the six men in the room filled with stand- alone hair dryers, hair curlers, curling thongs, rollers and other hair care nick-knacks. There was the body of a woman on the black and white tiled floor. The body of whom I presumed was the proprietor of the salon. I made a photographic memory plate of everything in the room. Of the six men, five looked like quick, heavy and brutish men. Rare and dangerous men, full of bouncy muscles, lean, mean, and seemingly extremely versatile. Two were armed with weapons dangling from their sides.

Only one was on his knees wearing a sweatshirt with jeans and black high-tops, groaning. I didn't need a video camera phone to tell me he was Marion Steiner, the man-child I had come for. He was sagging against the floor in his blue jeans, grey faced, hand clasped to his arm. His fine boned face and soft eyes were contorted in a painful frenzy. The enormous package of his family jewels I had noticed between his legs seemed to have shrivelled up. The man standing above him was a five foot four fatty who had eaten way too many Twinkies. A brute of a man with an untidy brown beard, short-cropped hair and a bull-neck. A dragon tattoo was prominently displayed on one of his forearm. He looked very flabby in his tan sports jacket and stubby fingers that held rings that were too small for his fingers. He was smiling down at Steiner with satisfaction at the pain he was causing. I noticed the man slightly to his right, also with a beard but coloured black grey and the numbers six, two, four, and eight tattooed on his fingers. I caught sight of the man behind him with long hair covered by a grey ball cap, a bling chain round his neck and a scar down his right cheek twirling a switchblade as he sat front to back on a hair stylist chair wearing a wife beater T-shirt. The fourth and fifth armed men were standing with half their backs exposed to me sipping on some cheap liquor. Each of two men was jeering on the spectacle before them and holding onto a Victory Arms MC5 semi-automatic parabellum pistol in each of their left hands.

I knew these sorts of men, businessmen of a sort. They knew the right doors to knock on, the right words to say, to punch and when, to get whatever they seek or want. Men ready to kill at the drop of a hat, for the right price, of course.

Su Chen, my Korean *Wing Chun* Sensei, had always advised that when fighting, one should use as few moves as possible that would bring complete subjugation of the enemy. Being only one of two Chinese immigrated Judo champions to turn down an Olympic medal, his advice was more than welcome. I put his counsel into effect.

I tossed my red *Bottega Veneta*'s Continental hand purse into a corner and took my first steps forward.

The two gunmen heard me and whirled. In the confined space, I used the *Shorin Ryu* technique, and showed the thugs how philosophical the fighting style of Shorin Ryu can be when combined with the three basic combination moves of Wing Chun. Spade, pin and sheath. With a tightened knuckle, I moved fast, a soft block of his soaring arm followed by a hard counter punch at the throat of the fourth goon, stopped him cold. Twisting his arm into an arm lock, I make the muzzle of his gun aim at his comrade and letting the force of my arm lock aid in his squeezing the trigger. I hear flesh tear and bones crack as the fifth goon goes down from a slug through his knee. The second shot from the goon's gun hits the fat man in his torso, close to his clavicle. He soars rather than bounce away in the air from Marion. His head hits the ground like a melon dropped from a third story window. I didn't pay any mind, I shuffled my footsteps and was already reversing the grip of my arm lock, making my captive's body twist around me, making him shield me like a spade as I rap the wrist of his gun hand with a pin strike from my knuckle. Several of the tiny bones in his wrist shatter. A bullet thuds into his foot as I crouch near to the ground, hand extended to let his MC5 semi-automatic pistol fall into my waiting hand. I fire two shots in rapid succession from that position at the second and third goon. They both screamed and hit the ground as the slugs found their marks. Their ankles.

My hair whooshed wildly across my face as I punched my captive and dump him flat on his face.

Content with my limited use of violence, I stood up and surveyed the carnage before my feet. I went over to the woman lying motionless on the floor. There was a crimson stain on her blouse in her chest, which I surmised was from a bullet. In any case, I still felt for a pulse. There was none. The fat thug, presumably the top dog of this little cadre was near the counter lying on his back in a pool of his own blood. He was alive, grasping hard on his chest wound. From the darts of anger spitting out of his eyes, I could tell there was plenty of life left in his body. Shaking and cursing bitterly, he watched me, with hate in his eyes, as I walked up to Steiner and crouched next to him.

Steiner was holding on to his aching arm. Shock and awe was across his face and not only that. There was blood splatter across his face and sweatshirt.

'Seems I got here in the nick of time, huh' I said to him, as I glanced at the groaning features of the second and third goon. 'Damn, I think I've painted a bullseye on both our asses'

'W-w-who a-are you?' he asked me shakily with a voice full of accentuated French argot.

'I'm …' I began as I put one bullet each into the knees of the second and third goon '… here to help, however if you rather wait for someone else to come along … well my dear Marion … you might have a long wait'

I rose and made my way towards the exit, dismantling the semi-automatic in my hand as I went, tossing the pieces across the room.

Over the moans and groans of the wounded men, I heard Marion scramble to his feet and scurry after me. I was standing outside the salon, sniffing the air when he joined me. He took a long note of me in my jogging outfit as I stood waiting. He was apprehensive and tense as he floundered after me. He wanted to speak but from my shoulders, he could tell this wasn't the time to speak.

It would have been prudent that we get in my Shelby and blown the town but I did not want my face plastered all over the police band with an "All-Points-Bulletin" amber alert trailing me. I thought it a bit premature to skip the town, at least for now, besides I had just gotten here.

Getting the truth out of the wounded jokers would prove fruitless, which meant I'll have to spend hours explaining to the local constabulary why I felt the need to act with such deadliness. My circumstance was not incrementally difficult because thankfully I had a witness. Best I confronted the police now, which I hoped wouldn't be long.

At that moment, I was thinking of Elena Shalamov specific hour for a call when my flip phone started to buzz. As iflike magic, Elena Shalamov's number and picture were displayed on the incoming call.

'Hallo Elena'

'Dax dis you … yes?' 'Yes Elena, it is I'

'Good. I ask question … like you ask … about grease ball …' 'Yeah yeah?'

'The families say they have nothink to do with death, in fact they wanna find out who do dis horrible and disrespectful crime they … er … ask if you do good for them … make any headway, inform them of your progre …'

'How'd they know I'm dealing with it?'

'They just know. They know your rep and ask you keep them … how they say … keep posted'

'You believe them?' I asked Elena

'I not know, it not uncommon … they not just lie like. They beg you take care good of your new protégé'

My new protégé? I wondered who that would be. She would not be talking about Bilquees and Nadia, my adopted daughters. No, she must be referring to Marion Steiner, my recent responsibility. Bloody hell!

I glanced at the man-boy stumbling beside me. He must be way important than I figured.

'Well tell them not to hold their breath' I said and hung up

I half believed the phone call but half a truth was better than none.

I was hit with a void filled with a matrix of sounds, scents, taste and texture as soon as I hit the sidewalk. It immediately informed me that I was hungry. In fact, I was starving.

Stepping past the bystanders and pedestrians, I headed east with the man-child Marion grudgingly on my heels.

You smelled Bowman's restaurant before you got inside. Despite its half-hearted renovation, it had an oldness about it. Maybe a hangover from its long past tree-logging days when it catered to truck drivers hauling timber through the town. We both entered the restaurant into a dining room of sorts that led directly to the bar. There was a large area for the bar and space for five wide seaters where you could drink to your leisure. The eatery space too was large but smaller by a metre or so. I choose a corner table away from the other diners wearing curious grins and inconsequential looks.

Marion Steiner was still massaging his arm when he sat down. 'W-what are w-we d-doin' here? S-shouldn't we be gettin' outta town?'

'I need some nosh' 'W-what?'

'I haven't had breakfast yet'

'*La vache*, y-y-you are English?' His question was more of a statement.

'Is that an issue, Marion? Marion …, jeeze. Do I have to call you that? It's too girlie for me and I'm giving you my honest opinion as a member of the fairer sex. No, Marion doesn't really sound normal to me'

'Wh-why i-in hell yo-you talk about?'

'Your name? Reminds me too much of Maid Marion … hey what does the R of your middle name stand for?'

'*Ferme ta gueule*' He cautioned me as a surly faced waitress came over with a menu. He leaned forward 'M-my name is Larry.

Larry Steinberg, mam'selle' he whispered

'Not with that accent you aren't and I doubt you aren't circumcised. Look don't get uptight because I really do not have time for games … hey … Robin … that's it. That's just up my alley. I'll call you Robin'

'*Ta gueule!* ' He snapped at me 'W-who are you?'

I got serious 'I'm friends of one the men that was killed with your lover Francesco'

There was a grimace of revulsion on his face before he answered 'Pa … Fra …. H-he was not my lover'

'I don't care. All I know is that the trolls you're running from know where you are. I cannot imagine why they would want to eliminate you, but they do. Dead or Alive, I have no idea. You need help and I'm here to provide it. If you don't want my help you're free to leave and manage by yourself'

He twisted his mouth 'W-why would you want help me?' 'Revenge, vengeance, honour … take your pick?'

'*Chapeau de ma tante, que tu mens*' he cussed at me in French believing I didn't understand.

'In reverence to your aunt but you're entitled to your opinion'

Both his eyebrows reacted to my reply 'Y-you are not with police and you not one of Ritchie's friends, who you are with?'

From my jogging pants, I pulled out the temporary FBI creds Prideaux had given me and deliberately placed it face up on the table 'I sometimes work with erm … the feds, but I'm not one of them'

Looking closely at the credentials, he asked 'Then who you are?'

'As you can see, my name is Susan Dax, my friends

call me Susan. You can call me Susan. That doesn't necessarily make us friends, got it?'

Nodding imperceptivity, he replied 'Yes'

Even if what I said brought a stirring of interest into his soft eyes, I could still tell he did not trust me. Hard to do when a strange woman kiboshes men twice her size. If I were in his position I might find it … well you know … "Kindda Hot" or "Cool". In either case, I wouldn't stare at her as if she were from outer space.

'So we understand each other huh?' I asked quietly but firmly. He shrugged and leaned forward 'Ok, Susan … not my friend … I have plenty complications in my life, I believe you charge me for your assistance, yes?'

I swore silently. For him to ask me that and I was only just beginning to enjoy his idiosyncratic gaudic use of the Queens's English.

If only he knew that I was the eighth Lady of Yelverton with a wealth that could launch a hundred shuttle missions, buy the US Presidency, the crown jewels, or even the Koh-I-Noor several times over. What would I need with anything he could offer me?

'You can't afford me' I revealed to him point-blank.

'I sure I can pay whatever day rate you thinking' he replied in a sarcastic voice.

I chuckled. Day rate huh! I suspended our forthcoming problems or no problems, I was starving. I needed to eat. When the waitress returned she wasn't surprised when I requested a rare thick steak with my eggs and orange soda.

Steiner just asked for some coffee, black with sugar. 'How you find me?'

'How would I know? Social media these days aren't

too prolific an avenue to bumble in and untraceable these days' I grunted in an ironic tone of voice.

As the waitress returned with our drinks, explaining that my steak would be a while, Marion Steiner's eyes brightened mischievously. 'I can be taking off again, you know'

I rolled my eyes 'Most morons don't look a gift horse in the mouth'

Steiner took a small sip of coffee and touched his mouth nervously. 'You not looking like a horse' he said literally. He sure didn't get my quip.

'But I look damn pretty in gift wrappers' Marion chuckled 'I betting you do'

When he leaned back against his chair to relax, I took it as a sign he was beginning to calm down and maybe loosen his paranoia. He was beginning to have faith in me, but only up to a point.

'Hey, can I ask you something. How good are you Frenchie's with riddles?'

He looked suspiciously at me 'Riddles?' he asked wondering if I were real or not.

'I heard this one the other day and it's been bugging the hell out of me' I said "See a man walks into a bar and asks the bartender for a glass of water. Instead, the bartender takes out a shotgun and fires at him, just missing him by ...."

The door banged and three uniformed cops burst in armed to the gills with automatic SIG Sauer otherwise known by American law enforcers as the "double tap gun".

Blue blistering barnacles! I thought, I was never going to get to solve this riddle.

I glanced at the coppers. They all were in their tailored uniforms, navy short sleeves, and close-fitting grey slacks. I examined their necks and hands for their ages. They were between thirty and thirty-five. The look and shape of hands and necks never lie. My snapshot of appraisal took less than a second.

Steiner sitting across from me for a moment stiffened, then when he saw how relaxed I was, he relaxed back, but by much.

The woman behind the counter, presumably the owner, regarded them with amusement. They looked around and fixed their eyes on us. The other punters looked on as they changed their stances and turned towards us without hesitation. With their hands firmly locked on their armed weapons, they approached us deliberately. Too bloody deliberate.

Two of the Deputies came to stand on either side of Steiner, while the eldest of the crew took up a position just behind me.

I discerned recognition in Steiner's eyes as the one with the Sheriff's shield settled behind me. His grip tightening on the butt end of his gun. 'You …Marion… you two must come with us'

There was a sneering kind of impression in his voice that told me, we had better obey. It wasn't just that he was seeing red, but there was also resentment possibly fury in his countenance.

Steiner quickly complied by getting to his feet. I smiled, placing my hands on the table next to my still open FBI Identification 'You're early, Deputies'

'Miss! … Marion!' he retorted, pulling out his gun from its holster to his side with a fervent I had rarely ever seen.

Normally, though in wronged lovers.

With my eyes and tapping thumb, I indicated the credentials on the table. The Sheriff barely took one look at it before ignoring it.

That was strange.

These were officers of the law all right, but they surrounded us with a certainty that is rare with officers of the court. Either they were just being vigilant or they had been informed of the mess I had made and had been instructed we be put on ice. Either way, surrendering to them was a bad idea, given the anger I was perceiving from the Sheriff.

'Officer, if you don't mind, I'd like to finish my meal before you get to arresting us'

With an effort, he managed to hide his irritation as he stepped forward, his gun drawn.

His cohorts also drew their weapons and stood on either side of us. They did not have the same demeanour of wrath as their Sheriff. They were there to do their job.

'Get your hands up' barked one the Deputies

'*Bordel de merde*' Marion cussed, shooting his arms into the air. 'Of course, Deputies' I muttered, getting slowly to my feet. 'We are arresting you under the suspicion of murder' raved

the Sheriff with venom in his voice. 'You have the right to remain silent, you have the right to an attorney, if you cannot afford an attorney, you will be appointed one. Do you understand these rights as I have …?'

I grunted 'Oh officer you are making me blush' I said raising my hands slowly.

'Do you understand these rights as we have explained

th ...?!' his voice raised

'Do you understand Marion?' the other deputy asked Steiner nodded vehemently.

Pointing very distinctively with a forefinger, I inquired if the Sheriff would not mind having a look at my credentials.

Not bothering to read what was on the credentials I indicated, he stood his ground with his gun firmly pointed at me.

'Hey!' The Sheriff protested furiously at one of his Deputies who was about to move towards the table to check my credentials. The other officer moved round the table and clamped his hand hard down on my shoulder.

The dazzling smile that was on my face a fraction of a second ago was replaced by a sternness that made him quickly withdraw his hand.

Turning slowly towards the Sheriff, he could see from my expression that I was in no mood for pleasantries and neither was he. I asked him again to look at the credentials and again he ignored it.

That settled it.

These Deputies could be on someone else's payroll and not the county of Prine or the State of Oregon for that matter. Either that or there was something else going on. There was nothing I hated more than a corrupt cop fucker. A corrupt copper was worse. It was time to close whatever deal they had made.

I twirled into action. Snatching up Steiner's steaming cup of coffee, I tossed the content into the faces of the three men in front of me. The two Deputies and Steiner. The hot liquid made them all stagger back two three paces off balance in different directions. Instantly whirling, I used my right hand to sweep aside the Sheriff 's gun hand making him outfling his stance for balance, without pausing I gathered power from my thigh and body and drove my knee into his groin while at the same time snatching the gun from his left hand.

It was a nice, loud kneeing.

The shock of my attack sent the Sheriff staggering back a pace. I braced myself by grabbing his collar and twirling him across my body and shoving his gun into his open mouth. With his body propped upright shielding mine and my hand gripping onto his neck while his gun was lodged in his mouth, I stood very adamant across from his two Deputies who glared at me through coffee drenched faces. They aimed their guns precariously at me, while Steiner half crouched by the next stall looked on at the spectacle through a coffee stained expression.

The punters in the restaurant, like Steiner all looked on in awe. Some were two three steps from the nearest exit, two were under a table and one I think had grabbed a coffee mug in anticipation of a struggle and was watching with amused, knowing eyes.

Shrugging mentally, I asked the man in my grip who put them up to this.

The Sheriff muttered indistinctively.

I asked his two officers. They just stared at me. 'Why arrest me?'

The oldest of the Deputies began to say something but the youngest one answered instead 'Y-you just killed a person' his voice was hoarse.

'Didn't my creds tell you anything?' 'You killed Polly'

'No she not do, Sheriff Tuskey' Steiner defended me from his hiding place.

'Polly?' I pondered

'His woman' Steiner whispered from the next stall.

The image of the dead woman lying dead on the Mayflower salon floor flashed through my head. 'Oh the lady?'

'M-my fiancée' grunted the man in my grip.

'Your fiancée? … Blue blistering barnacles' I cursed 'Blimey, I didn't know'

That explained his overzealous Gestapo routine. I instantly released the Sheriff and handed him back his gun. He staggered away, clutching his neck against his head. He and his two junior

Deputies looked at me with surprise as I turned my back to him with my hands raised 'My apologies for your loss but if you don't mind, my friend and I could clear that up' I croaked, glancing at Steiner.

It took a journey down to the police station and more than ten hours to clear up the errors between us. Given the position we were both in, there wasn't much of a tale to explain, really. It was our word against the hospitalised goons. Steiner had informed them of what really happened, excluding the details of his identity and why they were questioning him. For my part, I explained that I was just in the neighbourhood. A phone call to Deputy Director Benedict Prideaux's office and the hotel register confirming my check-in were enough to at least validate part of our story. Nevertheless, the Sheriff insisted we make a statement and that we were under strict instructions not to leave town until everything was cleared up. Five hitmen in his town and his fiancée killed under weird circumstances, and the FBI telling him to obey orders, shut the fuck up and bury the investigation, at least for now, was more than he bargained for when he was voted in as Sheriff.

Like I said, a killing stirs up things.

Given our state of affairs, I was beginning to worry about Agent Lionel Bandler. He hadn't shown up to enquire what had happened or got in touch and most especially, he had not at least tried to get in contact. FBI agents are nothing but prompt with procedure and punctuality. Sitting in the police station, I used my flip phone to dial his number. I sat there listening to the buzz with the feeling that events might likely take another abrupt change in due course.

Steiner and I left the station serenely, at least for my part. I was advising him that we should find someplace safe for him to go or stay to flush out those after him. He was barely listening to me. Steiner walked at a fast pace, glancing about him as he made a dash for his Datsun parked on a curb in the alley next to his workplace. A light mist of rain had begun to fall. I could see drops forming on the glazing of the surrounding windows.

'Haven't I earned your trust yet?' I asked

'Trust? Hah! *J'en ai rien à cirer*, you just get us arrested' 'I was starving'

We were about five paces away from his vehicle when he clicked on his fob key.

'You ...'

CHHA - KROOOOOMM!!

His complaint is abruptly cut. Cut, cramped and cauterised by a scathing eruption of light and fury. A holocaust made more awesome by its total, uncompromising detonation.

It is funny, when things like that happen, what you think of and notice first. His red Datsun exploded in an eruption of flames in front of us. I heard the roar of the explosion, like a volcano belching loudly and I heard myself swearing as both of us were catapulted up and outwards, across the alley, landing on the bonnet of a parked vehicle. The surging and burning of twisted metal sucked the air from around us.

My lungs felt like closing down as the rush of turbulent poisoned air hit me. I was sure it was the same with Steiner. I recalled large bits of twisted hot metal descending on us and trying to cover my head with my arms.

Then there was another explosion.

I was sure, I cursed in words a lady such as myself should never use. I was conscious enough to recognise for one brief flashing moment that the second blast was not a bomb but a reaction from the first detonation. Maybe from the engine block or gas tank of the Datsun.

I could not confirm it because blackness closed in on me as a sharp pain rushed through my head.

I came to, probably not more than a few minutes later and my blurred eyes finally focussed on the scene of the wreckage and debris. The Sheriff who had wanted me dead a few hours ago was supporting my head trying to make his Deputies keep away the small horde that had gathered around Steiner and me.

I lay there, my mind slowly orientating itself to who I was and why I was lying on the cold, wet asphalt, around this rubble. I felt the hot air, saw the orange flaring of flames and felt the heat from the air-licking blaze. It was sweltering, terribly hot. I pulled myself up to my hands and knees and glanced at Steiner.

Just beyond him, the horror of destruction remained cruelly intact.

Steiner had his eyes closed. For a second I thought that since he was nearer the blast that he might be dead. Then I saw him stirring.

'*Putain! Nom de Dieu ... mon Dieu*' I heard him mumble.

I pulled myself to my feet, helped generously by the Sheriff. 'Sheriff ' I whispered 'Get us out of here, now'

The Sheriff took one look at the abrasions on me, Steiner and the burning debris of the Datsun and issued orders. He had us escorted back into the four-desk stationhouse while he arranged for the fire department to investigate and then clear out the mess behind the Mayflower salon.

# *FIVE*

Between coordinating the fire department and the Sheriff chaperoning us to somewhere secure, I passed out again. When I woke, I had the headache bigger than that of all the Kardashians and Steiner

'Wh-where i-is he?' I groggily asked one of the Deputies.

'Who?'

'Whom'

'Whom?'

'What do you mean whom?'

'Marion?' the other deputy inquired 'Whom else'

'He wanted to go home to pick up some things so the boss let him'

I kicked back my chair and reached the door in three quick strides, ignoring the aching pain I felt nearly overcoming me.

'That's the fucking first place they'd look' I scolded as I burst through the doorway and hit the streets.

Could it be I cocked-up this whole situation by passing out?

It was still drizzling when I hit the streets but despite my throbbing head and weak constitution, I hurried to my hotel room, change my attire, grabbed my keys and my handy leather satchel, and raced down to my car. The desk clerk was dumbfounded by my rushed pace as I zipped past him twice in as many minutes. To an outsider, an observer would think I've lost the plot or lost my onions and I was moving for the sake of moving. It didn't really matter, I guess I was really feeling like I had thrown a spanner in the works. As a precaution, I checked under the hood and the chassis to  see if someone had improvised and bothered to plant a device like the one in Steiner's vehicle. The Shelby, for all intent and purpose looked untouched. I was thankful when the diagnostic screen didn't light up when I remotely activated the vehicle indicating a foreign object was on board. One of the features Brice had incorporated in the assembly. When I turned the ignition, I was pleased I wasn't blown to smithereens.

I drove fast to Steiner's address. However, again as a precaution, I parked a block and a half from his place. I didn't want to go barging into something unpleasant again, best to be cautious.

Thanks to Agent Lionel Bandler's chronicle, I knew exactly where to go. Approaching his place, I found to my delight that Steiner was for better or worse all right. However, something was definitely amiss. There was a sheriff 's cruiser parked in front of his two-story long-term motel but no sign of Sheriff Tuskey, former fiancée of Polly.

The large red green neon light of Ochoco motel flashing "Vacancy" sign, caught the glint of three motorbikes and their riders keeping vigilance on the place but especially on the vehicle. I ducked into a gloomy spot to watch the scene unfold. Maybe, I could get a first-hand insight on the whys and where forth of the murderers, I had tasked myself to seek out.

I watched as Steiner, rucksack and wheelie case in tow dash from a partially closed motel door towards a green coloured Pinto Hatch Back.

As he did, he constantly checked about his environment, looking over his shoulder, adjusting the rucksack across his shoulder and rubbing the nape of his neck. All were self-soothing gestures that demonstrated a sure sign of distress. He took care to open the car door, check under the hood and chassis before gently getting in. With the sheriff missing, I was hoping that Steiner had not killed him but had laid him out cold somewhere.

Nonetheless, I was hardly watching him. I was watching the three bikers, deciding which one of them was the ugliest or more precisely, which of them could handle themselves in a fight. I had already decided that all of them could win the ugliest biker contest. From the dirt on their bikes and in their hair, they gave the impression of a trio who hadn't touched a bar of soap in weeks, maybe months.

Not that the one with a knife scar curling down his left cheek was any disagreeable than the stocky dude wearing a red greasy bandanna to cover his dirty blond hair or the one that resembled a Caucasian Mr T. A bulky hairy ape with a copper-coloured beard wearing loads of bling around his neck. In my view, they could all do with a Jenny Jones makeover.

I had no clue as to their motives. Just their presence required me to pay attention, however their presence could all just be a coincidence or it could be an immorality play. A debauchery of silence to show the disparity of man's magnificence to his action, eons of evolvement, and we still seek the darkened corners to sate our lowest impulses.

Sitting on their parked bikes, two of them were smoking and whispering to each other, while the third, meaner, looked on.

As Steiner got into the car, the sound of their engines merged with the Pinto. I raced back to get into my Shelby. The bikes charged off without seeing me pull out of the curb and follow them. I was careful not to use my headlights, I drove by moonlight. In the distant, I saw the red of three single taillights follow the pair of taillights sweep around a corner and disappear from view.

Yep, they were on Steiner's trail all right.

I picked them up as they sped out of Prine in pursuit of the hatchback, which was moving faster than its recommended speed limit.

I cursed Marion Steiner as the town fell behind me, for not trusting me and setting himself up for whatever the bikers wanted with him.

I gave the Shelby more gas and closed in on them. One of the bikers had closed in on Steiner and had begun drumming a fist on the hood, gesturing for him to pull over and stop the car. Steiner ignored him and was trying to speed off much more faster, zigzagging absurdly across the highway. Between the black highway, the shoulder and the ditch across from the shoulder track there was not that much space to be playing hanky-panky.

Each biker took turns in trying to forge alongside the hatchback and intimidate him to comply.

It was time I intervened. I sped up to them and reaching them, I introduced myself very prominently. With the quick and sudden flash of my headlight beams, I initiated myself into their little game of cat and mouse. When my headlights plastered itself over them they instantly became aware that someone had unpleasantly horned-in on their party. One of the bikers, Mr. T, turned back, whipping into my path, so suddenly that I had to slam on the brakes and clutch to avoid colliding with him. His ugly mug smirked at me as I gritted my teeth and slid into a spin on the rain slick asphalt. Riding the spin out, I resumed the chase.

Two of them were still hounding Steiner. That meant they wanted Steiner out of the car by any means necessary, but they had no intention of killing him, at least it did not seem so. They just wanted him out of the car.

My headlights caught red bandanna guy first. He was purring his bike between the others, and me maintaining a slower pace to either keep me out of reach or see if I'll stick with them. As he glanced back, he made a crude burlesque grin showing his missing front incisor. It was almost as if he was glad to have a go at me. He produced a short length of chain from somewhere behind his seat and turned his bike. Dangling the chain in his hand he gunned his cycle and shot himself at me.

His deliberate action told me he wanted to play a game of chicken. I didn't hit the brake nor did I slow down. I bore solidly forward, the ray of my lights licking through the slick wet night. Bandanna rumbled closer. At the last moment when he saw that I had no intention of deviating from my course even though I was in his path, he veered the bike over into the other lane.

As he flashed past me, I saw his arm move as he snapped the chain like a whip.

I could have swerved the car and struck him as I passed

him or used one of the five concentric modifications in the Shelby to incapacitate him but on that slick asphalt, he would have suffered more injury than I would envision, besides I didn't want to go into another spin and my priority was to get to Steiner. Instead I gave the Shelby more gas and picked up speed.

The unexpected burst of speed I urged out of the Shelby caused Bandanna's timing on the lash from his chain to go awry. The hard-swung chain smashed off the rear bumper of the Shelby. I involuntarily grimaced as I heard the "*Thwack*" off the metal. Brice is going to be unhappy to see the Shelby with a bruise.

Speeding off, I saw his light hanging on behind me as I streaked round a corner and up a hill after Steiner's Pinto and his two other mates. The biker on the lead bike, the Caucasian Mr. T was racing alongside the Pinto. He was swerving into Steiner's path, causing him to pull over towards the shoulder of the road in order to avoid a collision.

He was so absorbed or perhaps fearful with the duel that he failed to pay attention to the on-coming curve. The car leapt off the road, careering across the shoulder as if it was not there. The Pinto bounced and swerved like a paper boat on an abrupt sewer stream. I was concerned the Pinto would flip over if it hit the ditch, but the jolt only slowed it down. Steiner had the good sense to avoid the sudden pressure of using the brakes. From the sideways the shimmy the vehicle made, I could only imagine that he had shifted into a lower gear. Then suddenly, the cars brakes came into play.

The Pinto bucked and slid on the shoulder but didn't flip over.

Steiner had precipitously brought the hatchback to a

halt in an open field. I guess he had had enough. The cyclists seeing the expected action spun their bikes around.

Scarface jumped the ditch with a beautiful piece of riding and raced across the field towards the Pinto. His wheels churning up dirt as he rode. Mr. T didn't have the guts or just did not see the need to jump the ditch. He stopped on the shoulder of the road and watched as I approached.

He killed the engine of his bike and got off.

I glanced at my rear view mirror to check on bandanna's progress as I turned onto the shoulder. Yes, he was still in the fight and catching up to me. I stopped the car, shut off its engine but left the headlights burning as I got out of the car.

Mr. T leered at me as if he smelt something dead but could not locate the source. He reached into his leather jacket and pulled out a knife. Light shimmered off the blade as he walked towards me. I picked up the glimmer of a violent need on his face. That erratic look of someone who has disregarded all that was instilled in them as a child and was now looking for a carnal release.

Two steps away from me, still brandishing the knife, he said in a very hoarse voice 'Babe, you'd better get your little arse lost and make it stay lost'

'And if I refuse?'

'Ever see a face sliced up like steak ready for barbecue?' he asked coming to a stop in front of me.

I half turned, with one leg bent, I drove my knee into his groin, with my right hand ready to sweep aside the knife. It was not necessary, he was already off balance with the pain to his groin. Nevertheless, with my left hand driving up with an impetus that started from my thigh, body and shoulder to explode in the heel on my hand as it took him under the jaw. The shock of my attack made him hang in the air for a moment, head back, blood running from his chin from a bitten tongue. Mr. T hit the ground and lay still as if the ground under him had been jerked from under him.

With my hair tussling in the wind, I picked up his knife, weighed and flipped it in my hand.

Bandanna arrived on the scene, roaring on his cycle, still twirling his chain, heading straight at me. I knew that if he hit me in the face or any part of my anatomy I'd be blinded or scarred for life or just plain decapitated. His chain whined as I ducked with him speeding past me. Ducking, I flipped the Mr. T's knife and threw, spearing him out of his saddle. While he flew away into the night, his bike kept going, careening off across my car's light beam before finally falling on its side and sliding away.

Without giving Bandanna another glance, I strolled over towards Scarface who was hammering with his fist on the windscreen of Steiner's car. He stopped when he saw me approach. He made a move towards his still purring bike that stood some feet away from him. He was three steps from it when I pulled out my Makarov and put a bullet through its engine block. Scarface, startled changed direction and started sprinting towards his friends, probably hoping to reach one of them. I aimed and with the Makarov shot the running man in the leg.

Marion Steiner shoved open the door of his Pinto. In his left hand was a .38 silver-plated revolver. Scarface didn't know it but I probably saved his life.

'Susan' Marion said in an awed voice 'You definitely something different'

I pointed my Makarov at the rear tyre of the Pinto and shot a hole through it. Walking past the staring Steiner, I did the same with the front tyre.

'You crazy, out your mind?' he demanded

'These motherfuckers left you a fucking bomb, almost killed you and you have the notion to run out on me' I said softly

'I-I not know if I trust you' 'Oh and now?'

'I sorry. I not …. Look I use to being on my own, I think it best for me'

'And you thought that pea shooter of yours could protect you?'

Glancing at the gun in his hand, he said 'Maybe'

'You tosser. You better get smart, mate. You need protection. So tell me now, you going to skip out on me? Tell me now, so I can go my way. I'd really would like to watch the series finale of Games of Thrones'

He thought for a long while before slowly shaking his head.

I made my way over to Scarface who was lying on the wet grass clutching his leg.

I examined his wound. 'You'll live' I said to him 'Only if I decide I want you to'

He licked his lip. 'Whatd'ya mean?'

I showed him the barrel of my Makarov. 'Ok mate, why harass this guy?'

His lips seemed sealed until I pressed the hot barrel on his wound. He screamed 'Fuck! Bitch' he screamed

'We wanted the fuckin' car, why the fuck else?'

'His car?' I asked knocked for six. I had no idea the

car was a rarity as put the barrel in-between his busy eyebrows 'Tell me something I don't know'

'Like what?'

I rolled my eyes 'Why after this car?'

'I dunno lady. Some guy paid us to pursue the guy and hijack the car, lady ...'

'But the car's a piece of garbage'

'Fuck bitch ... it's a '72 4-Speed Pinto hatchback. You'now how much that piece of beauty costs. Fuck yeah, we wanted it and this guy paid us to get it'

'Who was this guy?'

'I dunno, just a guy. A guy' Scarface hissed 'Where can I find this guy?'

'Bowman's' 'Describe him'

'I dunno. Thin guy with strange accent. Classy shoes' Scarface admitted forcing a shaky grin, as he looked up at me 'Who da fuck are ya?'

I wasn't sure I believed him but it just had that ring of truth and stupidity to be believable. Whoever had hired them would be long gone or close by. I definitely would not find a thin man with expensive shoes at Bowman's Restaurant.

'You should never ask that question. For now, here's some free advice. Stay out of my sight, I see you or any of your mates again, you'll wake up dead. Understood?'

'Understood, lady'

Steiner was searching for something within his luggage by my car. I had a glimpse of something shiny.

'Have nice talk?' he enquired when I walked up to him.

'I gave him the name of a doctor I have complete faith

in' I commented 'Now, why don't we get back to town'

He paused for a second before complying with me. He lobbed his luggage into the back then slid under the steering wheel and over to the passenger's seat. He grinned at me as I holstered the Makarov and got in.

As I got behind the steering wheel, he punched his .38 into my ribs.

"*Holy poo on a cracker*" I whispered to myself.

'I sorry Susan' he said apologetically 'I know this not what you expect, not best way to express gratitude but I better to look out for myself '

I had made the most naivest mistake any rookie police officer could ever make. I had holstered my gun while one was still visible. Now I was in what was at best an embarrassing position. At worse, it could end out to be fatal.

'I don't suppose we can discuss this?' I enquired to the man- child who was nudging my ribs with his revolver.

'Keys, please … I begging you' he pleaded.

'At least you said please' I observed, holding up the keys 'I not going back to Prine. They be looking for me there' 'And who are "they"?'

He nudged his revolver a bit further into my ribs 'I not know' he hesitatingly admitted

'Fine, we can go somewhere else'

'No, I go alone' he replied reaching for the keys. I held them back just out of his reach.

'You intend to ditch me. That's not very gentlemanly of you' 'I not care. I survive this long have I?'

'Not without my assistance, if you recall'

'I know' he admitted, his voice rising a tad higher 'But I prefer to not shoot you'

'Have you ever used a gun before?' I enquired

He was silent for a moment before he answered 'No'

While we were arguing, I was assessing my situation. My right hand rested lightly on the steering wheel, it would be a sure thing to bring my hand down and rap his gun hand to disable him. However, I didn't want to risk injuring him or myself for that matter. As an amateur, a blow to his wrist might jerk his trigger finger and let the gun go off prematurely. Piledriving a bullet into me at such a close range was not a possibility I wanted to consider. 'Alright' I conceded, taking my hand off the steering wheel and pocketing the keys 'Go ahead and shoot' 'What?'

'I said shoot. It's the only way you're getting my keys. From my dead cold dead body, so shoot away, boy'

Steiner stared at me, not sure of what to do next. Maybe he saw me as some Sheila, a bitch who thought she knew more than what she thought she knew or just some know-it-all bitch.

We both sat there staring at each other. He was unsure of what to do next or perhaps determining on whether to shoot me or not. I was considering whether to take away his gun, which would be easy enough or let him think his situation through or just plain knock him out. I finally settled on letting him think his situation through. Inside his head was a secret, whether he knew it or not, that got my friend Agent Tyler dead. I needed to know the secret that had caused several attempts on his life in as many hours of me learning where he was.

Despite the cold night air, beneath my tussling hair I felt a sheen of sweat form along my hairline.

After a long moment, he made a heavy ragged sigh and pulled the revolver from my side.

'You get … no … have … no … how you English say … 'ave brass, Susan' he grunted finally, 'I suppose, I should strang along with you, huh baby?' he teased, trying to use a British accent.

'No no don't do that. And it's string along … oh …'

I had a feeling that his teasing query was less of a question and more of an assertion.

'String along? Huh. Ok good, we go now.'

'Good decision' I said taking out my keys and turning the engine over.

As I turned, the vehicle around he asked 'Do we really need go back to Prine?'

'For the time being, but as soon as I can secure your safety then to a place where you won't be in danger'

As I drove past Mr. T who had started to crawl towards his friends, Steiner asked if they be all right. 'What do you care?' I mused 'They weren't going to leave you with much when they were done with you'

I shoved my foot on the accelerator and the Shelby leapt off the shoulder like a streak. Brice's mechanic would have been proud of how the vehicle performed.

'Hand me the gun' I demanded 'I need it' Steiner protested 'Not now you don't'

'But I …'

'You've never used one before and amateurs are dangerous when it comes to using guns'

'Probably why I not shoot you'

'And here I thought maybe you were beginning to like

me' 'I like you, just not that lots'

'How disappointing for me. Now hand it over' I insisted

After a brief pause, he dropped the weapon into my palm. A symbolic token of trust. It seemed like I was at least, making some progress.

I slid the .38 revolver into my jacket's left hand pocket, gassed down on the accelerator until the digital needle alternated between 65 and 70 miles per hour as we sped our way back to town.

'What do you want of me, Susan?' he asked me. 'We'll get to that'

'And why do you need my gun?'

'Just a precaution. In case you get jittery enough to point it at me again'

'Those men, they did not want to be killing me, do they?'

'Nope. They wanted your Pinto' 'It wasn't mine'

'Whose's is it?'

*'Je n'ai pas la moindre idée putain'* 'You stole it?'

He fell silent. I was beginning to admire his initiative. I took a long curve without letting off the accelerator.

'How the hell did you hook up with a member of the Cosa Nostra?'

It took him a while to answer 'I be in LA visiting Da Vinci's travel exhibition. I admire his great workings, it be one of my great passions. The other being archaeology, I adore dig for artefacts'

'Artefacts?'

'Yeah, I think you know. I doing postgraduate work in archelogy. Anyway, we be meeting, join head, he had stories …'

'And money?'

'Yeah, I not born yesterday. Yes, he have money and real good reputation'

'Reputation?' I grinned in the darkness 'You mean his line of business?'

Steiner was silent for a long moment 'He out of it. Or I think'

I dimmed my lights as a truck roared passed us, going the opposite way.

'Anyway, that my story, how about yours?' he asked me There was much more he was hiding but I thought not to press him, at least for now.

'I already told you mine'

'Oh yes, you work for big fédéral police, interest only to locate Ritchie's killers'

'That's about it'

'And you not with them?' His statement was half a question. 'Is that what you've been thinking?' He didn't reply. 'There was an agent there that day, Tyler Shaw, he was a friend of mine' 'Er … I remember name. Big man with little girl agent with him. They come see Ritchie, that all I know. I not ask Ritchie about his business. He know I not want any part in it'

During our conversation, I noticed that he spoke with a reverence when he spoke of Ritchie Francesco, especially when it came to his name. It made me think that there was probably much more to their relationship than just being mere lovers and lovers of antiquities.

'You already a part of it. Douchebags from hell have tried killing you thrice already'

He did not answer me. Instead, he asked 'You want me finger the killers eh, In returning, the fédérals guarantying my safety … or something like that for my witnessing?'

I spotted Prine's lights ahead and slowed down 'Do you have other options?'

He was silent for a while before saying 'I think it over'

I had to admit, I was a bit angry at his statement and I made it known.

'You think it's over? Are you kidding me? Men with guns and bombs are trying to take your life and you don't want protection? What the hell are you thinking?'

'Like I said, I think of thinking it over'

'You do realise you might not have a choice'

'Perhaps'

'If you are that adamant, you mind telling me what they want from you'

'Want from me? What you mean?'

'Hey, I'm not stupid. Those chumps at your place of work wanted something from you'

'What make you say that?'

'They killed your boss but left you alive for questioning' 'That not mean anything'

I let the question slide.

The town of Prine was down for the night. Only a couple of businesses remained open for business. A restaurant, a bar, a quickie convenience shop, and hotel. The Valero gas station I had stopped at the previous evening was also closed. I pulled into the darkened gas station hoping to get a glimpse of Agent Lionel Bandler with my headlights, but not even a cricket stirred. I was hoping he was all right and be able to contact his superiors for support. I was categorically concerned that Agent Lionel Bandler was at least 8 hours overdue to contact me.

Stopping the car, I pulled out my phone and engaged the locator app. I punched in Agent Bandler's number and did a hard- target search for his phone. It took less than a minute for the app to locate the GPS from his phone. It was located some sixty odd yards away from us, within the confines of the gas station. I pulled out my Makarov. 'Wait here' I instructed Marion as I got out.

With the pistol in one hand and the flashlight app enabled on my flip phone, I prowled around the gas station. It took me ten minutes of prowling before I found him lying in a discarded garbage bin about ten metres from the rear of the station in a field of abandoned tyres, cracked oil drums and superfluous rusted mechanical scraps.

The smell around the bin and me was bad enough to gag a maggot. I found Agent Lionel Bandler lifeless, rigid against piles and piles of old heaped refuse. His head had been split open by what seemed like a hatchet or axe.

He boasted he was Mr. Careful. He had not exactly lived up to his moniker.

Marion came up from behind me. He took in a sharp breath when he saw the body lying prone in the refuse bin.

'I know this man' he sputtered 'I see him around here'

I switched off my phone, plunging us into darkness 'I told you to wait in the car' I said softly.

'*Hey, je suis sans sissy Susan*. I can handle anything you

can handle'

'*Je parie que vous pouvez*' I replied, indulging him.

He stepped forward and took another closer look at the body.

He turned away and puked.

'W-who is … was he?' he finally asked after he was done upchucking 'Another friend of yours?' he added cleaning his lips along his sleeve.

'Yes. Another agent, sent to watch over you and now dead because of you'

'It not my fault' He complained, his voice riding high with panic in its overtone.

'Never said it was'

'And you expect me to be protected by these your friends when they not safe?'

It was a reasonable question, I thought to myself.

Marion Steiner turned and took off running through knee high grass. I had the assumption that he was running for the sake of it. He actually probably had no idea where he was going or why. He only knew he just needed to get away. I couldn't blame him.

I hated leaving Agent Lionel Bandler's body where it was but it couldn't be helped. I holstered my Makarov and took off after him. He didn't get far. I was about three feet from him when he began to slow down and eventually stop. He was breathing loudly when I came up behind him. 'You done?' I asked him

'I not going into protection' He panted 'You cannot make me.

I better without one, on my own'

I was not getting through to this milquetoast little man-boy or perhaps he had other reasons to be so temperamental. I was sure not going to get anywhere if I continued to coddle him, so I thought a change in tactics was exactly what was needed for this situation.

'Who're kidding, you're scared out of your wits, aren't you?' 'What you mean?' he asked stiffly 'Scare of what?'

'Oh not a lot. You know the Mob, bikers, bombers … hey maybe even me. You hate me right?'

His nostrils flared in anger '*Va te faire enculer*!'

'Fuck me? You are frightened off your wits but for some reason you're playing the tough guy act. You're not used to this kind of violence, but it now exists in your world ever since you met Ritchie Francesco. Not to mention the now deceased Anna Feldman and Bruce Windemill' I remarked, playing a hunch.

There was instant shock on his face followed by grief. There was no doubting from his expression that he knew the nurse and her boyfriend. He stared at me coldly, '*Vous n'avez pas putain me connaissent, donc cesser d'* être *un con*' he raged, then went on, 'Maybe I never think F-fa … Ritchie world would come up to me and if it did I would be knowledgeable to walk little carefully. But to me he not the man the world take him for and I knowing that ambiance he attract involve the brutal kind of violence and death'

In the night cold air, I could see by the pale moonlight that his face was paler than before. I had touched a deep and sensitive cord in him, for there was truth in what we were both saying. His felt like an element of accusation. Whether it was directed at Ritchie Francesco, or me I was not sure but I wanted to pull on this cord. 'His ambiance was how he lived and not the wisest choice for a friend'

I said making my voice chilling 'But listen my little hair dresser cum hooker and archaeologist doc, you got yourself into this. You met violence and murder all on your own, your friend Ritchie is dead as is my friend. If you don't want to or do blame him, he can't help you'

'Hooker?' he enquired sternly.

'Yes, weren't you that to him?'

'No'

'Well that's what the Feds think and probably your eventual killers, after all what relationship could you have possibly had with a former mob boss with questionable taste'

'What you saying?'

I moved three steps closer to him 'Whoever these buggers are, some old enemy, a revengeful friend, the Cosa Nostra ... whomever they are, they massacred my friend and your friend Ritchie. You barely escaped but they found you. They killed your friend in an attempt to torture and then kill you. They set a bomb for you to ensure your death. Now they've killed another agent looking out for you, so tell me, what is your response?' I stopped in front of him. I could see the anger and confusion bubbling on his face as he took in my body and especially my words. 'Run?' I asked distinctively 'And they might succeed in killing you ten minutes from now or in ten hours, I don't really give a shit'

'I – I ...' he began to mutter, shaking in the cold air where he stood.

'Then fuck you and go'

I flicked my hand across his face. In the psyched-up snapping tension that overcame him, his response was automatic, and what I had hoped.

It's not that I wasn't expecting it but still it took me by surprise. He whirled and with an open hand slapped me hard across my face. Maybe he was under the impression that I would block the slap or avoid the blow but to his surprise, I barely moved a muscle. The slap resounded in the night.

He seemed surprised by his actions because he stood there shaking and staring at me apologetically. A sound, a chocked cry emanated from his lips.

'Feel better?' I asked him.

'Susan … I … please! Sorry … I not mean … you been …please …!'

I smiled at him 'Don't worry about it' 'But … I …!'

'Don't worry about it. I was being a bitch but I had to be to get you to unwound'

I glanced around, there might be killers lurking around, looking for us. I had to get this man-child to a safe place as soon as possible.

He was still shaking when he reached out and took a hold of my hand. Marion gazed desirously at me, I could see in his eyes that there was an intense desire in him to plant his lips on me. This was a bad time for him to do that.

'Hey, this isn't the time' I bluntly told him.

The longing in his eyes was replaced with a disappointment that was shattering.

'W-who in hell are you?'

I grinned 'Let's get back to the car'

# *SIX*

We were in the car on our way to my hotel when Steiner overcoming his despair finally spoke.

'You think Ritchie's killers kill Anne and Brucie?' 'As sure as water is wet'

'And you think I can recognise them?' 'You were there so it stands to reason'

A bitter laugh emanated out of him. 'I not have clue as to who send the men but I do know it was not mafia. They not kill your friend or Ritchie. No, whoever they be … they want me dead not alive dead'

His revelation did not come as a surprise, it just confirmed one or two of my suspicions. If the mafia were not responsible then a third party, set the car bomb. Who could be that third party?

'You're full of surprises' I chuckled 'And why pray thee is that?' 'Whoever they are they believe I have something they want' 'And what is that?'

'Tell me something … please being truthful …' he demanded 'I'll try'

'Do you have faith?' he asked

What the hell was he asking? What kind of question was this? 'A faith? Do you mean a religious faith?' I replied, puzzled. 'Huh huh'

'Hmm that's an odd question'

'Do you have faith? You believe in God?' he insisted

'Um … well I do believe there is an almighty presence, a being that looks down over us but a particular faith … Methodist, Catholic, Presbyterian, Anglican … I don't know. No, I do not believe I do'

From the corner of my eye, I could see him staring at me as I drove. When a smile formed on his lips, it prompted me to ask why.

Still for a long while he stared at me then just as suddenly, he gave a heavy relieved sigh '*Oh mon aimable, Merci Dieu*'

I was confused, more than the chirping Cicada's or Coyote's prowling the empty streets of Prine. 'My lack of faith is good news to you?' I mused

'It mean you not be one of them' 'One of whom?'

'Those after Marie Dénarmaud's secret' The name seemed vaguely familiar. 'Who?' 'Ever hear of the Priory of Sion?'

In college, I did a thesis that dealt with mysterious organisations from the early days of Christianity to the present day. There were many, from the Grand Masonic "*Freemasons*". The American "*Skulls & Bones*," an organisation shrouded in conspiracies, the "*Rosicrucian Order*" founded by German protestants on the three Alchemist type documents published in the 1450s. There were the "*Paulicians*"; who believe strenuously in the Gospels of Christ and nothing else, the "*Knights Templars*"; the "*Illuminati*," a movement of freethinkers,

"*Opus Dei* " and the "*Order of the Temples of the East*" an organisation based around one tenement, "*Do what thou wilt shall be the whole of the Law, Love is the Law, Love under the will.*"

Of those societies, one of the most mysterious of groups was the *Priory of Sión*. A supposedly rumoured organisation, they boasted a history spanning hundreds of years with members to be from a secret order of Templars. The alleged instigators of the Crusades. Their main objective was to restore the Merovingian heir to the French throne. The heir who they believe is a direct descendant of Jesus Christ and Mary Magdalen. It is their contention and belief that when Christ was crucified, Mary Magdalen was pregnant with his child and was secreted off to France. The resultant offspring, the Priory of Sión believe is the true heir to the French- Merovingian throne. In my studies, I truly believed that the Priory was just a shade above being a myth. Dan Brown's bestseller book and subsequent movie starring Tom Hanks has made it all too believable now.

I played dumb 'Er … I think … no …yes … I … is it that Tom Hanks film … what's it called again yes … Da Vinci's Code?'

'A sugar coat for myth but yes' 'So, what about it?'

'You will not be pleased'

'From the dead bodies, I'm betting I won't'

'There is something you should know about Ritchie Francesco.

He … well, he … he was my father. The Papa I never know' I did not expect to hear that. I stared at him.

'What?'

Who the hell could have foreseen that? It did however

explain the reverence I heard in his voice when he spoke of Ritchie Francesco. But his father? How come the FBI didn't know? Could that be the reason why the mob had asked me to take care of him, my protégé? They knew about his heritage.

'He had me when he young and carving out niche for hi… well he just getting his feet wet with the Mob. He keep my existence secret from everyone because he … not want to appear weak in anyway'

'Is that what he told you?' I asked

'He try best to get involve in my life but … well … he try … He give me good education, send me to best schools, all anonymously of course and well … I almost to point where I can pick a major. I thinking of become an archaeologist'

'Congratulations. I should have known' The formed callouses on his palms I had noticed earlier on the camera video phone could have been formed whilst on a dig. 'I take it his antiquities fetish was from your influence?'

'*Donner ou prendre, plus ou moins*' 'The mob did not know?'

'He do best to make them believe otherwise'

'He may have but I think they know about your special relation' 'I not know how. Those that find out about me believe I was charity case, then benefactor. Later, because of strong connection,

I become inconspicuous lover. He do little to dissuade rumour'

His family tree and Francesco's colourful motive was dreary to me. I wanted to get back to the issue in hand.

'So what happened at the cottage?' 'I not sure'

'What do you …?'

'Look all I know is couple of month before, I was member of dig at *Rennes-la-Château* in western France when we unearth some documents clipped to two parchments that belong to Priest name Bárenger Sauniére' he paused.

Then it hit me. The name Marie Dénarmaud and why it was familiar.

I had heard of her name before, including the tale behind her.

I researched it during my thesis.

In 1896, a poor improvised priest found a number of parchments hidden in his church. Two of the parchments were encoded or in a language, he was unfamiliar with but he somehow decoded them. No one knows what the decoded parchment says but after a consult with Rome, the impact was that it made him a very wealthy individual. When he died, he bequeathed all his possessions to his housekeeper Marie Dénarmaud, including the parchments. She too, on the back of those parchments lived a very affluent and prosperous life until her death. Despite promising to bequeath the parchments to her family, Marie Dénarmaud died before revealing what was on the parchment or where they were hidden.

'Go on'

'My professor and our team discover it reveal fundamental truth that might upset not only Catholic faith but the Christian one, if parchment is revealed to be authentic'

'What truth?'

'It be not important at moment, fair say … we know it be religious time bomb. Sorry to say, someone must talk because as we start processing parchment for authenticity, some priest from some unknown church visit us. Afterwards, our professor characterise him as possible member of Priory. Someone understand something we not know, because strange things begin happen. Our *subvention* … uh grant is withdrawn, my professor face sexual harassment charges, and then he and three member of team begin mysteriously die from accidents. Before Rachel disappear she says …'

'Rachel?'

'Member of team and … Friend. Anyway, she say someone follow her. She labelled him as a man with sandals for shoes, beard and black hair. We were suppose to rendezvous but she vanished before she gets to me. When I see same man, I run and jump on first plane I find and contact my Papa hoping he know what to do''Good for you' 'I **was** lucky'

'Did he know what you found?'

'Yes. I tell him so he could make enquiries' 'I take it the parchments are …?'

'Hidden and safe in place I know they be found by right person' 'You know it could be fake? There are hundreds of scrolls, parchments, treasure maps and what nots, floating about the ether'

'It possible, but parchment have proof that … speak for itself ' 'So I take it that, this is what they want from you?'

He did not answer, he just stared ahead.

I digested his story as I turned into the car park of my hotel.

If any of this were true, then we were in a shit storm. Nothing provokes a man to murder than money, power or his faith. This was faith of the religious kind. "*Some*

*Secrets Must Remain Secret"*, the runic words carved on Francesco's chest would make sense if this were all true.

Something else also tickled at the back of head when he mentioned, priest. Something recent and quite important. I put it aside in the hopes it would come to me eventually.

'You realise the implication of this?' he asked me in a savage voice as I turned off the engine.

'So that's why you find it hard to trust anyone. Even someone who's saved your life?'

'You blame me?' 'Nope'

'So you understand?'

'Oh yes' I replied getting out of the car.

'Men of God are most dangerous people'

'Yeah, I get that, but I don't comprehend, why come here to this hick town?'

'Papa say if anything happen this be safest place to hide in plain sight. Something about intermittent blackout spots'

'I guess next time you should get rid of that distinctive car of yours. And the job?'

'I work in ladies salon during formative years'

There were three elderly gentlemen and one woman in the lobby of the hotel when we entered. I glanced at the desk clerk as I went past, he smiled at me with very supple lips. I returned his smile with a grin. A quick glance round the lobby informed me that there was no one there that was a threat to us.

'Did you know you unintentionally set your father up?' I asked Marion as we climbed the stairs.

'No' Marion said solemnly 'I not think of it. They kill him and your friend. They shoot them all, *mon Dieu*! Damn … *merde* it was a slaughter'

'You witnessed it?'

'I go into town. I just reach house when it happened. That poor *famille*, you know what happen to them?'

I recalled the folder Deputy Director Prideaux gave me 'The Ornithar's?'

'Is that their name?'

'The son, a kid of seven was the only casualty. I hear he is braindead'

'What was name?'

'Michael … I think' I said to him as we arrived at my hotel room door. I pulled out my Makarov, unlocked the door, and put on the light, the pistol in my hand leading the way. I glanced around then gestured for him to enter.

'*Mes plus sincères condoléances vont à lui*'

Marion went directly to the fridge and yanked out a couple of the complimentary mini-bottles ofliquor.

'You didn't know what they were going to do'

'*Ferme ta gueule* …. You think that making me feel any better?' he solemnly complained sitting down by the table and peeling the cap off one of the mini-bottles. '*Oui, le vieux con est un salaud du genre le plus bas*...but he good to me and he was … Papa. My Papa! And … *Je reçois... pauvre salaud a tué*'

'You can't help who your parents are or your actions involving them'

'You speak like faithless *crétin*' he grunted at me downing a bottle of bourbon in one gulp.

When he came up for breath, he tossed the empty bottle into the bin and selected another one. He held up a bottle 'You want?'

I shook my head.

I had to get protection for him no matter his tale was. I called Deputy Director Prideaux's number. A girl answered. After she scolded me as to the lateness of the hour, I told her I wanted to speak to the Deputy Director.

She said in a crisp, efficient voice that he'll call me back within the hour.

'Let him hurry. My panties are burning'

I hung up. Marion had downed three bottles and had popped into the bathroom. I heard him crying softly in the silence.

When he returned, he was all himself again.

'You said you had a visitor when you discovered the parchments, the person you suspect was a Priory member, who was he?'

He had to think for a moment 'Eh … Father … no … *Putain* … yes … Monsignor Halbert'

'Monsignor Halbert. He doesn't sound French' I remarked. 'No, he Italian, I think. I not sure'

'Italian, huh'

'He say he have Chapel in … near … the … ah *Golf de Sant Jordi* … Resu. That it, I think'

'Resu?'

'This Tyler, your friend? How well you know him?'

I never thought someone would ask me that. When I thought of it now, Tyler was a friend and that was just about it.

'Not well. He saved my once, I guess that made him a friend.'

'Your friend pick wrong day to visit, did he?'

'I guess so' I said stretching on the bed to relax.

He was silent for a long while. In that interval of silence, I closed my eyes in an attempt to relax. Then he asked the most obvious question I figured he had yet to ask.

'So tell me, what your story?' 'What do you mean?'

'What you do?'

I chuckled. 'Let's call me an out of work play girl' '*Jouer Fille*?'

'Tick tick tick'

'But you not work for the Feds or Mob or …, you not cop or Priory member, what your position in this?'

'I told you, I'm here for my friend' 'To avenge him?'

'If you say so. I just want to catch his killers'

'No, that not what I mean. I mean why you here? Why go to trouble to avenge a friend, he not special to you, eh? You two have … uh … *Comment vous dire - relation* ?… yes relationship?'

'Nothing like that, we never even held hands'

'It because you owe him debt, it is?' 'Not really'

'Then why do all this?'

For some reason, I got serious 'That's a good question' I paused then added 'When I figure it out, I'll let you know'

His question, though not inalienable to me, prompted me to think.

Why was I here? Why was I taking such large risks? For

my late friend Tyler, for justice, for creed, for prudence or honour? My flaws were plentiful, more than my character defects and yet I fight. Why? Why was I going through this? Was it because I like to fight? Why don't I just find a good man and settle down become a soccer mum, maybe join a carpool or the PTA of Bilquees and Nadia's school and run my empire from the safety of an executive office, just like Seymour wants me to? Maybe I was bored.

Why in God's name was I letting myself go through this? What the hell moves my values to pursue the bad and the wicked? Perhaps it was simple, I prefer justice in a certain way, not a business arrangement. Perhaps I did not believe a crime of passionate desires is a crime upon itself and someone or something must uphold a sense of justice or retribution. Conceivably, it could be because I enjoyed being the vigilantic arm of those unable to do for themselves. All these theories tingled within my mind and not one did I feel was exactly right for me. The shadows are no longer, where I strike but far away from me. I had no idea of what I was thinking. I had just the notion of doing well and being true to myself. Was this enough? I asked myself.

Marion dropped a bottle on the floor and the liquid spluttered across the floor. He stood up and looked yearningly at my body. 'Who you think send them butchers? The priory, the church maybe even Mob?' he asked softly

'Anyone is possible'

Still looking longingly at me, he whispered 'I hide from anyone who might find me, especially Ritchie's killers. You blame me for friend's death?'

It was true that the thought had occurred to me a few

times. The first time was when I first saw him in the camera phone Agent Lionel Bandler had shot. It still occurred to me that there were several questions still unanswered between us.

'Not as much as you blame yourself'

'I must to blame myself' he murmured 'Come here' I urged him rising from the bed

He fell into my embrace and leaned back so that we half sank, half fell together on the bed. He was whispering incoherently in French as I put a hand to his cheek to stop his lips with a kiss.

This was the time for *Kye-rumption*, a medieval word Seymour sometimes liked to describe as the commencement of a sway of appreciation between two people. Typically, an understanding between combatants.

'Don't, Robin' I whispered 'Don't be too hard on yourself'

He was taut and shaking at first as I made love to him, then passively grateful under my gentleness. Later came the tumult of release and then he became limp, with every nerve of his muscles unstrung. He slept with his mind empty, his breathing deep and regular, and a smile on his lips.

I lay there beside him, watching him breathe when my flip phone began to vibrate.

I snatched it up.

The same crisp, efficient voice of a girl answered me. 'Miss Dax, hold the line please, the Director will be with you momentarily'

A click and Prideaux's sleepy voice came on the line 'Miss Dax, what's the latest? No serious impediments from the car bomb, I hope?'

'Lionel is dead'

There was a brief silence 'How?' Prideaux asked suddenly awake.

'His head was smashed in' 'The perpetrator?' 'Unknown for now'

'Still no idea who your opposition is?'

'No'

I didn't feel it necessary to inform him about Marion's fanciful tale about lost and found parchments, the Priory and faith implicating religious beliefs.

'You sure it is not the Mob?' He enquired

I thought about what Steiner said he witnessed and the runic letters carved into Francesco's chest "*Some Secrets Must Remain Secret*". I tended to agree that it was not exactly the mob's style. Carving dead etymological letters into their Don was just a little too extravagant for them.

'It does smell and taste like the Mob but I'm not certain they're behind this'

'Marion Steiner?' 'In hand'

'You get results fast' Prideaux remarked favourably. 'I had some help. Now what?'

'I'm gonna send you an address of a safe house, please try and get there as soon as you can. I'll make arrangements. How hot do you believe your opposition is?'

'Scolding'

'Then you better get moving' He finished, hanging up.

# *SEVEN*

Half an hour later, Marion roused from his relaxed sleep and looked up at me with a smile on his face as I was putting on my lip-gloss in front of a mirror.

I had let him sleep because … well to me, it looked like he needed it.

'This nice of you' he said in his broken French English indicating the bed and the sex we just had. '*Je pense vraiment que j'en avais besoin*'

'Yes, you really did need it. *Elle* était *belle, n'* était-ce *pas* ?' I asked him as I splashed on a dash of make-up.

'Best I ever know'

'Such a shame because it's going to have to be short-lived' 'What you mean?' he asked rousing half-naked from the bed. 'We have to leave' I said glancing at my Versace patent-leather diva bag propped against the side of the door.

I had already parcelled up my stuff, which was not much, just my Versace patent-leather diva bag and Bottega hand purse that was tucked in one of the pockets of the diva bag.

I also attached one of the two microdot GPS bugs concealed in the bangle Brice had given me, to the bottom of Marion's left shoe.

I didn't want him unexpectedly stepping out on me again. After establishing and synchronizing the microdot frequency and signal to the tracking app on my phone I was satisfied that, I would be able to track him wherever he went or listen to his conversation if I needed. I did think of force pairing his phone to mine, in-effect clone his mobile phone, that way I would have the same effect. However, I had not seen him use a phone and even if I did, I would not put it past him to ditch his phone at the earliest convenience.

'Where's your stuff?' I queried. 'In your car' he replied

'Good, get dressed'

A sound pricked my attention. I cocked an eyebrow at the window. Something had alarmed my internal panic button because it tingled vehemently.

'There is problem?' Marion asked nervously pulling on his pants.

'Not really' I assured trying to sound positive 'Don't worry, everything is going to be OK'

'You believing that, do you?'

'Of course I do. I'm good at prophesising' I suggested as I moved over to the window.

I was trying to bolster his nerve. Actually, I knew we weren't safe until we were in the proper environment with trusted agents, like the newly received text message containing an address suggested by Prideaux.

I was over by the window watching, through a crack in the curtain, the scene before me that overlooked the hotel's parking lot. There were no lights, or figures of people or movement. My internal Spidey sense, however, was tingling rather fervently.

There was plenty we had accomplished and said, that at this moment, made us become a target.

In the silence, I put my senses into use, filtering out everything not strictly needed for our survival. My ears peeled, listening for faint sounds, my eyes watching, my mind was assimilating what could happen and calculated the responses. A scrap here, a chink there and I could almost tell where an enthusiastic assassin could be. To my gratification, there didn't appear to be any danger and yet my senses refused to hush. Somewhere I heard a toilet flush, a truck horn blowing nearby and in the distance, I think I heard a baby cry.

Something was off, but I couldn't exactly pinpoint where it was. Perhaps the problem was my blurring state of being. The condition where the scents, echoes and chills come less from my surroundings and more from within my head.

'There one question you not ask me?' Marion asked buttoning his shirt in the bathroom. I caught his reflected image from the mirror. 'You thinking to ask me?' he wondered.

'No' I bluntly said still seeking the environs for any strange movement. 'I figured you'll let me know in your own way when the time was right'

'You cool, you know. *Ici quelque chose que vous pensiez sur*'

'Excuse me?' Why was he asking about the is last thing I take off before you go bed?"'

'*Rien d'autre qu'un petit puzzle*. Just a riddle'

Ha! Another riddle. I was already racking my brain

with one riddle, I didn't need another one.

Marion tapped my arm 'You know why other faction who want me alive? They thinking I have Papa's retirement fund from Mob'

'You mean his million dollar pension?'

'You know about this?' He asked me as he switched off the light in the bathroom

'Yep' 'How?'

'Does it matter?'

'I supposing not' He replied turning off the lamp on the bedside table.

'Do you have it?'

'*Pour le meilleur ou le pire*'

'Good on you, let's get out of here'

He stopped me as I reached the door '*Hé!* '

'What?' I reached for the door handle and turned the knob. 'You not want any of this?'

I grinned at him 'I could care less, now let's get moving'

I pulled in the knob and opened the door. I didn't get to open it fully, a large shoulder rammed the door into me. I reeled backwards into Marion, my Versace bag flying from my hand as I plucked the Makarov from its holster. Still I did not get the chance to spring its safety and fire. A second body sprang into me hurling me over and into the bedside table. Before I could rise, the big man whose shoulder rammed into me caught me from behind and pinned my arms into my sides.

I heard a blow land on skin, followed by a thud. '*Merde*' Marion swore.

'Hold her' grunted a slightly built man who came

through the door and stood in the doorway.

Marion was on the floor a couple of feet between us.

I had been stupid. I had let my guard down and ignored my senses.

Driving my foot heel back, I caught the man behind me on the shin. He cursed but I failed in breaking his grip. He obviously knew what he was doing.

The other man scrambled across the room and struck me across the face with a .44 Remington Magnum.

Damn! He was strong, the blow I think busted my lip, loosened a molar and laced a cut on my cheek. Despite the blow, I brought my foot up, lashing for the groin of the man in front of me. Unfortunately, he had anticipated my move and stepped aside just out of my reach.

He chuckled to my surprise 'This chippy's a handful, Dan'

The big man named Dan was grunting, trying to hold onto me. I gyrated around and using my weight, I thumped him into the bedside table. The lamp crashed to the floor but Dan still held on. The other man moved forward and hit me again with a strike that felt like I had been smashed into a wall. My knees sagged under me and my head rang like a bell. I gulped in air and hung backward against Dan's tight grasp.

In a desperate move, I lunged backward against Dan's hold, driving him once again into the bedpost. He grunted in pain as I wrenched myself from his grip and brought the Makarov up.

His companion came in fast from my side and again cracked the barrel of the .44 Remington Magnum against the side of my head. I staggered sideways, dropped the Makarov, and would have fallen flat on my face if Dan's tight grip wasn't still holding me up.

'Kill the bitch' instructed the man in the doorway

'No! Do not. Do not kill her!' pleaded Marion from the floor 'I beg you not be killing her'

In physics, Newton's $2^{nd}$ Law, Force equals mass times acceleration. Interpretation, Put energy and determination behind any combat application. However, the $3^{rd}$ law of Newton states that for every action there is an equal and opposite corresponding reaction.

Action; I reeled back with every muscle in me with a determination that surpassed even me. Reaction; my opponent overcame my actions.

'Damn chippy' The big man Dan grunted, followed by a hit so hard with the back of his fist that I flew across the room, jarring and skidding against the wall before landing on the floor with my shoulders.

I tried to rise but I could not. He had literally blasted the wind out of me as I lay there between perception and oblivion. I passed out.

Slowly I struggled, out of a pit of darkness, slitting my eyes. I had no idea how many seconds I was out cold but I was still lying on my stomach against the wall.

My heart beat so loud, I thought it would burst out of me. The throbbing in my head was unbearable. I felt wetness drip from my nose and lips. I think I was blowing bubbles with every breath. My whole world is spinning. I try to slow it down but I can't so I resign myself to just listening.

Our intruders had pulled my jacket off my shoulders and half way over my breasts and down my arms to bind them. They had tied my wrists behind me with strips of the bed sheet. They had also tied my feet in the same manner. I moved my arms enough to know that they really did a good job of thrusting me like a chicken. I wouldn't be slipping out of my bonds that easily. I felt my forearm and almost grunted with pleasure when I felt Peko still strapped to my arm. They had not pulled my jacket down far enough to reveal his hiding place but they had inadvertently accomplished blocking its use.

'Paydirt m'man! This here brat will more'n make up for our troubles' one of the men was saying.

'You got yourself a damn tough missus here pal' I heard the thin man say with an accent I couldn't yet place. He padded towards me and prodded a foot into my side to see if I was still unconscious. I let him think I was.

'Do not be touching her' Marion pleaded shakily 'Leave alone' 'Or what?' He kicked me in the side, I barely moved 'Ah I see … you've knocked boots with her huh? Is that it eh … nice … was it good?'

Two of the men chuckled. The thin man to me seemed to have a perverse sense of humour. His accent now was at least identifiable to me. It was a cross between Italian and German. I watched through slitted eyes as his legs clad in dark blue cotton trousers, the size of tram rails and expensive Timberland black shoes turn away from me.

I observed without moving my head or any of my extremities and giving myself away. This must be the guy, Scarface meant about those who hired him and his cronies. Thin guy with expensive shoes.

'Just leave alone. This not her fault … she just showing up'

I heard a resonant slap. I was assuming the thin man had smacked Marion 'Who the fuck is she, Squirt? She a cop? Or from the mob?'

'I-I not know but she be good to me'

'Yeah we know. Know what she did to Nicky and his boys?' he hissed

'They … w-would have kill me if she not come to my rescuing' 'They were too easy on you. Know how much trouble they had in finding you?'

From the scuffle of feet Marion had done something that made the thin man shuffle back.

'Idiot' he cursed, followed by another hand smacking skin. '*Va te faire foutre*' I heard the milquetoast man-child hiss, followed by a spit.

'Goddamnit! Mr. Roche teach this French arsehole some fuckin' some manners'

I assumed the third man's name who had struck me with the magnum was Roche. I heard a tread of slow deliberated footsteps followed by a series of punches and slaps, then stop.

The thin man's voice became serious 'Katanga is very upset with us' he stated slowly 'She doesn't wanna hear any gimmicks we have in mind' he sniggered glancing at Roche

'I-I no-not know what you speaking a-about' Marion managed to sputter hesitantly.

'You like this bitch huh?' his voice grew more serious. 'You two make sheet music eh?'

'*T'es rien qu'un petit connard*'

'American, punk. Quit with the French stuff '

The slender man had no idea Marion had just called him an arsehole.

'Sh-she have no-nothing to doing with this' Marion complained 'Maybe not but she handles herself nicely'

Prudently, I shifted my limited gaze, trying to locate the men in the room. I could see to my right two huge feet and legs in dark pants and Obie type black shoes in a squatting position. The big man, Dan. The thin man was just off centre from me. I could not quite see Roche or Marion from my position. These men were professionals, just the type to perform a ruthless killing but they were not cold and/or efficient to perform a cold massacre.

I analysed the conversation. They talked with familiarity to Marion, a familiarity that seemed strained. Could it be these men, this Katanga, whoever she was, had entered an arrangement with Marion at some point for a share of his father's remuneration from the Mob or was it something else? Whatever the accord existing between Katanga and Marion, these men, maybe from the Mob were not associated with the murderers at the cottage in Castaic. I could be wrong of course, but then I could be right.

Dan, squatting nearby was searching through my stuff. He had already tossed out my underwear and change of clothes now he had dumbed the remainder on the floor. My make-up kit and brushes, my Sonic toothbrush, compact case, my Epilator, perfume, Straightening brush, nail polish, flip phone, my cocoa oil body lotions, Scholl Pedi, Vanity case and my *Javier Christian* No. 5 perfume which cost about £3500 an ounce, all lay untidily on the floor. I noticed he was inquisitive enough to sample the fragrance. Next, he went through my red Bottega hand purse. He took out the credit cards, inspected them before sticking them back in, the bundle of cash he found he appropriated it and then he found the wallet containing the special issued FBI credentials. The big man chuckled as he examined the creds.

'Hey buddy …!' Dan said tossing the wallet across the

room.

'Fuck! I don't believe it. Susan … Susan Dax' The thin man chuckled reading the FBI creds. I was not sure if his chuckling was in reverence or in superciliousness to me. I do know that he recognised my name. His feet turned towards me. 'This is Dax? Damn! The ball-breaking frikin' skank herself. Whoa … Mr Roche you remember?'

There was a pause before he answered 'God almighty, I remember. Jeeze, this that bitch Dax …! This her?' He queried in disbelief.

'What're you two talking about?' Dan enquired, his legs uncoupling as he stood up straight.

'You got the great Susan Dax covering your arse, boy?'

Looking up at the thin man Marion expressed his thought *'T'es un salaud'* Saying, "Fuck you" in French is not all that delectable. 'Geeze … I'm fucking impressed' the thin man said addressing

Marion.

'Like I say, I not know first thing about her. I just meet her and she helps me out of trouble with your men and she be around me since. I-I like her style'

'You don't know her?' he asked with scepticism in his voice as he squatted next to me.

'H-how would I?'

I wriggled my arm furtively, hoping to see if I could disengage Peko up my forearm. There was little chance I could because I was not in good shape. Despite my hair feeling damp from blood seeping out from a cut somewhere near my ear, my head throbbed with pain. I could also feel a cut on my lip and numerous little abrasions all over my body.

'Mr. Roche, should we acquaint our friend here about her?' 'Sure, Mr Silke, why da hell not?'

'We first heard about this bitch when she killed a Bravta boss, very lucrative business venture of ours in … where was it again?' The man Roche had called Mr Silke asked.

'Moscow …' Roche answered

'Yeah, the bookmaker' Silke augmented, grunting 'Yeah, him. We heard she shot him in the arse. Six years ago, she commandeered a boat of our former boss on its way to New York. It cost him more than $20 million in revenue and half his guys'

'Bad luck juju for him' Roche interjected 'We hear he no longer wit us'

'We also heard she once torched $50 million of the Albania Mob's cash because of a hooker' Silke remarked

'I hear it was $100 million' Roche corrected

'50, 100 million dollars what does it matter? She's a bitch troublemaker'

'That she fuckin' is. Did ya know she also took out the Quisqueya's couple of years ago' Roche added

'Quisqueya? The brothers?' Dan inquired turning his feet towards me 'I heard about 'em. This eensy weensy mud blood little bitch did that? Sheesh! You sure? … And she still fuckin' walks the planet?'

'Yeah because she's not that easy to kill, anyone tries and they disappear' said the squatted man next to me.

'She ain't fuckin' goin' nowhere now' Dan snickered

'No, she's not. Please get her up, Dan' Silke instructed as he stood up

The big man walked over to me and leaned down. He turned me over, running his hands down my body, pausing on my sensitive woman parts. When he was done, he stunned my face with a slap. Wheezing as though I was just regaining consciousness, I cracked my eyes open, then wider as a slap jarred me. I saw a neck like a bull resting on wide shoulders and atop of them was a face half mutilated by blows. His hand grasped at my blouse front pulling me up against the wall. The hand was large enough to cover both my hands and my feet.

'How're you doing, bitch?' Dan asked me.

If I could, I would have winced at the word "bitch".

When I spoke, the cut on my swelling lip made my voice sound as though I was wearing a pugilist's mouth-guard.

'I-I feel like I-I c-could take on Nicole Adams' 'Who?' the big man enquired

'N-Nicole Adams, our f-first f-female o-Olympic boxing champ' He chuckled.

Mr Silke stepped forward with a gun in his hand and for the first time, I saw the face tucked into the buttoned-down collar and necktie. He rammed the gun against my larynx, causing me to gag.

'Echhk!' I choked.

'What the hell are you doing here, slut?'

Ah! Was this Mr Silke about to pull a fast one against me? Pretending not to know of my intentions or who I was, was a good way to do that. 'I-I g-go w-where I'm needed' I mumbled

'Did the Feds or the mob send you?'

That question took me by surprise. I had assumed they were working for the Cosa Nostra or at least a dissident or disgruntled part of the organisation. His question put paid to that. Whom the hell did this cadre of bad guys belong to? This Katanga, perhaps. I flicked a glanced towards Marion who was huddled in the remaining chair. His fine boned face was precariously farcically pale and his soft eyes were filled with fright. He was worried not only for himself but about me.

'Talk, cunt or I'll put a slug through you' Silke requested angrily of me.

A glance into his eyes was enough to tell me he was not kidding.

I nodded 'Y-yes … the Feds' I hoarsely replied.

Jerking back the snout of the gun, he nodded at Dan who released my blouse front and let me fall back down against the wall.

There wasn't a hint of disappointment on Marion's inflamed face, which told me he didn't believe what I had just said.

'Hear that, Frenchie? You're in trouble with the Feds too. Not a good place to be'

Marion stared at me 'I-I taking m-my chances with them' 'You do that all right' Silke replied 'We just want our money.

Where is it?' he asked again.

'Y-you g-got Francesco killed' Marion complained

'The mob don't know that, at any rate we only pass on information. We had no part in his murder anyways whoever they were, they were after you, not him. Now where is our money?'

Their conversation hit me like a ton of bricks. If it were true, then Shaw's killers were after Marion. Why the hell

… it could not be for the money, could it be his tale of discovered parchments and the Priory of Sion had some substance?

*'Bê-bête comme ses pieds'*

If I could grin, I would have. Marion had literally compared Silke as stupid as his feet.

Silke held the gun to Marion's head 'You're an intelligent French little kiddie, aren't you?

'Tell me what happens if we don't get what we want?'

'Y-you kill us' Marion replied shakily. I could see by the chattering of his lips that Marion was terrified.

'Good boy' Silke chuckled, pulling back the safety of his weapon. 'Now once again, where is our money?'

'W-what if he doesn't know where it is' I interjected softly Silke turned to me and chuckled 'Ah Miss Dax, you finally get to join the conversation' he said picking up my wallet and tossing it over to me. 'Nice stich you got here, playing the Feds against the mob or is it vice versa. Which side are you on anyway?'

'Wwhat d-does it matter? A girl's got to eat'

Mr Silke chuckled, 'Nice one! Look, you are a smart woman, aren't you? Can you let this pile of crap know what will happen if he doesn't turn over our money?'

'He knows. Can't you see that he's scared to death?'

'Yeah he's scared, but I don't think he's scared enough. Most people would go through anything for a million bucks. I know I would' Silke gestured at Dan. 'Daniel, bring the car around, we may have to get serious with this punk. Somewhere out of the way might be a good idea'

'And if he doesn't talk?' Dan enquired.

'Dammit Daniel, you keep frettin' like this, you'll give yourself an ulcer'

'I won't get ulcer. What's more, I like fussing. Katanga doesn't' 'Hey, we've broken one of the Mob's law and about to break another. Then there's the Feds. We've spent months tracking this bastard down and now we have found him, things will definitely take a turn for the better, don't you think?'

'If we had the money, sure' Roche interjected

Mr Silke turned to Roche 'If he doesn't tell us, we'll find it some other way. We've killed for that money and I think we deserve it when we find it. Don't we?' Mr Silke turned to Dan. I noticed a glance pass between Silke and Dan. An exchange of understanding between the two that had been refined over years by a mutual trust. Much like Seymour and Me. 'Get the car' he turned to Roche again 'Relax … this will be worth it'

Dan watching the conversation between the two men paid more attention to Roche who was not really sold on Mr Silke's idea. However, the clicks in Roche's head accepted the idea and he nodded, turned, and exited the room.

Silke grabbed Marion by the hair and viciously yanked him out of the chair.

The last I saw of Marion, Silke and Dan were dragging him out of my hotel room.

# *EIGHT*

I heard a whimper from Marion before his voice was suddenly choked off. How they got him downstairs without anyone protesting, seeing or hearing was strange. Stranger still was leaving me up here to my own devices. I had no clue what they were going to do to him but I had a couple of ideas.

I heard another strangled cry, filled with pain and terror. I clenched my teeth and decided on a course of action.

First things first though, I had to get out of my binds. Peko was not only my option but he was the most convenient. A little flex of muscle at the right spot and he slid just short of my palm. Just then, one of the men came back into to the room, as I worked the blade down slowly then against my bonds.

'Look at you' he cynically said. It was Roche 'I thought you were a badass.'

'Marion is telling the truth you know, there's no sense in doing what I think you going to do to him'

'What d'you care? You're gonna die here any'now.

Besside's you don't fuckin' know those two. Especially Mr. Silke' I sliced off skin from my knuckle and winced. 'Bastard kindda enjoys this stuff and without beating around the bush so the fuck do I. Even if they believed the sonofabitch they still gonna enjoy themselves'

'How much does he owe anyway?' 'Plus the vig almost a million smackers' 'Jezus. He gambled a million dollars?'

'Gamble? What the fuck gave you that idea?'

'I assumed he got carried away … you know … waiting for that set oflucky cards …'

'No it was kindda of a loan to the Don' 'Loan? A loan to the Don?

'Yeah, we knew he was getting his yearly stipend that day which was meant for us but the arsehole stole it after the massacre. Our dough!'

'Your money?'

'Yeah, by all rights it's ours'

And if he didn't or doesn't have it?'

'He better, either way he meets his fuckin' maker' 'Is that what … Katanga would want?'

There was a brief hesitation in his step before he replied 'Fuck her! Bitch can go to hell. She doesn't play a part in this bessides she doesn't fuckin' care as long as she has her cut'

Could it be they were trying to pull a fast one on their employer, this Katanga?

'Boy, you guys must have got your jollies off in a twist back in Castaic when you came upon those bodies'

'Wish we did. All those bodies mushied up with severe lead poisoning. Damn whoever did that whoa …if we had weapons at the time Mr Silke would gladly have filled their bodies with more lead, all with a smile on his face, he's one crazy bastard'

'So you witnessed the bloodbath?' I enquired slicing into my bonds slowly.

'Nope, we arrived too fuckin' late for the show' he said sadly Despite his bombastic boast, I had confirmed my suspicions that this group of thugs were not responsible for the massacre at Castaic. Nor did they belong to the mob, but at one time, they did.

Marion's tale of unburied parchments and religious enigmas might just be authentic.

'Why wait till now to find him?'

'You should know? With the murder of a Don, there was gonna be a lot of heat about. Anyways, Marion was not easy to track'

I had almost forgotten the lie I'd told Silke, that I was sent by the Feds.

'I'm carrying out a contract for the feds, doesn't necessarily mean I'm with the mob'

'Whatever. We broke their laws. We heisted dough belonging to their Don, got him killed and interfered with their business. They've been looking for us harder than the Feds have. For Frenchie too, for different reasons I bet'

The prolific conversation was giving me precious time to slice my bonds loose and it had worked. The bonds cut loose. I propped my hand against my body so that the cut zip-ties did not fall and tried to prolong the conversation by asking him yet another question.

'How the hell did you find him? I thought I had the market on his whereabouts'

Roche walked over to me and with a matter-of-factly attitude, he slapped me across my cheek. 'You can thank the Feds for that. But enough of the stalling. You ain't getting loose, bitch' He produced a revolver and started fitting a silencer onto it 'Mr Silke gives me the jobs he ain't interested in. Meaning women and kids, he gets all-squeamish with those kinds of jobs. So he gets the Frenchie and I get you'

I had realised that the moment he had come into the room, he had come to kill me. The conversation was just his foreplay or perhaps, mine. If they wanted to be clear of the mafia, they naturally had to get rid of who they thought was their little errand girl. They weren't just going to leave me alive to report back to my masters. No way.

Squirming in my chair, I watched Roche back away from me as he tightened on the silencer. Beyond my arm's length. He scorned at my futile efforts to do something and raised the barrel of the revolver to point at me, like a cold and deadly eye. For a cursed second, I wished the turtleneck I was wearing had been fitted with my tactical laminated compacted silicon discs with ceramic matrices. It wasn't. With such a cutting edge body-armor that can take a pointblank 9mm gun blast, I would stand a chance against Roche's intention. It would hurt but there would be zero penetration. Unfortunately, this was goodnight for me, unless…

I heard more than saw the pop of the silenced weapon and felt the bullet tear into my chest like a blazing-hot bolt oflightning. I reeled backward as the soaring stab of pain hit me. My recoil was fast and as unexpected to him because I rose like a fish out of a pond, tearing away from my wrist bindings to pounce on him. It was an act of desperation on my part. It was either this or my corpse laying on the ground without fight in it.

His backing away did no good as my left hand took hold of his gun wrist, while my other hand, clutching Peko, sought his stomach. His disbelief was what I expected. He shot at me a second time but thankfully the gun's silencer was directed slightly away from me. His bullet was only good enough to sear the skin off my neck. It was like a bee sting, no more. Fortuitously, Peko's strike was much more intimate and aggressive. He slid with spearing force through Roche's tummy flesh, sliced into his kidney, upward and twisted the pulpy spongy organ before exiting. His second perforation, which was mini-seconds after the first one, went all the way through his belly button, slicing through the small intestines. My eyes stared into the grey pupils of Roche's eyes as he stared into mine with shock and dismay. Not quite believing what was happening.

We both stood there motionless looking into each other's eyes.

'T-the fuckin' rumours were true' he whispered as he stepped back away from me as Peko withdrew out of his fleshy skin, all bloody and wet.

'Rumour?'

'You really ... are a badas ...' he went limp as he dropped to his knees.

Slowly, he stretched out on the carpeted floor and lay still. Blood gushing out from under him. I stood there over him feeling the burning pain in my chest.

For some reason, my legs felt weak and my vision was fuzzy. I was paralyzed with weakness. I had to lie down and I did. Lying on my side, my turtleneck blouse blotted with blood. I gazed helplessly at the ceiling. Darkness was creeping in through the corners of my mind. I thought about Seymour and how he'd react when he learns of my death. I suppose he'd go mad with grief and probably go on a vengeance tour before he focused on my assets. As executor of my will, he would find it tedious trying to control a multi-billion dollar empire on behalf of my two wards, Bilquees and Nadia. I thought about Bilquees and Nadia. Bilquees at that moment was in the process of seeking a college of her choice while Nadia was at some computer camp. How would they react to my death? I had no idea. Yes, they would take it hard but how would they mourn? I thought about Deputy Director Prideaux and his reaction. I bet he would react the same way when he heard his agents luck had run out. Brice Darlow, Marion Steiner, all my friends, their disappointments, and the corollaries to the news of my demise. How will the stock market react to my death? It seem curious, but I had not really cherished the thought of anybody's reaction before now.

Before my mind disappeared into darkness, I pressed on the implanted bio-chip under my left arm, hoping the signal would alert Seymour in time.

Coalescence! Resolve! Form! Recognition! Focus!

Damn it! I was not going to die here. Like a swimmer bursting out of a pool to come out for air, I burst out of the darkness that had begun to engulf me. I couldn't explain it, but I think my appreciation for life or that spark of guile or alacrity to live, made me break out from the cloudy barriers that were seeking to pull me into that eternal night.

My eyes slowly fixed on the ceiling and brought it into a blurry focal point. I was breathing shakily and my normal concept of time was off. I had no idea how much time had passed, which was damn inconvenient. I had no idea how long I had been unconscious.

The hotel was silent, caught in an eerie stillness. A faint light had pierced the room as though dawn had arrived. Silke and the big man Dan had not returned. Roche still lay dead next to me. Since Roche had not returned they should have at least checked to find out what had held him up or just find out what had happened. Could this be good news for me?

From outside I heard a car, from the sound of the engines horsepower it was a powerful vehicle. It parked in front of the hotel. I lay listening, praying and hoping as the car's door opened and slammed shut. For quite some time, there was silence. Then I heard footfalls down the corridor, approaching my hotel door.

I worked my mouth, but no sound emanated came out. I tried to move but my muscles failed to co-operate besides I was too weak and my continuing blood loss was no help. Especially when I did try to move, the ceiling above me began to dint and palpitate and I almost passed out.

I heard the steady and soft footsteps approach. I was dreading the return of Silke and his companion big Dan. However, I was partially relieved when the footsteps stopped and I heard a tap on the door. Only someone who did not expect what was behind the door would knock. The doorknocker tapped on the door again before gently trying the doorknob.

The door slowly opened and a big man with broad shoulders in a ridiculous Hawaiian shirt with an Austrian Glock .24 in his hand, appeared in the doorway. He surveyed the room.

I grunted with relief. I must say the joy within me was extraordinary. I had no words to describe how I felt inside.

He heard my grunt as he stood like a colossus over me, inspecting the room with those steel eyes of his, while his gun covered everywhere else. Seymour was a good shot when it came to rifles but a poor one when it to handguns or revolvers. The pistol in his hands looked small in his big hand and his body even clothed in that ridiculous Hawaiian shirt looked hard and well- muscled. Satisfied, he closed the door gently behind him, slipped the gun into the small of his back and without a word, he stepped over the dead body of Riche and crouched beside me.

With his big hands, he ripped off my blouse and inspected my wound. My naked torso did not faze him neither did his examination bother me. Over the years, we've both had injuries that needed each other's knack of medical experience. His steel pale blue eyes scrutinised me thoroughly. He looked just like I last saw him.

My own personal butler with an automatic pistol for an umbrella and a hard right cross instead of scrambled eggs.

Seymour Reginald Krakauer was a big man, who was an inch shy of six feet. He was approximately fifty-two years old, with greying temples within dark well-groomed hair and pale blue eyes set in a face hardened by experience. An experience that I was not totally aware of. On the top ridge of his left ear was a two-inch scar that contributed to his sixty percent deafness for a good seven years of so. How he it got that way was a mystery to me.

With his aid, I shakily but painfully sat up. My pink caramel skin displayed blue-black wiry veins around the chest wound that troubled him. Seymour paid close attention to my breathing and circulation. Indications of my muscle paralysis were very apparent.

Snapping off the bed sheets from the bed, he began ripping it into strips.

In an essence to prevent any thoracic damage to my body, his first duty was to quickly and solely control the haemorrhage I was undergoing and prevent any contamination. He had to expedite and re-establish my possible survivable physiology.

He used a makeshift pad from the strips and placed it on my chest while using a strip to form a necktie for the wound on my neck. He slowly propped me against the wall and went into the bathroom and returned with a hotel first-aid kit, a glass and toothbrush. On his way back, he turned the key within the door lock because he did not want to be disturbed with the delicate procedure he knew he had to perform.

From the first-aid kit, he laid out all the remedial medical necessities he would need for a makeshift operating stand. Seymour directed me to open my mouth.

Breathing precariously, I did as ordered.

'Bite down' he instructed me, as he braced the stem of the toothbrush in-between my teeth. After smearing some lidocaine emulsion around the bullet hole, he went to work. Extracting the bullet within me was no easy undertaking. It took him several tries with me shrieking inaudibly for him to get the fragments of the bullet out. But out they came, with a great deal of blood following in their wake.

I was not pleased to say that with the room spinning, and my endurance for some reason was at an all-time low, I had to black out but pass out I did.

When I came to, I was surprised that in no time at all, he stopped the bleeding and had begun winding the bedsheet strips around my chest like a bandage. I noticed that I had almost bitten through the stem of the toothbrush before passing out.

After spreading over another solvent, this time on my neck, Seymour tighten the necktie over the gash on my neck.

'Him?' he finally asked, using his chin to point at the corpse in the room with us.

I nodded weakly.

He made a conceited little chuckle as he threw a blanket around me. I knew what that meant. He was proud of me. I had cleaned up my own mess even if it nearly killed me.

I caught sight of my reflection in the nearby mirror. I did not like what reflected back. I mean, it was no surprise that I looked like an ashen murky-pale sheet. However, to see the smear of blood on my chest and neck and the haggard nature of my hair was not one I'd like to see again.

I said nothing, I still couldn't. There was not much to say.

Seymour was inspecting the largest fragment of the bullet. He gave it a once over with his eyes then sniffed it. His reaction to the stink of the splinter told me that the slug had been coated with something other than gun oil. He put it to my nose. The scent made me wince. I knew that smell of calabash and bamboo or *D-Tubocurarine*, the main ingredients of *Curare*.

Seymour nodded. 'Yep, Curare.' he glanced at the corpse across the room 'Sonuvabitch' he cursed. Seymour rarely cursed but when he did, he meant it.

Curare! No wonder I felt this way. I had been shot before. Not once or twice, but many times. Once, I was even shot twice and stabbed, but compared with those injuries, the pain and my debilitating condition was much more worse. I had attributed my condition to the region of where I had been shot, but no. The toxic substance within my blood definitely was the cause of my delirious, paralytic, and weakened state.

I had unceremoniously been poisoned.

Curare was a poison that originated from South America and functions mainly as a competitively inhibiting nicotinic acetylcholine receptor. In other words, it wreaks havoc with muscles and if administered in sufficient dose it can cause death by asphyxiation due to muscle paralysis of the diaphragm.

Not many thugs varnish their bullets with a toxic substance.

Roche was indeed a singular kind of bastard.

Seymour hurried got to his feet and with his eyes searched the room for something but his eyes could not find what he was seeking. He quickly made his way to the door and disappeared for a couple of minutes. He returned with a half-filled jar of nestle coffee. I should have known. Coffee grounds were a quick and easy analgesic to Curare. He gently lifted up the improvised dressing and sprinkled half a handful of the coffee grounds over my chest wound. Then pleaded with me to swallow some of it. He knew I did not drink coffee but I understood that he was using the caffeine within the coffee grounds as an adenosine receptor or more specifically as a therapeutic inhibitor. It was a speedy and convenient way to halt the Curare poisoning within my system. It may even have the biochemical properties to possibly reverse it. With everything done, Seymour stared into my eyes with those flinty steel eyes of his, probing. He knew better than to say anything, besides he was quite incapable of saying anything at this moment in time because despite all his enduring gifts, he never spoke out of turn. To him, I was his ward and master, his responsibility and more importantly, according to him someone who should never question my will.

I turned my head in an effort to find my phone. I spotted it in a corner. I lifted a finger to point at it before glancing at Seymour. Finding my voice, I muttered 'Marion'

Seymour went over to it and picked it up. He fiddled with some image apps before turning to me with a contented grin.

I grinned weakly. He had found the tracking app and hopefully the signal emanating from the microdot bug I had planted on Marion.

He picked me up, carried me outside into the hot morning air, ignoring the looks we got and folded me into the back seat of a car. He disappeared for a couple of minutes maybe longer and returned. He climbed in behind the wheel and drove off. I closed my eyes.

* * * * * *

I cannot say how long we were in the car because I passed out again. Pain somewhere on my person made me regain consciousness in a strange room.

Everything hurt.

Sandpaper scrapes my skin, no not sandpaper, but sheets. Starched sheets.

I'm in a room somewhere, on a gurney. There are several smells, chemical smells of disinfectant, ammonia, antiseptic all that seemed part of a medical facility. I smell someone full of bathtub sweat quite close to me and someone with panic ingrained in their musky masculine smell. A smell I was familiar with. The bathtub sweat belonging to a feminine person injected me in the arm with a long syringe while Seymour, standing over her, kept watch. I can feel the long needle, but I was barely able to respond or move to reveal my discomfort.

I felt everything.

From what little I could make out from their conversation, it revolved over the novelty of my thoracic trauma and how I was the luckiest female she had ever met. Apart from the intermittent gunshot wounds that occurred over hunting season, I was the first to be treated not only for a gunshot wound but also from an exotic poison.

'She is damn lucky'

'She ought to be' Seymour replied agreeing with her.

All my mind could muster was the fact that I was lucky but Marion's faith was still unknown and that maybe he is not as lucky as I am.

I passed out again.

Next, I woke up in another room, another unfamiliar room.

Seymour was standing next to me, while I sat propped up in a couch. He glanced at me before turning to look at something on the floor. I turned my head and saw Marion, who lay motionless near a chair where he had been tied. The strips of cloth that bound him still dangled him from the chair's arm and lower rung.

'Robin … Marion …' I hesitated, 'Larry?' I called.

The fact that he did not move or reply to any of his names, real or imagined, did not surprise me. I felt a deep sadness and regret. I shakily got to my feet with Seymour's help. I knelt beside him and felt his pulse.

His skin felt cold. His fragile man-boy face was infirm, stagnant and bruised. With Seymour's aid, I loosened the bonds round his wrists and ankles. I could not help but feel a great feeling of disappointment as I untied him. Silke and Dan had really savagely worked him over.

Turning him over, I spotted a small black book under him. My fingers closed around it. Flipping through the pages, I could see it was an address book of sorts. I handed it to Seymour.

I touched his cold outstretched arm and closed my eyes for a minute to get my emotions under control and whispered a little prayer over his body. When I opened my eyes, I started inspecting the body.

I saw that he had been killed by blow so powerful it had broken his neck. The one man that could deliver such a blow was Dan. "That goddamn sonuvabitch," I thought.

I felt not only abject failure but also, a certain culpability. I had failed him. Failed to protect him. I was alive and he was dead. However, underneath my poignant cockup and remorse, there was an emotion that filled me with fortitude, and that was rage. I would come out of this and hunt down Silke and Dan. I would do it because I could and felt that Marion Steiner would deserve it.

I turned to look at Seymour.

Despite the pain and my weakness, I said to him 'Let's get out of here'

He cuddled me again and took me out to his car. For the first time I saw where we were. It was Marion Steiner's apartment building. I was here only last night. How time flies.

I did not know where we were going but when we got there, Seymour drew me a bath. He slowly showed me his eyes and methodically with his hands carefully probing the muscles of my body, he undressed me. After he was done, he removed his makeshift strappings, wrapped me in a full-length towel, then picking me up in his arms he carried me into a bathroom and immersed me in the three-quarters filled tub of hot water. He lathered my body and hair just the way I like it, then washed it. He devoted a lengthy time to my injuries before letting me float free in the tub. With my body floating free, he rose and looked me in the eye. He gave me a small grin then left.

With Seymour gone, I lay still until I think the water cooled. The old man came in, took one look at me, and pulled me up and out. My nakedness didn't bother me, neither did it bother Seymour. A testament to the faith we had in each other. Removing the stopper of the bath, Seymour let the water drain out of the bath then turned on the shower. It was chillingly cold.

I gasped with breathlessness as he held me under the shower for several minutes then slowly he added hot water to the cold. A few moments, later he turned the shower off, wrapped a towel around me and my hair then carried me up out of the bath like a teddy bear into a bedroom.

After placing me on the bed, I just lay there looking very despondent. Seymour had found another medical kit and towel. After he dried my hair, he tended to my injuries, renewing the bandages.

I looked up at Seymour and asked 'How am I doing, old man?'

He finished tending to my hair and walked into my sight. 'I think you might need a nurse'

'I have you, why would I need a nurse?'

'I'm not omniscient'

'You very nearly are' 'The girls send their love' 'You told them?'

'You never wanted me to keep anything from them' 'How did they take it?'

'You know Bilquees, as always she is very despondent' Seymour reported 'Nadia … well she can go through anything and still be able show no emotion. I bet that girl can be at the centre of a nuclear blast and still come out unscathed'

Chuckling faintly, I mused 'She's had a hard life. She still at that camp of hers?'

'No. Mrs Gillespie thought they it might be better if they were together in case the worse happened'

Mrs Gillespie was Nadia and Bilquees's nanny. A woman with three degrees, one in paediatric care, and the other in business management but whom for years had fallen on hard times. She was also the housekeeper for my homes in Bath and London.

'How very morbid of *Meme*' Meme was our nickname for Mrs Gillespie. 'What time is it?'

'Ten past eleven mi' lady' he noted 'Am or pm' I signed

'AM Susan, very AM'

I looked up at him 'When did you get in town?' I asked ignoring his last statement

'Last night'

'I take it … you … found …?' I did not finish the question but he understood what I was enquiring about.

'Yes. Polé'

I sighed, comprehending completely.

Polé Polé was the new name of Cancer. My organically bio-organic powered subdermal transmitter implanted bio-chip under my left arm. An updated zero emission implant made up of a rare isotope that can monitor me and my vital statistics through a GPS signal that can be picked up anywhere in the world by a low frequency encoded wavelength to a multitude of embedded relay receiver via the internet. A signal that Sir Galahad, my AI Homesaver Unit 6000 at my penthouse home in London, constantly monitors. My implant's tag is Cancer, while Capricorn was the tag of the subdermal implant in Seymour. Both implants were personal guarantees against either of us being seriously hurt, lost or kidnapped.

'Where are we?'

'Beltway Hotel in the lovely town of Concorde, two towns from Prine'

'Nice'

'I ran into three very bruised bikers' He paused pondering 'but it took a while for Galahad to lock onto you ... when he eventually did ... well you know the rest'

'Galahad alerted you yesterday and you rescue me a couple of hours later?'

'Actually, Susan I heard about the car bomb and was already on my way, furthermore I did have one advantage'

'Yeah and what pray tell was that?' I moaned

'You' he teased

I tried to laugh but couldn't muster the energy. Instead, tears welled up within my eyes and my body started to shake. Seymour knew I was feeling the sting of frustration and regret and wrapped his arms around me, just holding me.

After about five minutes, I let go and lay back on the bed. 'What's my prognosis?' I asked my manservant and guardian. 'Forty-two percent effective'

'Think I can make it?'

'You might want to fill me in on where you are at, at the moment'

He was right. He more than anyone ought to know what I've been up to. I filled him in with my investigation so far. He listened until I was done.

'You think they've got to the money?' 'Yeah'

'Including the vig … whatever that is'

'A commission of interest or tribute for the bosses patience in letting you have this time' I replied

'What?' 'Nevermind'


For the next day and a half, I relaxed as best as I could. It did wonders for me because I at least got half my stride back. Seymour had booked the whole floor of the hotel where my room was situated so he could both work and keep an eye on me without distraction. So while he worked on the financial stabilities of my various companies and creating a separate list of potential Operations Officers for our proposed Petronas Corp, I could move around and analyse the five female names in the black book Seymour and I retrieved. It got to a point when I was healed enough to exercise and even if it came down to it firing a weapon.

A day later, when I felt I was ready to get underway, I made the decision to leave. Yes, I was still weak but I felt close to par.

'Lagarde is still undecided about Germany's Brexit economic outlook' Seymour whined.

I thought for a moment trying to figure out who Lagarde was. Then I remembered, Ms. Christine Lagarde was the International Monetary Fund's managing director.

'I bet he's waiting for Chancellor Hammond to have a greater clarity about Britain's post-trade rules' I commented

Seymour glanced at me with approval. 'And here I was thinking you weren't paying attention'.

Out the window in the hotel's parking lot was my souped-up Shelby sitting there, waiting. Seymour, I assume had it brought over from Prine the day before. According to him the Prine Police were in the process of putting out an all points bulletin for my arrest. The rash of fatalities was making them very uneasy indeed. Prideaux had forestalled the questioning and pressure for now at least, but they still wanted explanations and answers.

I wasn't bothered with all that. All my energies were concentrating on finding my adversaries. Silke and Dan had two days head start on me, it was better that I get moving. I had no intention of letting their trail get any colder.

'Zeno-Tech and UIC aren't doing great this quarter' Seymour grumbled, trying to discourage any intentions I was in the process of having.

UIC Holdings is an electronic research, innovative and testing company that provide and test military equipment and/or components that include bulletproof jackets, cruise missiles and unmanned aerial vehicles. A subsidiary of mine that supply and test weapons for US and NATO nations, like United Kingdom, France and Germany.

As for Zeno-Tech, it was once a decrepit little bioresearch company that had nothing to offer except a staff that comprised of brilliant research scientists whom on Seymour's advice, I salvaged. It took a while but after an influx of funds, the result was an enterprise that grew out of the shadow of not only its competitors but also its rivals and now flanks them in its own right with about forty-seven commercial patents. Making it a trailblazing research organization.

'That isn't right' I said opening one of the drawers of the dresser and extracting my Makarov.

'I know what the problem is, it's getting round it and benefiting from it is the problem'

'Then get assertive within our rules'

'It might take two quarterly seasons to make …'

'Where did you say The Wilhelmina parked the jet?' I abruptly inquired, disrupting his thoughts.

Wilhelmina "The Wilhelmina" Sapir is my personal pilot who was once a grade A certifiable test air force pilot who fell on the wrong side of the law once up a time.

After she was shanghaied from the air force, she was a dope courier for some drug lord. Then she made an unforgiving mistake but the good sense to be prudent. She served time in Calverton penitentiary and was banned for a number of years by the FAA after flying under the influence. When I heard of her I figured, from my point of view, she was an excellent pilot and an instinct of mine told me she was someone who given the right impetus, I could not only trust but benefit from. For six years now, she has been doing the job excellently and as far as I know, she has lived her life clean with just the sporadic misstep here and there.

Pausing in his reading on a laptop, Seymour raised his head and peered at me with a flinty glare. 'You hate me, don't you? You want to see me suffer?'

'C'mon old man, whatever gave you that idea?'

'Whatever makes you think I'll veto any idea of you going after these killers from the wolfpack brigade, given your condition?'

'I doubt you will' I replied 'But you know I can handle this. If I didn't feel up to it, I'll tell you'

'Why do I find that hard to believe?'

I chuckled as I began strapping on my shoulder holster, Peko's sheath, and my other good luck charms. Not forgetting the two jackets that were embedded with my Ceramic and silicon next generation amour.

Sighing Seymour asked 'Tell me, this is simply a question of finding out what happened to Agent Shaw, is it not?'

'It started that with him, but I don't think it will end with him and you know it's not'

'Avenging Marion too?'

I stared across the table at him. 'You going to disagree?'

'No. Remember what the Chinese say about seeking revenge?' I grinned at his tight expression and said 'I've already dug my grave. Besides Mr Silke is a sadist who'll go on killing if no one stops him. You saw Marion's body. He and that mate of his enjoy

the rough stuff '

'I know. I just don't want you ending up as one of his casualties or by Marion's sandal wearing monk from the Priory, it they exist' 'It's very likely' I joked as I dialled the number of Deputy Director Prideaux's private line and set the speaker option setting.

When he was on, I said 'Director, Susan'

I am not sure, but I think I heard a sigh of relief escape his lips 'I'm glad you're up and about' he said over the line.

Hoping I didn't sound like a truant playing hooky, I replied 'Thanks ever so much for your platitude, Director'

'How the hell are you?'

'You know what happened, you don't need me to tell you anything different'

'Yeah, your man Krakauer informed me of the situation. You ok?' I glanced at Seymour who was watching and listening attentively to our conversation.

'If I weren't would you care?'

'When you didn't show up at the safe house, I got concerned. British subjects on my watch don't usually end up dead you know, Miss Dax. I did hope you were planning on calling me at some point to let me know you weren't among the dead'

'Well, I'm calling now' I replied glancing at Seymour. 'I was sorry to hear about Mr Steiner'

'Of course you were'

'Truly I was and I've been thinking of assigning someone else as reinforcement or to take over the investigation completely. Would you mind that?'

'No director, I wouldn't. I'd like to see this through'

'Alright Miss Dax, I'm going to allow you one more go

at this on your terms. Go get the bastards'

'Oh well' I said rolling my eyes 'Director you are aware that your security has been seriously breached?'

'I know and I did warn you. I've had a pack of mavericks from our advanced computer division nit-picking through our system. It's a direct challenge and an affront to us'

'Well your first suspects should be mafia cohorts with players working your system'

'I agree, they've been seeking Mr Steiner for a while not to mention a prominent member of theirs whom they promised security and retirement was killed on their watch. If he weren't already dead, they wouldn't be kind when they caught up to him'

'No they wouldn't.

'Your conclusions are a bit off target. Marion was Larry Steinberg … Francesco's son'

'His son?' the Deputy Director blurted with amazement in his

voice. 'You sure?'

'Would I lie about something like that?'

'His son?' he repeatedly exclaimed, his voice filled with incredulity.

'Yes. I think they were after him to provide protection or more importantly to see if he had his father's retirement money or  perhaps check out if he was a witness to those that assassinated his father but I think somebody in their coterie had other intentions'

'What does your friend think?' 'Friend?'

'Miss Golighty'

'You mean Elena? You think the families would allow such information to go blundering out to an outsider?'

'I see your point'

'Besides this Mr Silke didn't seem to be working on behalf of the mob. He once did, but it's a good bet he isn't now'

'I think there is something else you should be aware of ' 'And what pray thee would that be?'

'Have you had a look at Mr Steiner's autopsy report?' 'No'

'Well you should. Here, I'm sending you photographs of …' he paused 'Take a look. They are imperceptible to the naked eye. Our ME found them by a curious case of happenstance and ingenuity. This can only be view by using ultraviolet lighting'

'Black light?'

'Florescent lighting, that's correct'

My phone buzzed as three close-up pictures of Marion's corpse filled the 18.50 mm screen.

I sucked my breath through my teeth.

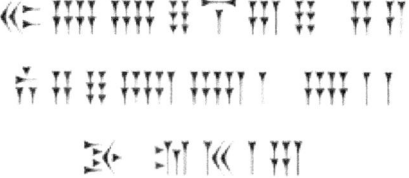

There were snapshots of a specific region of his body.

The sole of his feet. On each of them were tattooed writing of very weird symbols that resemble nothing I could identify. A linguistic script of some kind or just linear decorations. One set was on his right sole, the other on his left. What the hell persuaded Marion to do this to himself and why. They didn't resemble any language I have studied. They were not Greek, Erdogan, Sumerian, Latin, or even Runic. No, this was all Greek to me.

I let Seymour have a glimpse before asking the man on the other line what language was it.

The Deputy Director let out a resigned breath over the phone. 'We have no idea'

'I beg your pardon? Those poorly paid cryptologist and linguistic connoisseurs of yours can't ascertain their origins?'

'It's a complete mystery to them but they will crack it … eventually' he confidently replied 'Another odd thing, he only recently had them tattooed'

'How recent?'

'At least, within the past three months, about the time before he met his …' he let out a sigh of sorts '… his son? … I'm still trying to wrap my head round that one. Anyway … just before he met up with his … father'

First, letters of a runic origin and now an undecipherable one, I thought to myself. What would be the significant of this, I pondered. I was still deliberating within my head when it struck me, like a bolt out of the hell.

The connection.

'Three months … you say … Blue blistering barnacles … I should have figured it out sooner'

Seymour glanced at me with a cocked eyebrow. 'The boyfriend!' I exclaimed suddenly

Both men were stunned to silence.

'The boyfriend?' Seymour was first to ask. 'What boyfriend?' 'Bruce ... er ... Windemill. The nurse's boyfriend'

'Of course' chimed in the Deputy Director 'He worked part- time at a tattoo parlour, he was the tattooist. He did them and given Marion's disappearance within those months, he would have an inability to walk anywhere. Nurse Feldman would certainly know what medication to prescribe, what would be needed for him to heal and mend very quickly'

'Not only that, he was training to be an electrician or engineer. Someone with easy access to a mobile electronic jammer, like the one they used at the cottage' I added 'They were killed just for that?' I stated glancing at one of the photos.

'There are definitely some pieces fitting and missing from this puzzle' Seymour concluded

'I think so to. Maybe those mafia analysts of mine could figure out some of the pieces and come up with a theory huh?'

'Hey, you know how the mob thinks. They rarely dish out information unless it benefits them greatly' I reminded the Director again.

'I know but they just might be generous to someone with a reputation such as yours'

I was silent for a while before speaking again 'I'll look into it' I emphasized.

'Good and try if you're able, figure out our Marion's movements from the time he arrived in the US'

'Shouldn't you be looking into that?' Seymour interjected 'You're the FBI. The big grey overcoat G-Men of the law. You guys are pros when it comes to tracking and filing away useless junk like that'

'True, but we rarely have such aid as yours'

'It won't be easy' I stated glancing at Seymour 'But then two heads are better than one, and all that jazz. Right … we both check … a good place to start would be the renaissance exhibition in LA. That's where your surveillance first got wind of him, yes?'

'I think so'

'Marion must have interacted with the nurse and her boyfriend at some point. So we at least have a time reference point'

'And in the meantime, what will you be doing? Do you have any leads to follow from here on?'

I glanced at the table, next to Seymour's laptop where the black book we recovered from Marion's house rested and thought about mentioning it to him. Seymour's doubting look advised me otherwise.

'Maybe one or two. Any luck with the weird carving on Francesco's chest. Got anywhere with that?'

'No. Apart from it being runic and from some medieval society in Germany, we have nothing on it'

I wondered whether I should inform him of Marion's parchment story. Given the odd occurrences with the strange writings, it only seemed proper for me to inform him of all Marion shared with me. Only thing that stopped me was that he would think I was losing it and doubt my ability to carry on with this undertaking of mine.

'How about Dan, can you ID him for me?'

'From the witnesses description, he's the size of the iron

giant. When our hardware is back up and doing what its supposed to be doing, it shouldn't be too hard identify him or his cohorts and pinpoint their location'

'Great. Get back to us when you do' 'All right'

'Have a good one'

I tapped the "End Call" icon and turned my head towards Seymour. He was flipping through the pages of the black book.

'Tell me, are you really going to pay each of these girl's visits?' It was a slim lead but I had to start somewhere.

'How else am I going to track Silke? One of them is bound to point me in the right direction'

'If the other side don't get to you first' 'Then I better hurry' I said 'I need money'

'Five names, three cities' he remarked getting to his feet to make his way to his briefcase 'This guy had lady friends all over the country. Given your condition, can your system take it?'

'Not this again?' I complained reaching for the black book but Seymour was in no rush to hand it over.

'Oh please forgive me for my concern mi' lady' he bantered as he reached into the briefcase and pulled out a thick bundle of hundred dollar bills.

'Blimey, Seymour if you want to be my crutch, why don't you just say so?'

'I would but I've got too much to do. Your empire doesn't run itself you know'

Heading towards the dresser, I gripped softly to myself 'Pray thee for the head that bears the Crown'

'What was that?' he feigned asking 'Oh nothing'

'This is more than a book Susan. You do realise that?' he noted 'It's a sexual diary. You read this, didn't you?'

'Yes' I replied 'Pretty spicy stuff '

'It's like describing the Kama Sutra for depraved adults. Check out Lisa in San Diego, she sounds extraordinary'

'Maybe you should make notes and suggest using some of them with Martha' It made him think awhile before he chuckled. 'Anyway I like some of the references he made of Nora in Vegas'

'You are loving this, aren't you?' 'It will be a fun trip all right'

He closed the black book and tossed not only the book but also the thick wad of notes. The bank strap binding the money tipped me off to the fact he had just tossed me $20,000.

'What else, mistress? Anything I need to know?' 'No' I lied 'Whatever else could there be?'

'Just asking'

'Marion made a big impact on you, didn't he?'

'I wouldn't know. I didn't know him long enough'

What I hadn't mentioned was that there was another lead I was following and that was Katanga, Silke's female boss. Also, one of the names in Silke's book could belong to the person who actually knew Marion Steiner, personally. It was only later that I realized I was chasing Marion's ghost as well as his killers.

I was out the door before Seymour could think of other protestational expressions to stop me.

# NINE

In the previous days, since I was last in the city of LA nothing about it had changed. It's climate, like most Mediterranean countries, was still serenely beautiful as were most of its occupants. However, like most of its inhabitants, I could do without the smog, which I could swear had grown just a tad thicker.

My first port of call after booking into a third-rate motel was to Christina in LA. Not that it was closer but because most of my explorations began there. Marion said he was in LA before proceeding to Castaic. At one point, Ritchie Francesco was in the city shortly before he took up residency in Castaic. So were else was I to begin.

I was wondering how Christina, who had been rated eight in Silke's sexual *"Who's who"* register would compare with myself or the many blondes and brunettes sunning themselves in bikinis waiting to be discovered for the great American dream of stardom. It was early in the evening when a female voice answered the call I made to the number in Silke's black book next to Christina's name. The voice sounded disappointed when she heard my voice and even more so when I enquired after Christina.

'I'll get her' the female voice informed me. While I waited, I could hear in the background the clinking of glasses and the bustle of people playing cards.

I was sweltering in the heat and felt like I wasn't myself at all. The humid hot weather coupled with the wad of bandage round my chest wasn't making me feel any easier.

When I finally heard Christina voice on the phone, her voice sounded sultry, loud and rough. Maybe that was because her sexual talents as described by Silke in his little black diary had influenced my judgement.

I informed her that a friend had asked that I get in touch with her. She seemed mildly surprised that I, a female had been advised to look her up. Despite that, she invited me over. I had the impression that it was as easy as falling off a log 'C'mon over, I love meeting new people' she jubilantly remarked.

On my arrival, before she appeared, I opened my flip phone. My new android flip-phone was a Microsoft luxury voice activated unique grip mobile that had simple but complex operating systems attached to it. Sculptured in black steel and rubber with an OLED time display, 70.5 carats of sapphire crystal screen, slim and functioning adaptable display menus, it truly was one of a kind. Modified by Johnny Boyd, an employee cum acquaintance of mine, my flip phone was a precision-engineered electronic device that can combat almost any circumstances. The multi-purpose phone does everything from surfing the internet to X-raying and deactivating electronic safes or car security devices to emitting electronic magnetic pulses, downloading digital or analogue satellite images and disabling specific electrical appliances. Apart from the usual technical support a phone normally provides like taking calls, storing contact details, multimedia package, office tools and games, my smartphone operates on a modified inconspicuous mode with several installed Malware utility apps.

I readied the cloning malware app on my phone and waited for my guest. The malware was sure to clone any phone within a fifteen- feet range from the phone's radius. While I was preprograming the phone, I thought of Boyd, a computer genius with a passion for making complicated appliances. I made a mental note to call him, because beside being a friend with a brilliant mind who also had an amazing touch when it came to constructing gadgets like my android phones, he had mental problems which are kept at bay by his sister and my oh so infrequent visits.

When Christina appeared, I discovered instantly why she was crazy about meeting new people. She worked in a Bordello. Meeting new people was the norm in her world.

'What the hell happened to you hon?' she asked in greeting touching the bruised edge of my lip and the plaster sticking from my neck. 'You look like you've been ten rounds with Mike Tyson' 'I fell down a flight of stairs' I replied as I activated the Force

Pair utility on my phone.

'Must be some stairs' she commented

Christina was a composite of all the beauties in the place until you reached her eyes. Within them, you saw the depths, within those almost blue orbs that matched the silky sheen of her hair, the depths of disillusionment. She was a big beauty parlour blonde with lots of make-up. She wore a low-cut yellow blouse and a mini- shirt that could make JFK weep. Her mouth was a blossoming red flower accented by the even white teeth, one corner had a tiny grin appended to it. Speaking like a blue streak out of hades, she led me upstairs towards her place of business.

She had her phone in her hand and she was typing on it as if I was not present.

'It's not everyday, a beauty like yourself is recommended to me you know. But hey they did you a great favour endorsing me because I'm gonna give you the greatest time and, a massage that will fix you right up' she looked up from her phone 'I'm gonna treat you like you won't believe and you'll never never forget'

'Wouldn't that be fun?' Christina was a talker.

'I normally do not get female clients you know, certainly not Brits' I gave her a curiosity glance 'Your accent' she remarked as if she made it a point to notice it 'Not many of your country girls are enlightened to the touch of skin on skin, get it?' I nodded. Leading me up the stairs, she asked. 'So who was it that recommended you to me?'

'Mr Silke'

She let the grin slip wide for a second then made it reappear. She stuck her phone into the slip between her buttocks and panties. 'Silke huh? That's nice of him' She led me up some stairs then into a room and proceeded to take my jacket off, while I took a gander around the place. 'I have to check you over honey and give you a nice wash. My boss always says cleanliness is next to prosperity' 'Your madam must be a philosopher' I told her 'I prefer

Godliness though, what do you think?'

Whatever was in my voice made a lie out of the smile I wore.

Her attitude changed slightly 'What does it matter, we gonna do this?' she asked as she reached for the zipper of my pants. I evaded her nifty little reach. Her touch was firm and warm.

'I would like to meet your madam'

'No you wouldn't hon. Philosopher she might be, but her heart's as cold as Davy Jones' she paused when she saw my stumped expression 'Sorry ... my boyfriend gets his kicks from Pirate movies. What's the Problem? You shy? You have a problem with people touching you?' she asked as she reached for my jacket.

'Tell me about Silke?'

'Sorry?' she asked inadvertently.

I watched her for a good ten seconds, then asked again 'Silke, when did you last see him?'

'Who the fuck cares, I really don't care for the jerk. Is that why you're here? To find out where Silke is?' she asked. Her friendliness as expected tapered off sharply.

'You're a smart chick, what do you think?' She hesitated 'What do you want him for?'

'Nothing you should concern yourself about' I explained taking out a wad of bills from my black Lady Gaga wallet-purse.

She took a closer look at me and the fading bruises on my face 'He responsible for the stairs you fell down from?'

'Not only the stairs'

She shrugged, edged close to me and whispered 'Sorry hon, I can't help you but since you're here, you might as well enjoy the amnesties. What would you like?' she inquired, sliding her right arm round my shoulders.

I caught hold of her hand and turned it palm up and pressed two hundred dollar notes into her curled fingers. 'Silke, tell me about him. When did you see him last?'

She stroked the bills in her hand.

'I can't remember when I last saw him. I haven't seen him in the last several months. Honest. He only came here from time to time, that's all'

'How about a phone number, an address, swear I won't say where I got it from'

She rubbed her finger across the bottom of her nose 'Silke likes to knock people around and does a good job of it. He doesn't like strangers asking about him'

'I'm no stranger. We are … how should I put it … ah yes … we're old friends'

Her eyes steadily held mine in hers. 'Old friends eh?' She stuck the two bills into her low-cut blouse, between her large breasts. 'Look hon, don't con a Conner'

'Not my intention. Truly, no con' 'Then why're you looking for him?'

'To … erm … reacquaint myself with his … inhospitality'

She bobbed her head 'I bet' she turned to leave. I grabbed her arm.

Christina turned towards me with an annoyed and offensive look on her face. She glanced at the grasp I had on her arm. 'What?'

I held out two more hundred-dollar bills 'What would it take for me to get in touch with Silke?'

'You look too honest to be his … old friend. You a cop?' 'Would that matter?' I asked quietly

Scratching her neck with her index finger, she made a little shrug and declared it didn't matter to her either way. I noticed she insisted her neutrality with her fists balled. Her balled fist was a clear indication that she was not only becoming impatient with me but she was lying through her even teeth.

'You probably don't believe me but honest to god's truth I don't know where you can find him'

I turned her loose and grinned at her, pocketing my bills. I grinned at her. 'I believe you' I said to her.

'Great' she sneered at me with clenched teeth as she turned away from me with a funny expression on her face.

She could be telling me the truth but I didn't believe her one bit. She had displayed all the classic signs oflying.

'Thanks' I said as I made my way to the door. 'You bet!'

On my way out, I opened up my flip phone and grinned when I saw that my phone had cloned Christina's phone.

I ran through her list of contacts but there was no contact number or address for Silke. However, there were several unknowns in the contacts favourite list.

I waited outside, behind a café shop across the street from the Bordello's and waited for something to happen. For the next couple of minutes, nothing happened, then as I was just thinking that I might be wrong in my thinking that my supposition of her being a liar was fruitless, my phone began to hum from an outside dial tone. It was Christina's clone. She was making a call to one of the unknown numbers in the favourites list. There was no answer to her call. A few minutes later, she appeared and climbed into a beat-up brown 1997 Pontiac. I flung myself behind the wheel of the rented 2014 Navy Impala I picked up from the airport and took off after her. The Pontiac led me across town to a cheap apartment building. I followed her darting up a flight of stairs, two floors and went down a long hallway before stopping at a door. The busty blonde knocked on the door but got no reply. She knocked twice more, each time harder than the first. Then she turned to leave but she spotted me instead. Her surprise was evident because her eyes widened ever so slightly in astonishment.

'What you doing here?' 'You led me here'

'Talented as hell, aren't you hon?' she spat

I slipped by her and tried the door. 'Apparently Silke is not home. What do you think we should do now?'

She tried to make a dash for the stairs but I cornered her before she could make it. She scratched at my face and called me some names I hadn't heard in quite some time. Considering how widely my travels have been, that was saying quite a lot for her vocabulary.

I grabbed her neck and forced half her body over the edge of the banister.

'Let's hear the truth'

'You wouldn't?' she dared me 'No?' I ventured

She chuckled 'You're not gonna push me over. Silke would, but you ...' she shook her head

'Why do you think that?'

'Like I told you before hon, you are too honest to be cruel'

I took hold of her left leg and using it as a level with her neck in my chokehold grip, I heaved and shoved her indiscriminately over the banister, sending her falling two floors down.

'Aarrgghhh!' Christina screamed all the way down. Landing in the courtyard next to the sidewalk below, she hit the tarmacadam ground hand first with a resounding crack of something breaking. I leisurely made my way downstairs and approached her.

She was clutching her leg and sobbing from a broken ankle and sprained wrist. Two bystanders in the courtyard had gone up to her to aid, but I waved them away. They reluctantly hurried away.

I crouched next to her 'Silke killed a friend of mine' I

hissed at her 'Not to mention trying to kill me, so I'm finding that nasty git with or without you. Best with you or damn you, if you don't'

She was staring at my face and something in my expression scared her.

'Katanga … Katanga …' she yelled with her palm outward Katanga. A name I recognise. Now we were getting somewhere. 'Katanga?' I enquired with doubt in my voice.

'Yes … yes …' she muttered

'Am I supposed to know who the hell is that?'

'He's a big deal, loaded with dough and lives like a solid citizen, but Silke has bragged that he put up money for some of his jobs'

'Why should I believe you?'

'Ask anyone' she panted 'Ask my girlfriends back at the shop, they'll all tell you the same. He's a repo expect but he doesn't retrieve cars. He recovers money. He often boasts about those he tracks and just one person he works for. Katanga'

'Know where I can find this Katanga?'

She informed me that Katanga had offices at the Pregerson Tower in uptown LA, but she didn't know which one and that's all she insisted she knew.

I thanked her, left her moaning on the courtyard and returned upstairs to check out the apartment Christina was so interested in. The cheap lock on the door was not that hard to spring open.

The rooms within were vacant and about a quarter inch of dust lay on most of the fine but cheap furniture. The current lodger hadn't been in for quite a while.

Apart from the number of junk mail at the door that suggested the tenant had not been present for more than two months, it also informed me that the resident's other name was Edwart.

Edwart Silke. Weird spelling for an Edward.

The next day my chest burned like a son of a bitch in the mid-morning workday as I made my way up the mirrored elevator of Pregerson Skyscraper and announced myself, first to one of the three attendants about the place, armed with Glocks and then to the receptionist behind the desk of Colburn Group and the offices of a Mrs Ursula Conic otherwise known by her street moniker of Katanga.

In the Colburn office, there were two businesses under the same organization, a real estate business, and a loan investment establishment. The thick carpeting, the refreshments, and the magazines that were no older than a week, indicated she made money from both companies. The slim, red haired permed secretary with man type hands and dark blue-velvet nail polish on her gnawed fingernails behind the receptionist desk smiled at me as I approached. I noticed there were no obvious surveillance cameras but beside the receptionists was a terra cotta bowl with a handful of phone's in them. I had never seen such security except in a government run SCIF building.

The smile on the receptionist's face eclipsed with red blush was all teeth with no sincerity behind it. She informed me that Mrs Conic never saw anyone without an appointment.

Her tone was bland, but conclusive.

'And how does one make an appointment?' I asked

She showed me her insincere smile again, 'If she doesn't know you then you rarely ever get one'

'Well then, tell her I know Katanga' I said 'That should do it' She froze. The smile on her face slipped off as she shifted nervously in her seat, glancing at one of attendants or should I be more precise as to call them bodyguards. She gave me a curt nod before standing up to gather some papers and head down an office hallway to drop the name. When she returned, she told me that Mrs Conic was very busy at the moment and that she had never heard of the name Katanga.

I grinned 'In other words, I should go to hell' The receptionist shrugged her shoulders uneasily.

For fun, I winked at her and the attendants with a "like maybe I'd be back" twinkle, before turning away.

It was not easy locating Katanga. I had been up all the previous night, slogging on my phone, and playing phone tag with a number of secret service official types trying to find her. From what I knew, Katanga was female, cautious, and judging from Christina's reaction, her identity was known to most as a man but besides that she was a force to be reckoned with. It was possible, she perhaps had ties to the mob and now from what I have now observed was that she was paranoid when it came to any surveillance device.

That must be why the LA county police did not know of a "Katanga". There was no evidence that whoever this person was, even existed anywhere. Yes, they were familiar with the name but unconfirmed reports of Katanga could not or would not be verified. According to their Confidential Informants and unsubstantiated reports, "Katanga" was big muscle in the criminal underground circuit. Rumour was that he bankrolls most high profile criminal activities in the south-west region. Activities that included high priced hits and heists. They however could not associate the name with a face or perhaps they were unwilling to mention him because she was paid up with the right people. I found it unbelievable that in this day and age of electronic surveillance there wasn't a snapshot of Katanga anywhere in their files.

Thankfully, my NSA contacts who were not bound by such obligations or restrictions, they had a more comprehensive investigative report on the endeavours of Katanga. It included some of Katanga's undertakings and most importantly Katanga's true-identity.

'She doesn't exactly talk to anyone off the street you know' one of my contacts advised me.

'Well, I'll just have to try to be a little persuasive then'

My persuasiveness or charm had failed me but I was not out of the running just yet.

I exited the building into the hot sunshine and headed to my car, making my way through the parking lot. On my way, I spotted a black limousine sitting behind the nametag of U. Conic. A uniformed chauffeur with a face from the second season of Kojak was doing his utmost to polish the bonnet. In the blistering heat, I found that counterproductive.

I leaned forward to speak to him just as I passed 'Isn't it a bit hot for that?'

He just grunted. As I passed him, I noticed the bulge under his arm stand out like a bump on a tyre.

With my Chevy Impala parked half a block away, I was in a perfect position to keep an eye on the limousine that was obviously at Katanga's disposal.

Three hours later, a big man with broad shoulders in a black suit with the business edge of a sporty shade appeared followed closely by a big figure wearing huge dark glasses that covered half her face and a headscarf that covered the rest. She appeared carrying a yellow seasonal Prada handbag. Cornrow hair peeked from under the scarf, as did her dry jade skin. On her feet were black ked shoes and her chequered tailored pantsuit could barely contain her watermelon breasts as the big man opened the rear door to the limousine and let her climb into it. The big man, obviously a bodyguard of some sort, followed by getting into the front with the driver.

When the limousine passed me, I fell in behind it. Our destination turned out to be a swanky country club in the O.C. suburbs of the town. The bodyguard kept his distance as Mrs Conic went on ahead.

Katanga seemed to be a well-liked and well-known personage in the club. She was greeted with respect, knew almost every one and almost everybody knew her. A waiter led her to a very reserved area while I watched her some hundred yards away through binoculars. She was a card player or more specifically, a baccarat player. From what I could tell, she was fairly good. A group of over indulgent females played with her until she joined a more eclectic group who for obvious reasons let her win.

The long hours made me reconsider my move and made it. Strapping my beige Cartier leather happy birthday satchel over my shoulder, I went up to the chauffer and clipped him behind the ear. He slumped against the steering wheel. I yanked him out and relieved him of his car keys and the bulge under his coat, a .38 revolver, which I promptly tossed into a garbage can. The bodyguard was much more easier to contain. A pinch of a

*Chloral Hydrate* dose from my 9-carat black gold thumb ring made him pass out within three seconds. As an organic compound, his sedation should not be that long, probably an hour or two. However, his headache will last just a little bit longer.

When Mrs Conic emerged from the clubhouse with an entourage of female hoity totties, she didn't immediately notice her missing driver and bodyguard. However, she did notice my suspicious figure next to her vehicle. She courteously bade her group a good night and headed towards me with my Makarov pointed surreptitiously at her.

She did not flinch or even lose a beat in her steps as she approached me.

'I don't believe I've had the pleasure, Miss Dax' she greeted me in recognition.

'No, I don't believe we do, Katanga' I emphasised her non-de plum with specificity.

'Where's Howard?' she inquired with concern as she walked up to me.

'The driver or bodyguard?' 'Driver?'

I glanced at the row of cars behind me, indicating where he might be. 'His neck hurts rather painfully'

'That's rather kind of you. You didn't kill him' she replied in relief.

'Not my style' I replied 'Unlike your man Rodney Shahe' 'Sorry about that. We didn't know the lay of the land when he

was commissioned with the contract' 'And now you do?'

'Howard's my husband's second cousin. I wouldn't hear the end of it, if anything happened to him' she mumbled with appreciation. 'I understand. Men are generally not the happiest sort when they complain'

I was dumbfounded when she threw back her head and burst into a laughter that sounded like the throttle of an F1 engine.

'No they are not' she agreed with me, chuckling.

Chitchat over, I gestured with the gun 'Please get in behind the wheel please Katanga, or would you prefer Mrs Conic?'

She moved deliberately slowly towards me and stopped, standing gallantly in front of me. I noticed the smooth tan of her jade skin and the confidence in her eyes. 'I'm an independent woman, just as I believe you are. So why continue with pretexts?' 'I'm glad we understand one another' I hoarsely said. 'I rather like your anonymity and your pseudonym …'

'It serves a purpose and comes in kindda handy for unseemly eyes'

I did not know it, but I felt like I understood her and that in different circumstances, I'd be partial to this woman. I knew without question that if she were forcibly challenged, she would definitely be able to handle herself.

'Slowly' I cautioned her as I got in beside her in the passenger seat still brandishing my Makarov.

She eased into the car and settled back behind the wheel. She glanced down at my gun hand 'This is very impetuous of you. I didn't think you were the impulsive type, Miss Dax'

'It sometimes bodes well when jaded'

'Ah' she commented 'So what is it you want?' 'Your man Mr Silke and his faithful sidekick Dan'

She grimaced 'Oh them. If you were acquainted with

Silke as others have been, you wouldn't want to find him. He isn't exactly right up there if you know what I mean. He enjoys hurting people' 'Don't you mean he likes killing people? That I already know and why I'm looking for him'

'Well, we never did exchange addresses' 'You recently had a deal with him'

'Yes, but he has failed to show up' 'What was the deal?'

'To collect a debt?'

'From Ritchie Francesco?'

'No from his son, Marion Steiner'

It came as no surprise to me that she would know that Marion was Francesco's son. It only confirmed for me that she was part of the mafia. Maybe not a fully-fledged member but she did have certain dealings with them.

'I understand Francesco kept that relationship concealed?' 'He did but not hard enough'

I ran a hand through my hair 'So what did he do, steal the money or was it just for services rendered?'

'Exactly' she replied without a pause. 'What services?'

'I can't reveal that. I'm sure you know confidentiality must be maintained'

'Silke killed Marion. Did you and your friends know that?' 'Yes, we are aware' She solemnly responded, confirming my suspicions of her connections to the mob 'From what I understand you barely made it. Curare huh?' she scrutinised me 'It's amazing you are sitting here with me'

'Resilience is not something I take likely' 'I can see that'

I thought for a moment, shook my head, and got back to the matter at hand.

'Someone like you would know where to find such an acquaintance even if you didn't exchange addresses. I want to know where you can find him, if you wanted to'

'I assume you've checked the housing project where he stays when he's in LA?'

'Yes'

'Then I hardly know where to look'

I sighed. Another dead end. A wasted day, except for the pleasure of getting to meet Katanga, which I could do without. I was about to get out of the car.

'Is that it?' she asked me. 'What else is there?'

'Didn't you ever learn to never settle for half ' 'What else can you give me?'

'I hear you never go back on your word, is that true?' 'Why would you ask that?'

'Because though I don't know where you can find Silke, I do know where you might find his friend Dan and another of his associate Mr. Roche'

'Dan? You know where I might find the bugger?' I asked trying not to sound excited.

'And Mr. Roche'

'Roche is dead'

'Oh' she sneered with understanding. 'That leaves the big man Dan then'

'Yes it does'

'Then, in exchange for his possible whereabouts we would like the opportunity to take care of the situation ourselves. Would you agree to that?'

'I can't. He and his mates didn't kill Francesco. My interests are just ...' I hesitated before continuing 'For selfish reasons'

'I see'

'However, if I do catch up to those responsible for your man's death, I might, might … give you guys a heads up. Will that do?'

She contemplated for a short while then began speaking. 'He's a gun for hire, and despite his appearance of being a dimwitted buffoon and gargantuan outlook, he's one of the best with a profound loyalty to Mr Silke and his ways' She was telling me something I hadn't already guessed.

'Is he on the mob's payroll?'

'No' she promptly replied 'but I do know he's not here in LA' 'How can you be sure?'

'Oh I am or else he would have been dealt with already' 'That doesn't help me'

'No, it doesn't but may I suggest a visit to Haemin Café in New York. You might find what you're looking for'

'Haemin Café huh?' 'You never know'

I put my Makarov back into his holster before asking her the question that had been bothering me since she sat in the car. 'Why?'

'Why what?'

'Why the assistance?'

'Oh that?' she thought for a moment 'Well, I can assume for now is that we both have mutual interests and I rather not have you for an enemy. I've heard how furiously vengeful you can get when you get upset'

'If that's the case, the FBI's computer has been on the fritz for some time now. You might want to let your compatriots know the Feds won't tolerate stragglers. Get your people out, at least for now'

She grinned at me. 'I will see to it'

I opened the car door and climbed out of the car 'Well thanks for all …'

'Er … about my obscurity, Miss Dax I wond…?' 'Don't worry, I can keep a secret'

'In that case, have you seen Christina since your last visit?' she asked

The mob had been keeping tracks on me. I half suspected they would. I had led them here. Like most organisations, they were patient, tenacious and deliberate in their questions when they need to be.

'And if I did?'

'I would imagine you weren't too hard on her'

'Not really'

'Good. She's a loquaciously good earner' she replied in a matter-of-factly way. She had ended the conversation.

I expressed my gratitude by thanking her and walking after handing her, her car keys.

* * * * * *

Katanga's inquiry about Christina had made made me curious, as she knew it would. The lateness of the hour, I made my way back to the Bordello.

A burly Korean greeted me at the door. He was not there on my previous visit and I could see why. His expression wasn't exactly friendly and he was built like a bulldozer. Two conditions that would put any client off their sexual fix.

'Is late miss. Dis no drive-through. You not have appointment to be here you should not be here' he remarked 'You go now missy'

'Tell Christina, a friend is here to see her' 'Ya friend of hers?' he asked scowling at me. 'We've met'

'Sorries, but she be not seeing nobody for good long time. She have accident' he said closing the door in my face. I smiled at him as I stuck my foot in-between the frame and door.

'Well, she is seeing me' I adamantly maintained.

He glanced at me and at my foot. He chuckled, 'Little girl, you not try no rough stuff wit me, you lose … bad'

My response was giving him one hard shot to the kidneys with my fist to punctuate my argument. All breath went out of him in a short huff as he went down letting the door swing open. Another strike with the chiseled edge of my right hand at his throat and he was out for the count. I stepped over him and went in search of Christina.

A yawning and stretching blonde-haired young woman appeared at the head of the stairway Christina had led me up the day before. She was much in appearance to Christina except she was much younger and leaner in the hips. She was wearing a purple negligee that concealed enough of her body to matter.

'What'd you need, babe?' Her voice indicated that a person like me could get whatever I wanted just for the asking.

'Christina'

'Ah. Maybe you should talk to Madame Nova first'

She led me into a room where the blinds had been drawn tight. Cheap incense fouled the air and the incongruous furniture inside reeked of teak cigarette residue. The blond closed the door behind me leaving an inch from it really closing.

Madame Nova, the woman I hadn't intended to meet looked nothing like the blondes. She was in her fifties and looked like a certain type. She had little hooks you could hang certain possibilities on. From her appearance, she had more than an oriental ancestry in her genes. Her eyes were barely slanted but from what I could see, they could pick you clean in seconds. Her skin had a very sallow hue, which I suspected was due to lack of sunshine. Her brown hair was closely cropped to her head. Her long silver fingernails glittered through her very clinging mandarin robe. In the shadowy room, her green eyes shone like the eyes of the black Siamese cat curled on her lap.

She stared at me with a friendly smile but there was a frigidity within them, that could possibly see through me. Assessing my body and my looks like a lamb to the slaughter, she finally surmised me. 'Hmm … yes I could use you. You have nice hips darling … you could drop the tomboy look dear, … but yes, you have great potential. You have a name, darling?'

I told her.

Her mood instantly transformed. Her eyebrows shot up, querulously with an unspoken challenge.

'Ah I remember now, you're Christina's troublemaker. You're not welcomed here' she snarled. Cold cynicism was instantly cut into a corner of her mouth. 'Kenny' she bellowed. Kenny, I assumed was the Korean bodyguard.

The cat in Nova's lap raised its head and flicked its tiny tongue around its chops.

'I have come to see Christina'

Caressing the cat, she probed me with her green malignant eyes. 'No can do' she abruptly commented.

I wondered why someone who had been so available

yesterday was so problematical today.

'May I ask why?'

'You've brought us nothing but trouble'

Trouble? I pondered. What trouble? 'Trouble, what sort of trouble?' I solicited, voicing my thoughts.

'Sorry we can't help you. Kenny?' she barked again. When Kenny failed to appear, she stared at me.

'What'd you do?' she asked jumping down my throat.

'What trouble could I have wrecked on you and yours?' I enquired again.

'The worse kind. Look whatever business you're involved with … is none of our affair. We don't want no part of it'

Kenny, the Korean bouncer burst into the room and grabbed my shoulder in an effort to spin me round and use his fist. I flinched because his grip was just close enough to my chest wound to cause me some discomfort. Also above and beyond, it violated my personal breathing space. 'I kill ya myselflitt …' he barked hoarsely and angrily at me.

I had no time for this. With a savage back motion, I slammed my elbow into the niche just above his hard tummy.

'Ugghhh' He snorted with distress.

As his face took on an unfathomable façade, I pivoted and skewered him in the groin with my knee. Lines of pain rippled across his face as he sank into a stoop like a squirrel trying to crack a nut between their knees. I was hoping it was enough for him to stay down, but it wasn't. He again reached for me, I feinted to the left and chopped down hard again with the edge of my right hand. The strike, which should have felled a drunken Ox, only angered him more. Fortunately, I had beaten the fight out of him. On the ground with eyes protruding, breath whistling hard from between his teeth, he knew he was done for. I took mercy with him by pinching his *Chun Joo Hyul* nerve centre, two points at the back of his neck, sending him off to bye bye land.

Madame Nova watching, sprang to her feet and threw her cat at me. I watched the Siamese cat sail past me, a ball of spitting fur and fury, as I evaded its target and land on Kenny's back, claws and all. I promptly pulled out my Makarov and pointed the muzzle of the pistol between her vile sea green eyes.

'No more foreplay, where's Christina?'

Madame Nova uttered such profanities at me in Mandarin that I would not want to listen to it in polite American society.

Still cursing me, she took me up another flight of stairs. Christina was sitting on a bed counting cards, playing a rough game of solitaire. She looked up, squinted tying to see my face. When she recognised me, she clicked her tongue and turned her head away as we walked into the room. 'Look who's here, my own Brit Calamity Jane. Come to hurt me some more, huh?'

Her bland tongue wet her pale lips as she coughed into her bandaged hand.

She did not look as voluptuous as she did yesterday. She looked like a tired old shopkeeper in pink dressing. Apart from the swathe of bandages on her ankle and an arm strapped in a tourniquet, she had two black eyes, and swollen lips. Fresh injuries, that never occurred during our little dalliance. It wasn't a bold stretch to think that she had undergone a serious beating.

'She has a nasty bite, Chrissy. Couldn't stop the cunt' Madame Nova asserted to Christina while sneering at me.

I walked over to her and tilted her chin. 'I didn't do this, did I?

What the hell happened?'

'Don't tell her anything' Her Madame advised.

'She is going to tell me' I replied calmly, glancing at Madame Nova with a penetrating glare

Christina swept the cards together into a pile on the bed 'It wouldna hurt to tell her. What'd it matter anyway' she declared, glancing at Nova.

'So tell her, it's your funeral'

She turned to look at me 'I got careless and your friend taught me the error of my ways'

'My friend?'

'He must be, he came here last night and asked all the questions you did'

'You tell him about me?'

'Everything. Your friend wasn't much for procrastination'. 'No, not a friend of mine and I don't think the mafia would be interested in roughing you up for Silke's location' I thoughtfully said. More to myself than to any of the women.

'No, the mob didn't do this' Madame Nova chimed into my thoughts 'Yes, we know a capo got hit and the mobs money got lifted, a job Silke could have pulled'

'Huh huh. This man, like you didn't care about money, only his whereabouts. So I assume he must be a friend of yours' Christina added

'No, not mine'

'Then who was this clergyman?' Madame Nova demanded from me.

Both Christina and I turned our heads to face the Madame. 'Clergyman? A priest?'

'Yeah, priest?'

Priest! Marion did mention a member of the clergy had visited him and his colleagues at their dig. The thought resurrected a nagging thought within me. A thought, I couldn't quite dig up or remember why I had it. The thought was so viable within me, that I knew it must be important but I set it aside and enquired from Madam Nova her brilliant insight on how she could figure Christina's intimidator as a member of a clergy.

With the scowl leaving her face all at once, she addressed Christina 'Didn't you know Chrissy?' Madame Nova asked.

Christina replied quietly 'I suppose, but wasn't sure. What does it matter anyway, he got what he wanted' she answered bitterly.

Madame Nova turned to me 'Her bully was a man of the church, that you can take to the bank' Madame Nova declared in a very positive pragmatic way, even without her pretentious assurance. 'Man of the church?' I questioned, turning to glance at Christina. I had also heard that before. From Marion. 'Are you sure?' I enquired rather forcibly.

'Of course I'm sure. I know a man of the cloth when I see one'

'Was he wearing a cassock?' I asked as her Siamese cat sauntered into the room and jumped onto the bed. It meowed and curled itself onto the bed next to Christina. Madame Nova picked it up gently as it purred and licked its paw.

'No, but if you've spent time in seminary school or with clerics who are indifferent to our amenities' she cocked an eye at me 'You'll understand how they move, talk, even smell. I know how they carry their damn bags. Trust me, if he wasn't a priest I'd eat my cat. Your man was no different'

'You got all that?'

'Like devout religious men, his eyes never look you in the eyes, and if they do their eyes are always judgemental or remorseful. Always crossing themselves and speak in a certain way. But I must say your man was a bit different. His fashion sense was the worse, unless straw sandals are making a comeback. What's more, the bastard had a rosary wrapped round a wrist. It was a dead giveaway'

My mind clicked back. Sandals! Priest? Francesco and Tyler's killers? Could they be priests?

I thought of Marion's parchment tale and the runic writing on Francesco's chest. Was it possible?

'All I wanted was Silke's location' I acknowledged to myself and to the ladies in the room 'I didn't mean to bring mayhem into your life or establishment'

Madame Nova caressing her cat's fur looked at Christina. 'I think I believe her'

'I went to see Katanga. He didn't know either'

By using a male façade, I had chosen by default to keep Katanga's anonymity.

'Then this man, if he's what I think he is, he will burn you' Madame Nova assured 'And burn you good. Even those close to you'

'Why do you say that?' 'He's a man on a mission' I grinned at her.

From my satchel, I retrieved my Lady Gaga wallet-purse, peeled off a couple of hundred dollar bills from the wad of bills within, and handed a couple to Madame Nova. The rest I gave to Christina.

Before leaving to go down the stairs, Christina stopped me 'I didn't exactly tell you the truth'

'What do you mean?'

'At least not everything I know' 'What don't I know?'

'Silke is a New Yorker and so is his friend, Dan'

New York, again. Katanga didn't prevaricate. I guess I knew my next port of call.

'You tell this cleric that?' She nodded.

I thanked her, apologised again for my intrusion and informed them of where I was staying, in the event the priest returned asking for me.

Kenny was grimacing and hanging onto the frame of the front door when I walked by with a hearty good night for his prayers. He eyed me menacingly as he painfully closed the door behind me.

# TEN

A couple of minutes after I had climbed into the Impala, I noticed I was being followed by a blue Toyota Camry. My attention was on the clergyman Madame Nova had mentioned, so my concentration was a bit lagging to notice the vehicle three car lengths behind me.

It was dark now and the LA traffic had thinned out considerably since I journeyed to the Pregerson Tower that morning.

I moved into the nearest traffic lane, keeping my eyes on the lights of the car following via my side and rearview mirrors, which I hoped would lead me one step closer to the elusive Mr. Silke or give me a first glimpse of the clergyman, whom I've heard so little about. I was heading towards the direction of Rose Hills as I moved into one of the outer traffic lanes before turning onto one of the radial roads away from the business lights of the city. From my subtle drive, I could identify two individuals within the Toyota Camry, I couldn't make them out but with the aid of alternating streetlights, I could make out a bearded man in the passenger seat. I was glad of it, I was at last getting some traction, and now

Susan Dax was much less anonymous than I cared to admit. It was at the end of a wide dusty avenue that it hit me like a ton of bricks. That thing that tickled the back of my head when Marion Steiner and then just now when Madame Nova mentioned something about a clergyman. That something recent and quite important I could not quite put my fingers on.

It was the organic stains on the foreheads of Shaw, Francesco and the others. The oleic, linoleic acids and scented balsam. Olive oil on their foreheads and hands. A priest giving last rites would be the only ones able to apply them on their corpse.

Damn! Could it be possible that they were given last rites? It seemed improbable, but the facts bear out any other probability.

I should have realised this sooner. One or more priests were present at the massacre or perhaps carried out the massacre themselves.

Priests! Whoa!

Why would priests commit murder? And not only a murder but a massacre of such ruthlessness. This must definitely relate to Marion's find in the south of France. If this were true then his tale was no more such a fantasy as I would like. I kicked myself in the stomach and focused on the situation at hand.

At the end of the wide dusty avenue, with my stalkers still following closely behind me, I maneuverer my Impala down a street lit up with an open marketplace. I slowed down and pulled over.

I studied them for a minute as I sat in the car before sliding out the car and strolling into the bazaar, glad of the cover, which not only the darkness but the higgledy-piggledy commotion around afforded me.

At this point in time, I was glad of Angelinos who did not rightly care about who did what, to whom or had the basic of inhibitions. Angelinos who would sell or buy anything. This night market was such a place. It was lined with souvenir stands, print kiosks, erotic American miniatures and the usual array of food stalls.

I wasn't a tourist but I acted like one in an effort to identify my stalkers. I lingered over some of the wares that were being hawked using the cover and reflective surfaces to identify the lone individual who had gotten out of the Toyota Camry. A man in black trousers and a dark patterned shirt, there seemed to be something in his left hand but I couldn't make it out. Most importantly, I was quiet interested in his footwear. When I finally got a look, I was doubly appreciative. He was wearing straw-coloured sandals, which I must say in this heat and the fashion period was quiet a statement.

Up ahead, I spotted the end of an alley, with a narrow wooden booth and an amphitheatre identified as the "Pantages's Room". It had a sign below it, stating that the *"Why Does Anything Go?,"* production was about to start. The perfect spot, I thought to myself.

I stood squarely in the faded neon light of the ticket booth and purchased a ticket to the show. I had no idea what the show was about but I took my time making my entry.

My stalker didn't think twice about joining me.

A spotlight slid its yellow-white beam over the audience and onto the wooden structure of the stage. I could hear a taped narration being broadcasted over a loudspeaker system, introducing us to the show. Then all the lights except the spotlights went out.

The debonair of a show was about to start.

The play functioning as a musical was a history lesson of sorts, a journey of a naïve guy called Gabriel, going on a cruise without the benefit of understanding the simplest oflife's notions. His adventure was full of sex, booze, gangsters and for what it was worth God. Despite the "*Blow, Gabriel, Blow*," and many other show-stopping tunes including toe-tapping routines that spilled out from the cast and crew to raise the audience's spirits, my thoughts were on my stalker and his intentions.

For a moment, I had lost him in the darkened audience. As my eyes began to search the darkness, I all of a sudden heard the almost silent shuffling patter of feet hurtling from behind me. I turned my head over my shoulder and found myself being introduced to the glinty edges of a double-edged steel athame. The blade was larger and longer than Peko, I noticed that detail as the blade came down for a sharp slicing cut, almost slitting off my left ear. Instead, it sliced off a good chunk of the left arm of my jacket. My tracker was good, I had barely noticed him. He had chosen an opportune time and his attack was not only sudden but also vicious.

Without thinking, I lurched backwards, thrusting out my left hand in a jiujutsu *sohn-nal mak-ki* knife-hand thwart. I missed. My tracker did not pause to perceive if there was not a need for a second try. He lunged at me again.

His white teeth flashed a sardonic grin as the blade of his athame hovered in the air, waiting to lunge for a second try. It was definitely my lucky day, because somehow at that particular moment the spotlight caught the glint of the silver crucifix attached to the rosary wrapped round his left wrist. The flicker oflight caught him full in the eyes, momentarily blinding him. My second sohn-nal mak-ki smack hit its mark. It made him fall to the side, he hurriedly picked himself up and began to run down the narrow aisle between the rows of the cushioned folding chairs and exasperated viewers. The spectators that were glued to the action on the stage gave an applause here and an applause there, just as the cast jaunted about, having no idea what we were on about. I was running then, racing after my assailant.

Even if I did not know how he figured me out, I could still hear the blade of his knife hissing and slicing through the air, shredding the left arm of my jacket and narrowly missing my skin.

As I ran after him, I slid a hand into my jacket to retrieve my Makarov and slid the safety off. No one in the audience seemed to find our actions disconcerting as the spotlight swept across the friezes of the theatre, its flash virtually pinpointing both our locations, luckily it didn't.

My assailant had found his way behind the stage, through the stage door and out the loading bay. I sprinted after him and suddenly found myself out in a condensed passageway. A damp earthy smell of musk and age permeated the open air, smacking my nose like a jackhammer. I could not find my assailant but he was out here, lurking in the darkness, perhaps waiting for me to tumble into the impromptu ambush he had possibly laid out for me.

I halted, scanning the darkness. I walked slow, turning a corner to hear an unfamiliar sound and halted again. At the end of a short tunnel was a faint rattling *chug-chug-chug* sound. What was that I wondered? As I drew closer, I wondered if I could identify the sound. Yes, it was the chortling grating sound of a machine but what kind? The sound of an apparatus I did not recognise. I did know it was neither a generator nor a water pump. I lingered at the corner, hoping to identify the sound but to no avail. I turned my wandering ears back to the matter at hand.

Why was I here? I thought to myself. Yes, I could have turned back, return to my motel room to figure out my next move, but I chose not to. This was my first glimpse of the men in sandals. I wanted to know as much as I could know, so he had to be found as soon as I could. The sooner the better.

I slipped off my wellington boots. The Bottega-Veneta leather boots were just not going to cut it, if I wanted to sneak up to him through the columns of wood in the way and the bare chippings of concrete beneath our feet.

I thanked the stars that it was now less difficult to hear him over the sounds bubbling over from the unnerving chug-chug- chug reverberation, the theatre and the street market. In contrast, the darkness was more engulfing. I heard the fast accentuated hollow thuds that accompanied the moving feet of my assailants hurried footsteps. He was running again, just ahead of me. He was moving fast, further and further away from me. I felt relieved about that. Pleased, that no bystander or night tourist shopper would be threatened by any violent confrontation which could take place.

I raced silently after the running footsteps, running from post to another post, alert to every sound he made. I had already accustomed myself to most of the sound effects in the area except for the faint rattling *chug-chug-chug* machinery. So when I heard a low-pitched groan merge with the rattling reverberating sound I was grateful to pinpoint his position. I caught sight of him rising from the ground. It seemed he had tripped over some stone steps.

My finger was already on the trigger as I set my Makarov's sights.

My aim was to disable. Killing him was not in my scheme of things to do, he would be useless to me dead, but if I had to kill him, I would. Alive, he could be a veritable fountain of information. The Makarov's hammer slipped back, the instant I squeezed the trigger. A bark of gunfire pierced the echoing darkness. The slug chipped against a stone pillar sending a little cloud of smoky white dust rising up into the air.

I had missed my mark, good, but I still hurried forward. My assaulter had already gotten to his feet and disappeared. Vaulting over the steps, he had tripped over in my stockinged feet, I found myself standing in the middle of a circular grassy path. From behind me came the sharp hiss of someone inhaling snappishly. I didn't have a chance to put the Makarov to use. Instead, I rammed both of my elbows back, twisting my body around at the same time. One of my elbows made contact. I caught the assailant behind me with a glancing blow to his ribs. I should have been pleased that I'd got the upper hand. I hadn't. Though he seemed temporarily out of breath, he still managed to sidestep me and get out of the range of my pistol.

Suddenly, a slurred and barely audible voice spoke from the darkness from across me 'Well done, Michel'

I snapped my right leg straight back behind me in a back kick, which sent the ball of my feet crashing into someone's knee. My second assailant let out a bellow of pain and reeled back. I clobbered him with a punch that included the butt of my gun. Bouncing away to the side, I inhaled a breath, backing away but training the Makarov on first one and then the other of my two antagonists.

Now there were two against little ol' me. The first assailant, my tracker and the second, I recognised as the bearded man in the passenger seat of the Camry.

The six foot one man looked faceless, his features were handsome but also somewhat unrecognisable. His hair was brown with grey tresses on left brow, was his white priest-collar between his neck. What made him dangerous was the smirk on his smooth face and the Heckler & Koch machine pistol tucked in his trouser. I tentatively relieved it off him and threw it away into a corner. When he spoke, he spoke English with a perceptible Italian accent. 'We finally meeting Signorina Dax' he chortled with a coarse and a feeble attempt at hilarity.

'I'm sorry ... have we met?'

'No we not yet, but we should be having'

Keeping the pistol's deadly trajectory on either of my assailants, I asked 'And why should we have met?'

'Ah ... this ... welling ...' he started to say. 'Who are you and what do you want from me?'

'Ah! You no clever as they be saying huh, Piccolo uno'

I immediately disliked him, especially when he referred to me as "Little One".

'Maybe not. You know my name but I don't know yours'

'Ah! Excuse me, Piccolo uno. I am Father Theodore Halbert and this be Father Lew Michel' he imparted, introducing us. He gave me a little bow. His accented pidgin words came out of him dauntingly and slang-like.

'From Rome?' *'Infatti'*

I understood that the Vatican is not exactly a place of love and peace but of politics, faith and banking. I didn't think it was a place of dark rituals and great secrecy or especially a place where some priest or cardinal could order a person's death.

'Why does the Pope want my death?' 'Because of companying you being keep'

Was he talking about Christina or Marion? Was it possible that the Priory with its incriminating faith, might be at last making its appearance?

I decided to test my hypotheses 'You.'

I decided to test either of my hypotheses 'You were the one who messed with Christina?'

'No my dear. Michel having that arduous undertaking'

'Then whose company have I desecrated?' He stared at me, daring me to figure it out 'Marion Steiner?' I whispered under my breath. 'His discovery?' Halbert lingering in his stare, gazed at me as if I had signed my own death warrant. In all likelihood, I think I just might have. 'It's genuine?' I asked half in incredulity.

'You will kindly be providing us with document then letting us dispose of you now or else' Father Halbert kindly suggested. It was as if he was telling me to pass the peas but first swallow the hemlock.

I chuckled 'Hey padre, who has the advantage here' I reminded him, glancing at the gun in my hand.

He sniggered with that weird smirk on his face, stood straight up, brushed down his clothes and turned to Father Michel 'Michel, *girati, ragazzo mio*' he instructed

'*Padre*?' Father Michel queried, confused.

'The Senorita is verying capable young woman but

she not kind to being able of shooting two people or any person in cold blood, *Soprattutto nella regione posteriore*'

Father Halbert turned around and stood with his back to me.

His colleague quickly followed suit.

This was a strange turn of events. Yes, the Father was right, he had turned the table on me. I wouldn't shoot anyone in the back. At least, not without cause.

'You've got me Father' I surrendered 'But please stay out of my way. I'm on the trail of some very nefarious individuals' I warned, applying yet another hunch.

'We knowing of this. Still we regreting to telling you this … Mr Edwarto Silke is dead' he informed me. He told me like he was reciting the weather. God was this man such an arsehole. 'But his *complice Signore Daniel Friedlander, vive ancora, signorina*'

His information wasn't exactly mind-boggling, but it did tend to ask how he knew any of this. Unless he and his happy go lucky subordinate were the ones responsible? Who were these guys and what were their motives?

I did not know how I felt. Silke dead! On one hand, I felt cheated and on the other, I felt angry. I did not believe this Father Halbert was lying but I hoped he was.

'So Silke is dead but Dan still lives?' I asked. With the back of his head towards me, Father Halbert nodded indelibly 'How would you know all this? Who exactly are you?'

'All verying good questions, *signorina*. You shoot now?'

Then it occurred to me that I was not only looking at the butchers from the Castaic cottage, but also Anna Feldman and Bruce Windemill's murderers. Now, I was reconsidering, the "not shoot in the back" principle I had.

'You killed the capo?'

'*Piccola mia, voglio chiederti qualcosa*' The bearded Father enquired, disregarding my question.

Why would he want to tell me anything, I pondered to myself. '*Cosa vuoi chiedermi?*'

'You believe in God? You believe ...' This was the same question Marion had asked me but it seemed he was searching for the words to complete his thought '... *alcuni segreti devono rimanere... segreti?* '

Secrets, to my mind are those for the beholder, unless it protrudes harmfully on others.

Before I could finish my train of thought, in that split second of time, something thin, colourful, dangling and metallic flew across my field of vision. I spun around and squeezed off a round, before I realised it was Michel's rosary. The high calibre slug droned off through the air. In that instant, Michel took the opportunity to duck back behind one of the wooden posts, momentarily escaping my pistol's trajectory. Just then, the Makarov itself was unceremoniously knocked out of my hand by Halbert.

I lurched forward, unbalanced but I recouped nicely. As I spun around in anticipation of an attack, I let Peko fall into the palm of my right hand in anticipation of his impending assault. I turned to face the blackness of the darkness. They had both disappeared. I scanned the area for any sounds of running footsteps or movements but strangely, there was nothing.

I tried to consider the meaning behind Father Halbert's question of "Secrets Staying Secret". There was no doubt in my mind that these jokers were the ones responsible for Agent Shaw's murder and had also carved those runic symbols into Francesco's chest.

However, all I could think of was this eerie feeling within me that informed me that despite the advantage I had, I was not only lucky to have survived this encounter but someone had just stood over my grave and was about to take a piss on it.

# *ELEVEN*

I went to bed early with plans to sleep until dawn but an unfamiliar hissing sound awoke me. Eyes partly open, I reached under my pillow and let my fingers curl itself around the butt of my Makarov. I lay there listening until I felt a sudden burst of heat against my nude body.

Kicking off the sheets, I twisted and hit the floor in a crouch. The Makarov in my hand. Scanning the room, it took several seconds to figure out that the orange flames licking its way up the wall of my motel room was the hissing sound I had heard. The flames were curling into black tinder and the fire was burning the wallpaper on the wall creating the hissing sound.

I hastened over to the closet where the Fire Extinguisher hung hooked on a nail at the bottom of the cabinet. I wondered why the fire alarm had not gone off. I flinched at the heat as the extinguisher made quick work on the wall. Moving into the next room the story was quite different. The room was in the second stage of burning. The curtains at the glass door and furniture on the patio where already gone. The fire had already found its way into the front room. I glanced at the fire alarm unit in the centre of the room and noticed that it had been quite professionally disabled. It was not smashed or anything like that, but the diminutive amber blinking light that flashed intermittently was no longer blinking. Someone had either removed the battery or disabled the wiring. Like I said, someone had gone to great lengths to disable it. Only a profession or someone who knew what they intended would know what to do.

The fire in the front room was almost beyond the effects of the extinguisher, but eventually it did win it over.

While I stood there naked, gazing over the charred remains of the room, a bullet pierced the patio door near my head and thud into the far wall. An instant later, I was on the floor behind the bed with the gun in my hand. I quickly scrambled for my pants, and waited, listening. I could hear the murmuring chatter of the other guests of the motel outside. In the distance was the wail of a fire truck nearby. In my vicinity, I could hear nothing of the person who had taken a silenced pot-shot at me.

Tracing the trajectory of the bullet, I could only venture that my assassin was somewhere outside beyond and between my patio and the swimming pool that was positioned within the motel's hub. The likeliest of places would be the mounted barbecue hob at the near corner side of the pool.

In the pale light of the dying flames, I could just make out the shape of a black windbreaker and the snout of a gun equipped with a humongous silencer. Whoever the shooter was, he had done this before. Except he had missed my head by mere inches. It was possible I moved at the instant he fired.

I did not return fire because I could not make him out clearly and if I missed, I just might be giving away my position. My assassin also could not get a clear read of me, either. It was a matter of waiting who flinched first. A waiting game. Who would move before either the motel's guest or fire crew arrived to check on my condition? I decided to take the bull by the horns. I was tired of people taking pot-shots at me.

Hugging the floor, I began to wriggle backward. When I was well away from the bed I stood up and moving quietly on my bare feet I made my way through the connecting door of my motel room into the next room. It was empty. Trotting on through its main door, down the carpeted corridor, I climbed up a flight of steps to the next floor. With any luck, I was hoping to get a shot at him from above. However, by the time I reached the railing overlooking the barbecue hob he had vanished from his hiding place.

Clusters of herbaceous vegetation on the motels ground provided excellent cover for him, but he had to dart from one to the other if he needed to target me. Eventually he would make a break for it and then I'll spot him.

The sounds at the front of the motel were growing louder and so was the fire truck's siren. A couple of male guests watching the spectacle from the floor above caught sight of me and whistled or whooped suggestively at me. The gun in my hand held no fear to them.

I stood there waiting behind the railing in the cover of the stairs overlooking the pool, the shrubs, and its surroundings, shivering in the night's cool air wondering why the hoots.

I was unaware of the cold or my condition until I gazed down at myself and noticed that apart from my pants, all I had on were the bandages wrapped around my chest covering one of my breasts.

I raised my gun hand at them and they fell silent immediately.

Finally, I spotted a crouch figure, as expected, making a break for it. Before I could fire at him, he had disappeared round the corner of the building. I went after him. Descending the stairs, past a couple of credit card operated vending machines, guests, onlookers and parking lot. My assailant in the black windbreaker was in full retreat mode.

I spotted him, jumping into a car parked in the front space of a convenience store beyond the motel property. His weapon leading the way into the car. I could have snapped a shot at him but he had a good lead on me and I did not want to attract a crowd more than I had already. I plodded my way back to my room not the least worrying how they could have found me. It was a mute question. Christina and Madame Nova undoubtedly played a part in disclosing my whereabouts, just as I had hoped.

It took several hours before the fire crew could douse the flames and leave. The police were another matter. Their questions filled me with frustration until a call from an unlisted number put paid to their enquiries. The motel manager tersely asked to check out. I couldn't blame her. I had created enough damage that even my deposit wouldn't cover. After arranging for her compensation, I packed up my unburned stuff, made several calls and left.

I drove to the Gray Butte airfield and arrived just after nine that evening. My destination was New York and the Haemin Café. Wilhelmina was waiting as usual when I arrived. She asked me our destination and I informed her.

I entered the wide-body cabin with its generous elements of comfort. The acoustics, the custom crafted interior furnishings were a comfort to my weary state.

Without saying anything, I headed towards the shower cubicle to get the grime and ash off of me.

Within thirty minutes, feeling refreshed I I asked Wilhelmina to join her requested consent to join her from the cockpit. She helped me change the dressing on my chest and after some small talk between us, she made her way back to the cockpit. I referenced the location of the Haemin Café. The address corresponded with an address I had previously seen. I had noticed the street in Silke's little black book. After consulting the book and the goggle map, I had a good idea where Dan might be hanging out.

To make sure I wasn't missing anything, I grabbed my next generation laptop and began a formal search for the whereabouts of one Daniel Friedlander, inputting all the parameters I was aware of. The laptop was one of only two prototype computers. Equipped with liquid gel coolant, in a titanium housing and an overclocking AI chip processor was able to encryptively link up to Apollo in seconds.

Apollo was my high performance SOPHOS dedicated twin omega systemic memory server that was linked to a secure, hacker proof and supposedly reliable failsafe satellite system. A proprietary system that had significant communication network access to a couple of algorithmic programs that activates Alpha. A heuristic databank that can hack into most digital computers on any network. Alpha is fully equipped with full photo and forensic programs designed with digital and analogue hard back door heuristic data crawler programs. Upgraded with a Schneider Cryptology system and a J-Dam satellite unit, Alpha was specially designed to by-pass any commercial or government electronic database and link into the live feeds on any grid in the world to seek out any information I might desire.

With constantly updated facial recognition and GPS targeting software that is tied into most of the World's intelligence and law enforcement databases, I inputted the name and description of Daniel Friedlander. Alpha began searching all international social media network databases, intelligence databanks like the American AFIS, DIA, and CIA. Alpha was also synchronised with most bank, police and government surveillance camera footage. In point of fact, Alpha can synchronize with any automated database that could locate the barest of electronic footprint needed to track Dan's whereabouts, like credit card uses, ATM walk-bys, cell phone uses etc.

As the plane banged west, I wondered what Halbert and Michel were up to. I sat behind my desk punched a couple of buttons on the Vista Pane Display Unit surface, and a holovid plasma screen slid up into view. I was linked directly to Deputy Director Prideaux. He was in a car when he took my video call. He looked worn out.

'Director?' I began

'Miss Dax'

'You okay, sir. You look a bit tired to me'

'I'll be Ok ... thanks. I've just heard about Mr Silke. You didn't have anything to do with it by any chance, did you?'

I wondered what he meant. I had already notified him a couple of hours ago to make a quick search, because I believed Silke was no longer among the living. I didn't inform him of how I knew that or where it might have occurred or who might be responsible or even if it were true. Why didn't I? Well, because I already knew. Not all but the major facts.

'What have you heard?'

He leaned forward and tapped a button on his screen. Apart from several maggots clinging to his head, Edwart Silke's body was unremarkably unspoiled even if the positioning of his corpse looked somewhat odd. All that weirdness evaporated when snapshots of his backside slid into view. His backend was messed up with almost the same exact etchings from Francesco's chest.

'Where was he found?' 'At a potter's cemetery

'A potter's cemetery somewhere near San Pasqual, Los Angeles. He was somewhat ...' He hesitated for quite some time. I wasn't sure if it was for dramatic effect or he didn't really know how to voice what he wanted to say.

'He was what ... Director?'

'Victimized .... No ... that is a loose term. Silke was six foot one but at the time of his death, he was six foot eight. He was elongated ... bones dislocated, cartilage, ligaments were sort of .... Remember the inquisition?'

'Hmm'

'Well, they used some sort of device to torture alleged witches ... your man Silke, was executed almost the same way. Whoever did this used a method we can't seem to put a handle on yet. According to the Coroner's report, he had massive dislocation to virtually every bone in his body, serious ligature marks on his wrists and ankles and his ... a synovial capsule reading indicated that his trauma happened bit by bit over time'

'Karma is a bitch, isn't it?'

Prideaux rolled his eyes 'Miss Dax, really?' 'Have the locals released the news yet?' 'No'

'Where are you now?' 'On my way to New York'

Prideaux sighed, then got thoughtful. 'Miss Dax' he paused 'Is there something you wanna tell me?' The Director asked

I felt that now was the time to inform him of Marion's wild theory. I started slow and finished with my confrontation the previous evening. I even explained my theory on the oleic, linoleic acids and scented balsam from his toxicology report his people found on the corpses.

'Hmm' he grunted at last when I was done. 'That could explain the oils on Silke's forehead too. You sure about this? I have no need of implicating or antagonising the Catholic Church with wild theories'

'You believe this tale?'

'Do you have any ideas where these parchments are?' I was surprised by his question.

'No'

'Huh' he mumbled again 'You do realise this might be a fantasy'

'A wild one. If you believe this'

'Hold it. Don't go so overboard. It's been more than proven that some myths are based in some form or the other as fact. Are you aware that this office has a department dedicated to the investigation and study of the weird and inexplicable?'

'You're saying you believe this crap?'

He beamed a coquettish grin at me 'I would be a fool if I dismissed this or at least not have an open mind about this' Now and again, I was surprised by his reaction 'This Father Halbert seems to believe in it and just for being aware of it, he has chosen to silence you'

In all my thinking, I had not thought of that, but I should have, considering what happened to Anne and Bruce. I was a danger because I was in Marion's purview, a condition that had exposed me to knowing whatever secret he had discovered, I knew religious enigmas would be a problem. Not this much, but a problem'

'I knew this was going to be a problem' I grumbled into the screen.

'This shouldn't be our concern' 'No'

'Silke is dead. There is no longer any reason for you to continue this hunt'

'Yes. But if what you believe has any bases, Monsignor Halbert and Michel need some painful reminders of how religious people should behave'

'How are you going to do that?'

'I have a hunch they will be on the hunt for big Dan and even take another shot at me. I'll be waiting'

'And the mob?'

'I think I've settled things with them' 'How so?'

'If you ask nicely you'll find out'

I tapped a button and the holovid image was replaced by photographic images of Apollo's search.

As of four hours ago, there were ATM depictions and security camera images of big Dan in nineteen of the thirty-four images. All centred around a spot in, at or near Brooklyn. Displayed on the preview pane was Daniel Friedlander's rap sheet including recent electronic activities. His rap sheet read like a primer for bigtime criminality, B and E's up the whazzo. Racketeering, kidnapping and armed assault, but it seemed not much could be pinned on him. He must have had an angel perched on his shoulder overlooking his good fortune.

One of the last electronic activities was an ATM capture somewhere in the east of Brooklyn and his bank statements. They included the purchase of a set of luxury travel cases, *Dramamine tablets*, durex condoms, and a bundle of cigarettes packets. There was a deposit but no indication of a sale of two tickets at a travel agency. This could only mean he was running, and possibly running with a female person. A likely assumption if he had retrieved the money Marion was hiding. The Dramamine anti- sickness motion tablets meant he was trying to use the sea to escape. Probably a ship or boat on standby.

I had to get to him before he skedaddled for good.

# *TWELVE*

**D**aniel Friedlander truly was not my quandary, he was a means to an end. The means to find my problem, my problem being Monsignor Halbert and his Confrères. I needed to find them or let them find me. Whichever was convenient, preferred me. I didn't care if they were men of God, they were, like Dan, going to suffer the same fate as they deemed others and as I deemed fit.

But where to begin and how?

I turned to my computer and began researching the Priory while I began a search for Father Theodore Halbert.

The Priory of Scion had recently grown a certain notoriety since the publication of Da Vinci's code by Dan Brown and the movie made based on the book. However, the Priory wasn't so lamentedly interesting as portrayed in the book or movie. Some argued that though it may have been founded around 1099 with grandmasters that included Isaac Newton and Leonardo da Vinci, in all likelihood, the society was perhaps a hoax. An elaborate one but still unfounded.

I searched for a biographical data of Father Theodore Halbert. Alpha informed me he was born in Ferrara in 1964. His father was a physician and his mother a fourth grade teacher. He has two other siblings Nicola and Michele.

From a young age, he was indeed a man of God. A principled child who was an altar boy and who attended a catholic school, then a catholic college where he received a Master's in Mathematics and Sacramental Theology.

One winter day it seems, influenced by the works of a Dominican Friar, a *Girolamo Savonarola* who prophesied civic glory and the continuation of Christian ethics, he knocked on the door of a catholic nunnery and begged to be admitted.

He was ordained as a Priest two years later. Much of his life after that is vague. From what I could piece together, he was at one point invited to the Vatican because of his Dominican ideals. He was later invested as a knight in Malta and by the Holy Sepulchre in Jerusalem. He was appointed as the auxiliary Bishop for *Santa Giulia*, a church in Lucca, Italy and there he has remained. The biographical data did not tell me about the man himself. His beliefs, his hopes, or more importantly his motivation for doing what he was now doing.

I called Seymour and asked him to search for someone from the Catholic Church that he can speak to pertaining to the man, Father Halbert. As soon as he informed me he'd do what he can, my thoughts went back to Marion Steiner and his tale.

If Halbert and his minion Michel were after me for what I might be aware of, then, it stands to reason that I'll be better suited to find the one thing I had to have. I have. I continued to mull over the meaning of Halbert's words

"Secrets staying Secret" and its relation to Marion and the parchments. There must be something damaging within those parchments, if they were authentic. If they were in Marion's possession, he would want to keep them safe from those that would create harm. I did not know much of the man-child to know where he might hide any valuables of his. If indeed, they were in his possession. He did assure me of that, even if I wasn't interested at the time. I doubt he would have mentioned it to Mr Silke or big Dan. All they were interested in was the money.

Marion would not have hidden the parchments where no one would ever find them. As an archaeology student, he would have left behind a clue, hints, just in case he did not make it.

But where, what or how? Where would he hide it?

I thought for a minute then it occurred to me. His riddle! The one he shared with me when we were just about to leave my hotel room, just before we got jumped by Silke and his pals.

"What is the last thing you take off before you go to bed?"

It took me ten minutes of hard thinking before I realised I was perhaps thinking too hard and perhaps a bit too metaphoric. When I understood that I didn't have to be too literal, the answer fell with surprising easy into my lap.

The last thing anyone takes off before going to bed was one's feet off the floor.

His feet!

It hit me like a ton of bricks. I should have known.

He had just recently had squiggled illegible tattoos inked on the sole of his feet. That incomprehensible fowl's scratch must contain a message or clue as to where he hid the parchments. Once decoded, of course.

I tapped the screen, downloaded the autopsy photos of Marion Steiner, and paid particular attention to the writings on each sole of his feet.

I tackled the one his right sole first.

《Ⴀ ᛁᛁᛁᛁ ᛁᛁᛁᛁ ᛁᛁ Ⴕ ᛁᛁᛁ ᛁᛁ  ᛁᛁ ᛁ. ꐨꓷꙥ  ꓤꓼꓨꞏꓚ.

After an hour, I tried the one on his left.

ᛊᛁᛁ ᛁᛁ ᛁᛁ ᛁᛁᛁᛁ ᛁᛁᛁᛁ ᛁ  ᛁᛁᛁᛁ ᛁ ᛁ. ꓔꛟ  ꓤꙛꓶꙭ

For almost two hours, I stared at the writing, trying to make sense of them. They still didn't resemble any language I recognised. They were not Germanic, Erdogan, Sumerian, Mandarin, or even Runic. No, this was still incomprehensible to me.

Then I thought of using Galahad to decipher them. I tapped a button.

'Call Galahad No. 3' I voiced into the vista pane.

Sir Galahad the third, is the nickname I gave the semi-functional Interactive Artificial Intelligence Residential Automated Habitat system of my smart homes. The Homesaver unit closest to my current position was my smart home No. 3, located in Seattle.

Like its parent Homesaver unit in my Penthouse home in London, it had a detailed chip matrix designed specifically to anticipate all my personal preferences with advanced algorithm programs linked to the multimedia and telecommunication software that was second to none. Except for a few minor programming, it was almost identical to its parent homesaver.

Over the drone of the plane, I waited until a soft tone

bleeped and before long Galahad's electronic voice that resembled Jerry MacDonald, a Canadian newscaster whose voice I loved hearing, came on. *'Please identify yourself'* it said

'Rumpelstiltskin has a name' I recited The tone on the other end went quiet.

*'Hello Miss Susan; your last remote contact was today …*
*9.27am.*

*How has your morning been?'*

'Just fine Galahad. Please re-initiate Apollo?'

There was a short pause *"Apollo priority command nexus located and contacted. Prepare for security identification"* Galahad informed me.

Another pause. *"Miss Dax?"* 'Yes?'

*"Apollo is coming online"*

'Thank you Galahad. Apollo, you there?'

*"Good Afternoon this is Apollo secure server"* A feminine synthetic voice that had a striking similarity to Vivian Leigh's voice came on-line.

I spoke softly. 'Apollo this is Cancer, confirm identity'

Without warning, a blinking light flashed at me, taking a snapshot of my image, then started running a facial and retinal identification program. It didn't take more than 3 seconds for it to acknowledge me.

I despised having to go through the process of identification but it was a security protocol Seymour and Daniel Anderton, one of the few men I trusted, had long ago insisted should be in place in the event of hacking or some other form of exploitation into Galahad's system.

*"Identity challenge verified. Voiceprint ID authenticated.*
*Retina scan authenticated. No indication of stress. Imprint*

*scan not obligatory. Identification confirmed. Password required"*

'Humpty Dumpty sat on a wall' I replied making myself comfortable in one of the planes sofas. The thirty-inch holovid screen didn't flicker.

"*Challenge evaluated and authenticated. Retinal, voiceprint verified. Identity assessed, established and confirmed. Cancer authorised to access Apollo secure server system. Good morning, Miss Dax"*

'Apollo, get ready for another query protocol with specific attention to ancient languages and writings'

"*Command acknowledged'*

' Identify and decrypt writings on autopsy image three two'

'Command acknowledge. Satellite tasking priority eminent. Running script. Primary link, established. Wireless link, strong. Signal and uplink protocol, strong. Overriding admin access. IP address 935.631.25.8 inputted. Connecting to primary secure port. Securing port. Linking with Sunshine satellite. Penetrating system security . . . Port command, on . . . .

Key found . . . Processing . . . Loading data decryption . . . Processing . . .

*Processing* " There was another brief pause before Apollo began

again. "*Processing . . . Processing The     writing    is     . . . Enochian … processing … and Zarathustra"*

'Zarathustra? Enochian …?' I glanced at the image of Marion's feet. Angelic script and a dead language? 'Is your battery running down, Apollo? That isn't Enochian … neither does it look anything like Zarathustra'

"*The writing is a combination of Enochian and Zarathustra*" Apollo stated emphatically.

Apollo must have blown a fuse. I know Enochian, Zarathustra ... well not so much but I can recognise it when I see it. The writing on the sole of Marion's feet was definitely not Zarathustra neither was it Enochian.

'Check again?' I argued

A pause, followed by a beep. "*Writing is a combination of Enochian and Zarathustra*" Apollo again insisted, unequivocally stating that the writing was Enochian or Zarathustra. He must be developing a fault.

'Boss, four minutes' Wilhelmina's voice notified me over the intercom

'Ok decrypt writing' I challenged Apollo

For a long minute, it was silent. When it did speak it was with an resolved resolute it answered. "*Unable to decrypt Enochian or Zarathustra writing*"

'Ha! If the writing is a combination of Enochian or *Zarathustra*, you should be able to decrypt it' I argued with Apollo.

"*Unable to decrypt writing*" 'You're useless' I grumbled '*Yes, Miss*'

'Don't get cute' I cautioned 'All right, begin a new search, all parameters, social media, the works for Marion Steiner aka Larry Steinberg and his red Datsun license plate AT 498 C. Commencing from arrival in Los Angeles, his visit to the Da Vinci exhibition and subsequent journey to Prine. Inform me when you have the results'

I rose to join Wilhelmina in the cockpit. 'Something wrong boss?' Wilhelmina enquired

'Something has been bothering for almost a week now. A riddle. Would you believe that?'

'Riddle? What sort?'

'A man walks into a bar and asks for a glass of water. The bartender takes out a shotgun and fires at him, just missing him by inches'

'Shoots at him?'

'Yes, the bartender shoots at the man. The man thanks the Bartender gives him a huge tip and leaves.

Why does the man thank the bartender and give him the tip?' Like me, Wilhelmina was stunned for an answer.

'Why thank the barman and give him a tip?' she pondered 'I'm sorry boss, I have no idea why'

'Neither do I. Why would the man thank and tip for being shot at? It's been bugging me for ages'

Shaking her head, Wilhelmina made her final checks and told me we were coming in for a landing.

\* \* \* \* \* \* \*

We landed in La Guardia just after eight in the morning on one of its several private terminals, where I asked Wilhelmina to journey to our Upper East Side home.

'Let Vincent know I'm on my way'

Mr. Vincent "Vince" Samberg was Seymour's live-in valet and manservant.

The mornings in New York is always in full tilt and sticky. I hailed a yellow cab.

I asked the Ukrainian cab driver to take me to Brooklyn. I gave him the name of the street where Dan had made one of his last credit card purchases. There were two names in Silke's little black book that lived in New York. Sonia and Patricia. Sonia lived on one of the streets in the vicinity of Haemin Café and where one of Dan's last electronic purchases was made, eleven hours ago. That was where I intended to go.

349 W 86th St349 W 86th St. The driver glanced suspiciously at me in his rear view mirror then his attention was directed to the hefty roll of dollar bills I had pulled from my purse. He grinned then tapped on the charge metre and engaged his gears.

New York is one of the most widely held happening cities in the world. Most people would consider as the most industrialized, cultural, financial, and luxurious city in the world. A place where you can find anything, at any time or price. Unfortunately, none of those eccentricities applied to me. I hated New York, I always have, even if I've spent several months in and out of the city. Maybe, it was too belligerently insensitive for me. To me, even the air was hard to take in. I do not know why I have an abhorrence for the city, but I've always tried to give it a wide berth when travelling despite its popularity.

To me it smelt grubby and full of dirt. Although I admired the activities, the bubbling inability of the inhabitants to pause, I felt it a tad too bustling for me. Given the designation as "The city that never sleeps", I guess it was too damn appropriate.

To me depending on the time, it could smell like stale rot, at times cold and fresh with a hint of wet mud or dog. However, every so often it was like a pleasant spring Thursday afternoon. That was not today. Today, it was like a wet Wednesday morning even if the day was Friday.

The rush hour was in spate and nobody was going anywhere fast.

The driver moved slowly into the nearest traffic lane on the Interboro Parkway, while I leaned half off my seat, keeping my eyes on the shops and buildings, which I hoped, would lead me one-step closer to the elusive big Dan.

The cabby glanced up at me via the rear view mirror, openly admiring my beauty.

'You meetin' someone, lady?'

'No, but something like that' I assured him. I leaned forward and whispered in his ear.

'Someone like you but much burlier'

He blushed under his copper complexion. 'Ah, I see, lady.

What you call it? A rendezvous, yes?'

'Precisely' I grinned, having implied that I was meeting someone for a romantic encounter.

'This not your first time in town, is it lady?' 'Nope'

'You watch out, lady' he cautioned 'We New Yorkers very tricky' he said flicking his thumb against his index finger several times in quick succession.

We moved into the outer traffic wheel, and then turned slowly onto one of the slip roads, away from the business centre of New York. Driving east along the Jackie Robinson Parkway, then the Eastern Parkway and finally my journeys end, the Jamaican Avenue. I took the opportunity to take in the sights. However, neither the Cypress Hill cemetery, nor Highland Park held any appeal to me.

'Last stop' the driver informed me as he pulled to a

halt.

It took the cab almost an hour and thirty minutes to reach Thomas S Boyland Street the adjourning road next to Sonia's place and a stone's throw away from the department store of Dan's last automated acquisition. Peeling off a couple of notes from my thick wad, I handed him more than the cost for the ride including a generous tip. His tip included a glance at my Makarov sitting pretty within his holster, in case he had other designs on me, other than driving his cab. Wishing him well, I slid off the seat and strolled down the street. I waited until the driver was out of sight before reversing course and headed towards St Marks Avenue.

It took me seven minutes of walking before I reached St Marks Avenue.

I looked up and down the street. It was as inviting as a cellblock, a neighbourhood where one is likely to be rolled in a church. I knew instinctively what might lay behind every dirty apartment house, front or behind each of the alleys, by the smell of piss in the alleyways, clothes on the lines or pigeon poop on the roofs. People working, dealing drugs, studying, taking tests, fucking, were having a lucky break, sweating their bad luck, or even being scared silly.

Thanks to the goggle map, I knew exactly where Sonia's place was. Fifty feet from the iintersection, a 2011 black Chevy Sedan with tinted glasses was parked, the doors locked. After my initial glance at it, I walked past it and down the street, casing Sonia's buildings as I went.

There were other cars on the street but there was something ominous about that Chevy that made me want to pay particular attention to it.

No. 1641A St Marks Avenue, Brooklyn, Sonia's

apartment was located in a brown, partial renovated detached three floor apartment building. It had been razed by fire, years ago and was only now, to a degree being restored to its former glory. If it had any glory before.

Activity on the street was busy but light. There was a Dunkin' Donuts franchise up the street and a couple of "mom and pop" stores littering the street. I found a diner called "Been There" a couple of blocks down and entered. The diner had an oddness about it, an air-conditioned mustiness of stale smoke, beer and burnt coffee grounds. The front entrance let you into a dining room of sorts with a bar adjacent to it.

I smiled nicely at the patrons within the half-filled diner who would meet my glance, which was more than half of them, before settling behind a stall near the front window where I had perfect view on the door to Sonia's place. After positioning my beige Cartier leather happy birthday satchel next to me, I ordered some hash browns, eggs and bacon from the Albanian waitress in the pink white uniform. Finding a discarded copy of the days early edition New York Post lying on one of the seats I reached over and started reading some articles from it while I kept an eye on my target.

On the headlines, apart from another Russian Curler in the Pyeong Chang, South Korea's Winter Olympic failing a drug test, there was a replicated church shooting in Russia, just days after the Florida school shooting incident. This time, five victims were killed in contrast to the seventeen killed by the student in Florida. It was beginning to be a theme with young disturbed individuals. If you're fed up with your life, buy a machine pistol, eat a satisfactory last meal and go blazing at those you hate. Strangely, there was no news about the

Yankees or Red Sox baseball teams but there was another major headline suggesting that President Trump was going after Oprah. By what means, why and how, I did not care. Neither were his attempts to slam down on his predecessor's nuclear payment deal with Iran. The man, Trump was hardly a politician and more a Kardashian. I know, I've met him twice before. Obama was several times the president, Trump proclaims himself to be.

As I continued to read, I noticed a theme. Obesity. Apart from the discovery of a famous pirate's bones, there was an article criticising Fat cops weighing down the resources of the NYPD. Another fat story was played in the air. An over-weighed farty passenger seemingly forced a plane to make an emergency landing. When the waitress returned with my order, she had an odd expression on her face. An expression of concern, not for herself but for me. I glanced behind her to fathom the source of her discomfort.

It was the Caucasian men sitting at the bar with black leather jackets and intense sneering expressions on their mugs. The two wise guys at the bar with half-filled Pabst in clear glasses in front of them staring into space. One of them had a cigarette stuck between his teeth, his black leather jacket displayed a bulge, which could only be one thing. He, for some reason was paying a particular interest in me. His greying counterpart looked like an old-style ward heeler and had a nose, which someone had long ago knocked out ofline.

The surly faced bartender behind the bar had his head down, eyes fixed on his rag as he wiped the counter making an half- hearted attempt to ignore what he knew was about to happen.

'You should leave' whispered the waitress to me.

I should have known. Since the mafia knew almost as much as I knew, I had hoped Sonia's place would be the ideal place for me to begin my search instead of the Haemin Café. I had chosen Sonia's place because I had hoped for less interference. I did not think the mob knew of her place or that they would have had their own guys monitor her, in the event Dan showed up here. The only superlative spot within five blocks to keep an eye open for him. If they knew this, then not only would Dan be aware of it, but probably Halbert and his entourage would figure it out too. Also my outfit, makeup and my highlighted contours made me stand out. I should have drabbed down from my dark turtleneck, black leather jacket equipped with my body armor, tan overcoat, brown slick thigh leggings tucked into my ankle boots.

I grinned at them.

'Yeah guys, take a picture. I'm a girl, I'm curvy and dress in frilly' The one with the cigarette blurted half-way across the diner

'You sure are, lady?' when I looked up at him, he shifted the cigarette in his mouth with two fingers 'You lost? Sure you're in the right place?'

'I'm just having breakfast, mate'

Noticing my accent, he sneered at me. 'Hey Johnny, babe's a Brit' he said. As he tagged me for being a British subject, I instantly tagged him as a Cugine. A young Italian tough guy or earner for the mafia looking to be taken serious in an attempt to be "made" someday.

'Leave her be. She's only having breakfast?' his much older companion Johnny complained softly to him. It seemed he was the man, the voice of authority of the two.

I tapped the waitress 'Who's he?'

Before she could answer, the bartender interrupted 'Marie, better get the filters from the back huh'

'You have nice piece of ass, lady' Cigarette smoking guy snorted at me whilst he stubbed out his cigarette.

I didn't need this. Not now.

Then a point suddenly struck me. An idea occurring to me then and there was the last thing I needed to have, but it had happened.

Stirring the pot.

I almost kicked myself for not having thought of it earlier. Since Halbert seemed to be privy to information the mafia had, it wouldn't hurt to make as much a commotion as I could. Presuming this was true, then the more commotion I made the faster they will be able to track me.

I got slowly to my feet and walked over to the wise guys. 'Am I missing something guys?' I asked both men

'Nah, I'd like to help find you something though' the younger of the two jokingly giggled at me as he eyed my groin.

'You think you're man enough to find it?' I asked him with a broad simulated smile on my face

'You bet'cha' Johnny's companion reached up and cupped my arse. 'But this ain't a place for such things, babe' he suggestively said with a leering grin as he caressed his hand up the length of my torso.

This was one of the things I cannot stand at all. The presumptions of males. Italian males, especially. I think it's something a hell of a lot of girls learned never to get used to.

'We should go someplace, have a drink … talk … you

know ... get to know each other. Tell me all about that Queen of yours ... your teas .... What'dyou say?' he asked as his hand finally stopped on my breast, cupping my breast with his palm to emphasise his point.

I cocked an eye at him 'You yanks all act butch but in fact you're much like Freddie Corleone'

'Who?' he curiously enquired just as his other hand reached up to touch my cheek. I grabbed his index finger, twisted and broke it straight back without moving his arm. Before the surprised pain reached his amazed face, my fingers curled round the butt of his gun tucked in his coat, while at the same time I hooked a leg under his stool and kicked it from under him. His knees jerked as he collapsed in front of us.

Pulling out the gun in quick succession, I aimed the snout of the Colt gun inches away from prying eyes but firmly at his companion Johnny's family jewels.

For some reason, Marion's dead body flashed through my mind. I wondered why that was. It had been happening every so often since I left the delightful town of Concorde.

I turned to face Johnny 'Your friend, Freddo has trippy legs, what do you think?' I remarked.

Johnny tried bringing back his sneer, saw the expression in my gold speckled eyes and thought less of his intentions. He cleared his throat 'I regret he never learned when to listen or shut up'

'That's what I thought' I said releasing the clip from the Colt Combat Elite gun and clearing the chamber of the bullet already in it. 'Perhaps he should go back home to Corleone'

Johnny noted how efficiently I handled the weapon.

Handing the steel pieces of the gun and cartridge over to the bartender, I turned away from them, sat back down to finish my breakfast and keep an eye on Sonia's door.

I ignored the argument and commotion behind me as Johnny pulled his subordinate out of the diner.

The disturbance put paid to my stake out. It was time to change tactics. The diner, not to mention me, was now compromised. Maybe with a new found approach, I might just get lucky.

# THIRTEEN

Iapproached Sonia's apartment house bypassing the ominous black Chevy and pressed the buzzer set in the half-charred doorframe. I was checking the time on my Breitling wristwatch across my left wrist when the door opened.

A woman with white hair peered out. Her hair had dyed out years ago, and her painted eyebrows looked like batwings. Once she may have been pretty but her beauty had long since vanished along with her dreams. She glanced up and down the street as if to make sure I was alone.

'Yah?' she suspiciously asked, as she looked up at me. Her faded blue grey irises had the look of glaucoma. There was caked secretion between her tear ducts.

'Sonia please'

She gazed at me. Maybe because I was not the usual type to grace her front door.

'Ya're nat one of her regular friends, are ya?' 'I would like to be'

'Nah, ya wauldn't wanna be'

I discerned the confusion with the "a's" and "o's" of her Midwestern accent.

'Ah please ma'am could I at least try it?' I asked in a jeeringly Oliver Twist way.

The woman decided to grace my presence with a smile. A mouthy smile with brownish blackened teeth.

Her head disappeared as she snuck her head back through the door. I heard whispering and then after a minute she re-appeared. She swung the door open, just enough to allow me to squeeze past her. I smelt her oily aged sweat over the cheap perfume she liberally splashed on herself. For the first time, I see what she was wearing. She had on Labour Day white boots, skin-tight thigh pants that gave way to her bulging tummy and a pullover blouse with blue spot dots drawn over her copious breasts.

She slid a bolt after she closed the door. My ears were greeted by music.

The music I heard was the kind you hear in department stores. There was something obscenely about the loudness of it, I was mildly surprised the whole building didn't shake. And loud as the music was, it was not enough to drone out the other sounds within the orchestration of resonances. Like the stupid reality show of housewives. Of course, I do have a problem about disliking reality stars. The grunts and heaves of a couple, a few doors down the hallway also offended my ears.

'Expecting trouble?'

'Ya ne'er know these days. Hanest living ain't what it used ta be'

I wondered if she would recognise what an honest living would be like.

'Ya a nice-sized girl' she said, running a quick and experience eye over me, spotting the carefully concealed bruises on my face. 'I bet ya nat so sweet. Ya been knacked 'bout a bit? Dan't 'orry chil' we all 'ave been'

I forced a grin. She had a cynical wisdom, which I bet stemmed from years of experience.

A man came out of a door at the foot of a stairway that ran to the house's second floor.

'Ah here's Otto' she said, laying a hand, with fingers like sausages, on my arm.

Otto's face was moon shaped with fat pinching the corners of his small eyes. He had had the sleeves of his shirt cut off, exposing his broad upper arms. He had metal studs gleaming from his wide belt. His pants were as fit and tight as a woman's, showing the bulges in his powerful legs. Including the package between his legs. 'What you want Sonia for?' Otto asked me barring his teeth that were in worse shape than the woman's. 'Woman business'

'What kind of … woman … business?'

'Let 'er go up, Otto. What 'arm kan it do' the woman insisted. Otto shook his head. 'I get feeling she ain't playin' 'ith full deck' he complained 'She 'oesn't look like she belon' here. You hear that voice, she a fuckin' brit' he hesitated then asked 'You get any references, lady?' 'Silke' I replied

The woman smirked and scowled, nodding her head in acceptance. Obviously, Silke's name carried more than weight.

'That a fuckin' good reference' Otto said, then he stuck out his hand 'A hundred smackers, tha' our cover charge'

I reached into my Cartier satchel and peeled out two

hundred dollars from my Lady Gaga wallet-purse.

'No disturbances' I pointed out to him as I crossed his palm with the notes.

Otto grinned widely as he led me up the stairs.

The first thing I saw when he opened the door to let me through was the array of whips, belts and other sex toys laying on a leather covered bench covered with silk trappings. The second thing was the girl. Even from a woman's point of view, she was lovely.

Lying against a stack of throw pillows on an unmade bed, her black her was sprawled across the pillow. Her olive complexion, high cheekbones complimented her lean taut face. She was younger than me, lithe and petite.

The door closed behind me. She assessed me slowly.

'Who are you darlin'?' she asked in a husky voice 'You Sonia?'

'Huh huh'

I peeled off three hundred dollar bills and held them over her. 'No small talk'

She slowly rose to her knees 'What's your game?' 'Dan Friedlander'

'Him?' she frowned, reaching up on her knees to take the bills 'I'm surprised and a little disappointed'

I tossed her one of the bills 'Why's that?' 'You don't look his type'

'I'm not. I'm just looking for him'

'Did you mention this to Otto?' she asked reaching across her bed to pick up a pack of cigarettes and slip the note into the space between her breasts.

'Nope, would I be allowed up here if I had?'

'Good thinking. He was in a panic when he was here' she advised as she bummed a crudely rolled cigarette in between her teeth and lit it up with a zippo lighter. The yellow slip across her shoulder slid down her shoulder revealing her small, round breast. She blew smoke in the air before giving me another tantalising smile.

'He was here?' 'Yesterday'

'He was in a panic, why?'

'Don't know, don't care … something about his father coming after him'

'And Silke?'

'You know Silke?' I shook my head.

'Why are you trying to find Dan?'

'My business'

'He's not a person you wanna go looking for' The odour from the cigarette informed me that this wasn't the kind she'd offer the Chief of Police. 'You don't look like a gangster and not a cop. Even cops have second thoughts when trying to find him'

'Are you trying to scare me off or tell me you care?' 'Maybe'

'Just tell me what you know'

'Well, you find Silke, you find Dan'

I walked closer to the bed 'How do I do that?' 'How should I know, but I do know they left town' 'If you wanted to find Dan, where would you look?' 'Hell. That's where I'd start'

The door to the bedroom burst open. Otto and the white- haired woman rushed in.

Sonia straightened up, her lovely mouth twisting.

'You should have waited, Otto!' she yelled 'I could have gotten her to tell me more'

'Shaddup' the woman snapped at Sonia.

'We hear' enough' Otto replied, picking up the biggest bullwhip from the silk covered wooden bench. 'Missy, if Danny or Mr Silke ever found out one of us set you on his tail, we'd all be sorry'

'Don't worry I'll be silent as a mouse'

'You won't be sayin' anythin'' He snapped the bullwhip as he moved towards me.

I sighed. Not again. Trouble seemed to be following me these past days.

'Hon' han' over your purse, guys 'atch what I see 'he have nice hunk of chunk in it'

I realized that they were perfectly willing to kill me for the money I carried or even just a favour for Dan.

Otto drew back the bullwhip. I see the heat form on his flushed cheeks, the flush of unsullied aggressiveness. The form of antagonism that belongs in a South Street bar.

I react first. I snatched up the straight-backed chair near the bed as the bullwhip sings through the air, towards me. The bullwhip snaked around the legs of the chair as I raised it to protect me. Otto cursed and tried to pull the bullwhip back.

Taking two steps forward, spinning the chair in the air, I twirl the bullwhip ends round the legs of the chair and smash it down over his head. The chair splintered as he spassed down to his knees. I wasn't done. I belted him in the face with the back of my fist making blood spurt.

Sonia squealed, bouncing on the bed to reach under

one of her pillows. She hauled out a .22 calibre Taurus pistol.

This crowd were ready for bare, not taking any chances.

Sonia didn't give me any warning, like stop or put my hands up. She pointed the gun and pulled the trigger. The slug hit the wall behind me. She was too agitated to shoot straight.

My opinion of her had drastically changed in the last twenty seconds or so.

'Shoot her!' Screamed the white haired woman.

I stepped towards her and punched the old woman in the breast.

Sonia was aiming again, collecting herself and feeling a measurably sense of control when I dived at her. We both landed and tumbled wildly across the bed, the weight and force was like charging a rugby ball across the goal line. The bed collapsed underneath us as she managed to squeeze off another shot. It went up and through the ceiling. Sonia made a sound like a sick bird as the small calibre gun danced from her hand to careen across the floor. Otto wiping his bloody face got to his feet and staggered for it. I reached for my Makarov but white hair jumped on my back. I spun her 160 pounds around and threw her over my shoulder at Otto who was having trouble locating the Taurus pistol because of the blood on his face. The white haired woman collided into Otto with a resounding thump.

When Sonia came at me again, I backhanded her to send her flying across the bed.

I pulled out my Makarov and surveyed the carnage before me.

White hair reared up from the heap she was in. 'Otto,

she hurt ya, Otto?' she cried, genuinely concerned for the brute of a man. 'No, I didn't' I replied 'He loves rolling johns. A woman might just be beneath him huh Otto?' I ridiculed.

'Ya bastard, if ya hurt …' her voice choked off as I pointed my pistol at her and fired a shot into her thigh. 'Aaaarrrrggghhhh' she screamed, with shock. I made sure it was a through and through, nowhere near her femoral artery or any major blood veins.

'Shut the fuck up' I said quietly.

Whelping in pain, she crouched back down into the heap she arose from and padded her wounds with the cushions she could get her hands on. I ignored her fidgeting as I grabbed Otto by the hair and lugged him onto the bed.

'Don't shoot Otto' Sonia pleaded loudly from across the room.

I pointed the pistol directly at Otto's ugly mug, in between his eyes. 'Give me a reason not to'

'Danny! I tell you about him. That's what you want huh?' she asked

'I'm listening'

'He and Silke left town a few months ago on a job. Trailing this guy who had gone into hiding. Rumour was this guy had loads of money due one of their bosses. So they went hunting for him. Yesterday, when he came, he was like I said he was worried, looking for paper. With his father looking for him, I can't say I blame the arsehole'

'Not his father … but a father' 'Oh' she muttered

Paper! He was looking for someone who forged ID's. Driver's licence, passports, and special IDs. Any sort really.

Dan may have already gotten hold of his special passport. The activity of a travel agency involving ticket sales on his debit card was an indication, unless it was a ruse.

'Paper, where would he go for that?' 'How should I know?'

'Fake Passports, where would you go?' 'I don't know'

I cocked the safety off my weapon 'You better think hard, luv' 'CFSix'

'What the hell is that?'

'CFSix is where'd I'd go for him to pick up his stuff and mine'

'CFSix?'

'Yeah, ask for Simmon's … yeah. The best paper guy there is. Top shelf, top charges. It's a estate agent shop down in the village' 'Where?' She quoted an address to me on Roosevelt Avenue.

'Are you lying to me?'

She glanced at my gun on Otto's head 'Why would I?'

I looked down at Otto. 'If she's lying' I hissed at him taking the gun off his forehead 'I'm coming back here and I won't be coming through the door' I said squeezing the trigger of my gun, putting a bullet through his kneecap.

Sticking my face in his, I said 'That should keep you from rolling johns for a while huh?'

I wanted to make a lasting impression and not only prevent his coming after me but to at least curb their fraudulent activities for a while.

As he screamed and flailed his legs, I dug through his

pockets and fished out my two hundred dollars. I also relieved Sonia of the bill I had given her. She stared at me with terror in her expression and eyes.

Before leaving, I injected a bit a humour into their lives by telling them they should really have to work on their *Joie de Visré*. I left them with not only a subtle threat, which I hoped, would cause them several sleepless nights, but also a ruckus that might send ripples through the underworld.

Descending the stairs, I ignored the sharp looks from the eyes of the other female residents and one or two johns and let myself out.

The menacing Chevy Sedan was nowhere to be seen.

# FOURTEEN

I hurried down the street, found and hailed a cab. In the cab, I updated my sketchy description and had it tag seaports, ferries or any transportation by water with the possibility that Dan could use to get out of the city.

Then I put a call through to Prideaux and asked him to do the same from his end. The FBI's resources could match mine but of a much wider ranger.

'How's your progress?' he asked 'Slow' I reported.

'So what's next?'

'I'm working on it' I told him before hanging up to put a call through to Lieutenant Stephanie O'Connor of 16th Police Precinct of New York. The Lieutenant was a friend who commanded a homicide squad of eight detectives at the precinct. She was married to a Costa Rican Executive immigrant named Victor and had a daughter named Judith … or was it Julie.

It was not always so. When we first met, she was a five foot nine brass Caucasian brunette who was almost as tough as nails, with smarts and a dedication that impressed both Seymour and I.

Several years ago, Seymour and I commandeered a cargo ship with some unsavoury goods and an unpleasant crew. When we found our way into New York harbour, indignant Officer O'Connor was on duty. At the time, she was studying for the detective exams and wishing something would happen to secure her transfer from her current beat. Fortunately, she was exactly at the right place and the right time. The perfect person you want to let take credit for a huge bust. Over the years, we have kept in touch, not that often but enough to promote and witness her rise through the grades.

'Lieutenant'

'Sue!' she bellowed over the phone 'Girl, it's been some time' 'Not too much time I hope?' I chuckled

'Don't be audacious babe... where are you?' she asked 'Somewhere close'

'Any chance you might swin' round and see Judith this visit?' 'I have no idea but it's a distinct possibility'

'Yeah right, pull the other one'

'Sorry Steph ... by the way how is Judith now? Still in kindergarten, right? She must be looking forward to the holidays' 'She is but she doesn't show it. She beginnin' to act like me but talk like her father. No inhibitions at all' 'Still has Bubbles?'

Seymour and I have a Christmas list for birthdays, anniversary, and remembrance dedicated to our friends around the world. We use it mostly to earn favours by sending personal gifts to them. My last gift to her daughter, Judith was a grizzly teddy bear she named Bubbles.

'Never sleeps 'ithout him' 'And Victor how is old boy?'

'Same ol' same ol'' she remarked with a slight touch of

tension in her voice 'How's your old man?'

'Seymour's just fine. Busy with work'

'Good. So babe, what's up? What has you makin' this call?'

Shop talk over, now to business. That's one of the things I loved about Stephanie. She almost never ever waste time.

'What makes you think that …?'

'You wouldn't be callin' unless somethin's up. What is it?

'I need a BOLO put out and be notified if any credible results show up'

'A Be On the Look-Out order? You don't ask for much do you?' 'I wouldn't ask but …'

'You don't need to ask. I take it trouble is a-brewin' somewhere abound huh?'

'Huh huh'

'What's the name for this BOLO?' 'When I have the time I'll brief you' 'Yeah I know'

I expressed my gratitude to her then told her. 'His name is Daniel Friedlander'

'Big Danny boy?' 'You've heard of him?'

'Our paths have crossed once or twice. Tell me you didn't get involved with that ape and that slimy pal of his … Silke?'

'I did'

She cursed 'Shit!'

'Language, Steph' I chastised

'You do know how to pick 'em, eh Sue?' 'Seems so'

'You sure you wanna mess 'ith these guys?'

'Well I need to find him first and it's kind of urgent. He might be on the run, so he'll be looking to get out of town'

'I get it'

'Good. You have my number'

'I'll let you know' she assured me then hung up. I felt satisfied.

If big Dan were running, he wouldn't get far. With all bases covered, all that would be needed would be the false name he was traveling under and he would be done.

Marion Steiner's face again flashed through my mind.

For some reason, I had been daydreaming of Marion Steiner. I had been reliving the moment we found his body in his apartment in Prine. Since his death, he had been on my mind more often than I would have wanted anyone to know. I had known him briefly, but it seemed despite my efforts, something had rippled between us. An electricity that was more than sexual and held the promise of more.

Accompanying his face were the images of a couple lying on a sidewalk on some unknown road. The images of a navy coloured nurse uniform worn by Anna Feldman and her acne-ridden boyfriend Bruce Windemill. Their relevance, which was now apparent to me except for the senselessness of their murderstill baffled me. It couldn't just be contact with Marion that decided their fate. However, I doubt it could be something else entirely.

After manoeuvring from a piazza through a maze of honey coloured colonnades on Roosevelt Avenue, I found myself in front of CFSix.

The CFSix estate agent office was part of a attention-grabbing nineties block out of which almost anything goes. Being on a popular street in the village did it no favours. Its entrance melted into the masonry behind it but its dark orange painted office with a plexi-glass tempered door huddled between a laundry matt and a pawnbroker shop stood embracing customers.

It was quiet inside, quiet and cool. I had a nasty feeling I was walking into trouble again. There was a world of difference between my mood and the reason I was here. I had a name to find and a friend to mourn or to curse, if I survive this. God help those who made me combine the two.

Within the offices of CFSix where large pictures of buildings up for rent, lease or buy. A large plasma advertised each of the buildings for occupation. Prize, cubit feet, neighbourhood were all distinctively publicised. Prizes that seemed too exorbitant for native New Yorkers.

A guy dressed in a dark-blue business suit and open neck maroon shirt that emphasised the blackness of his hair as well as the robin's-egg blue of his eyes with a stencilled nametag on his chest was seated at one of the four official looking desks, munching away at wop clam chowder and some breadsticks. The stencilled name was Harry. I found the meal somewhat appealing. He watched with interest as I walked up to him, give him a gestural nod and at the two other occupants in the shop. One was a girl wearing a purple beret sipping on a smoothie, the other a man agonising and fidgeting over the tightness of his shoes or belt, I could not tell.

When I said hello, he nodded with appreciated ostentatious on his face. It was something I was used to.

'Can I help you?' he asked me after assessing me with his eyes. 'Is Simmon's here?' I asked.

His disposition instantly changed.

His eyes flicked sideways at the curtained back door, shaking his head, trying to conceal a self-conscious smile.

'Who's asking?' he asked as he bit into a breadstick. 'So he's here'

His face tightened 'I didn't say that' 'I need to speak with him'

'Who are you?'

'No one you would want to know' I told him 'But I have to speak to him about a personal matter'

'What! You a cop?'

'I need to speak to him'

'Simmon's on the clock' he said bending his face towards the plate 'What's this about?'

'It's a legal and personal matter' I replied 'Call him out please, Harry'

He glanced at the stencilled nametag 'I'm gonna have to see some ID and ...'

'Call him out Harry'

He leaned back in his seat, folded his very proportioned arms 'I'm gonna have to see something'

'How about a bloody nose? Yours?'

His neck reddened, eyebrows went up and a masticating smirk formed on his face.

'Ok you better get the fuck out ...'

I reached up fast, grabbed a portion of his black fuzz of hair and yanked up, slamming his head hard onto the desk. Chowder spilling out of his mouth.

'I'm sorry, you were saying …?' 'Fuck …'

I slammed his head down on the desk again. 'Yes …'

He pointed earnestly towards the back room. I let go of his hair and was about to walk behind the counter when a too- brunette woman with freckles on her face, porcelain skin that had apparently was untouched by the New York sun with gorgeous white teeth and manicured hands wearing an baggy grey sweater and black cropped trousers came hustling through the curtained door. I immediately liked the long and lustrous and very conspicuous cut of her hair.

'What the hell is going on?' she barked. She saw me, then caught a glimpse of Harry, hurried over to him 'Harry what …?'

The two other occupants watched on with amusement. 'Sorry, just a minor disagreement' I said to her 'I tried asking for Simmons nicely'

'Well you found her'. She explained as she began consoling him like a mother towards her child 'Shit! What the fuck did you do to him?'

I don't think my surprise showed, however my voice did contain a little incredulity 'You?'

'Who the fuck are you?' she spat at me.

I caught a glimpse of her wristwatch left wrist. It was an expensive one. Informing me that she was the one in fact in charge of the place.

'The name is Dax'

Ignoring me she began fussing over the big man 'Oh … ooohhh … how come you did this to poor Harry?', she asked taking out a napkin and applying it to his nose.

'My impatience was larger than his perseverance'

'Don't worry sweetheart … oooohhh … I'll fuck her up bad' Simmons cooed over Harry 'Ooohhh … she's a bad girl isn't she …' she said glancing at me with venom in her eyes as she led Harry back through the curtained door.

'Someone will be with you soon' she said to the waiting customers before turning to me.

'Don't try rousting me, bitch. We're clean' 'I'm not a cop'

'Yeah, right' she spat dubiously at me

'Hey hold on, I know first-aid' I said following both of them through the curtained door.

This back office was darker but much more stylish and larger. For the size, I expected two doors in the back room but I saw only one that led to either a bathroom and/or storage space. However, there was something wrong with the dimensions. The floor creaked as I made a quick survey and figured it was much smaller than the landscape of the building allowed. I filed that fact away.

Apart from the odd shape of its architectural design, there was another set of Posture and Mesh back chairs in the backroom but unlike the front office, the walls weren't covered by an array of apartment or studio buildings of most kind of buildings you can ever find or on offer. Swords, Dragons, Klingon letters, Symbols, Faces … all kinds of writing was displayed on the walls. At first, I thought I had walked into a tattoo parlour. I was guessing that this was where the costly or perhaps the illegal kind of work was imparted from. It made me think of the soles of Marion's feet again. I could see from her eyes that she was trying to work up a tirade of curses to throw at me 'What right have you got to … don't you need a search warrant or somethin'? If you're …'

'Like I said, not a cop'

'Then you better leave before I call someone' 'The cops?' I asked

'Yeah' she snapped

'Go ahead, I'll wait' I replied, taking my sweet time to sit in a chair next to Harry and his bleeding face. I found a piece of rag and told him to tilt his head. He gingerly did as he was told. As I placed the rag on his face and told him to leave it on for five minutes, I noticed a sliver of red light peeking from just under one part of the wall. A door-sized red sliver.

'Who are you again?' Simmons asked I told her.

'Have we met?' 'I doubt it'

'What do you want?'

'A massage, a pony … what the hell do you think girls like us want?'

'How the fuck would I know?' 'You're a woman like me'

'So what do girls like us want?'

'A good man and money in the bank' 'Good for us'

'You got a good man yet?'

She folded her hands and glanced at Harry 'What do you think?'

'And the other?' 'Working on it. You?'

'For now, I just want one thing' 'What's that?'

'Information. In particular, a name' 'Name? Who?'

'Daniel Friedlander or Big Dan, whatever you call him?'

She shifted uncomfortable, then shrugged 'Never

heard of him'

I reached into my wallet-purse and peeled off five hundred dollars. I held it in the air.

Bribery is a delicate art. Success really depends less on how much cash you're offering than on how you offer it. Even a most ethical person if they see you as likable, even difficult to get on with will not blow the chance of earning a few bucks from your stupidity.

'This will be for your troubles, lie to me and Harry here won't be nursing just his nose. He'll be nursing you'

'But I don't know …'

I pulled out my Makarov. 'Will showing you this help?'

Simmons tried to swallow but her mouth was too dry 'I-I … what makes you think I know …'

I got to my feet, went over to one of the panels next to the walls, and tapped on one section. When I heard the hollow tap, I pressed on it and the panel swung outward revealing the smell of heavy chemicals and a dark room. Safety papers, special different coloured ink-dots, a desktop computer, a colour photocopier, and some photographic equipment littered the small room. The musty air held a gentle rumble of working equipment.

I turned towards Simmons and snapped the safety off my gun. She shook her head trying to understand what was happening.

She tried and failed. 'What do you want to know?'

'The passport you made for him. What name is on it?' 'Joshua Brandt'

'When did you last see him?' I asked over my shoulder 'About six hours ago when he came to pick them up' 'Them?'

'Yeah. Two passports. One for him, the other for a girl'
'Girls name on passport'

'Evelyn Brandt' she answered without hesitation. I checked the time 'Good for you'

I holstered my weapon and handed her the money. 'Are you really the best there is?'

'Excuse me?'

'I hear you maybe the best paper forger in New York?'

She thought hesitantly for a moment. 'I don't know. There's Rigoberto, Perenyi and Zuckerman oh and Philippe in the west end'

'So one of the top three then?' 'Perhaps'

I peeled of a twenty more notes and handed them over to her. 'What's this for?'

'A retainer'

As she counted the notes, her eyes grew wider with each note. 'For what?'

'Your brand of business'

'For this you could get the real thing' 'Maybe. I do have three imperatives though' 'Rules? I-I don't like rules'

'Me neither, but you'll be able to follow mine' 'Yours?'

'There's no if and there are no maybes however if you ever give me up as easily as you just did for big Dan, I can promise they'll never be able to find all your body parts'

'I-I … won't …'

I turned my back to leave 'I hate questions, so they'll be no questions'

'And your third rule?'

'You'll figure it out' I said to her as I walked out through the door and then outside.

I was excited because now I had a name. Joshua Brandt. I didn't care about the girls name.

It did not take me long to update, Apollo's parameter search on Daniel Friedlander or pass on the information to Lieutenant Stephanie and the Deputy Director.

I spent the rest of the afternoon hitting a couple of wise guys haunts, dive bars, Pupusa and Taco shack, strip clubs, hooker joints or any place I knew where even a tinkle of corruption might be. I made no bones about who I was seeking, but the news preceded me anyway, so it didn't make much difference. I met with many sore faces, new faces and even hard faces. I did most of my talking with my hands than my mouth. There were a lot of winks. Big winks, broad winks and sly winks, I accepted and returned some of them with a wink or a grin back. I did have to use my booted heels a few times and on occasion, the almighty dollar, but it didn't achieve much. A few thought it might be beneficial to talk and some rattled off, but not enough to steer me onto a direct line to Dan. However, I let it be known to all and sundry that I was looking for Daniel Friedlander aka Joshua Brandt. Not one, if truth be told, knew they were blazing me a trail to find or be found by Halbert and his associates.

Those who saw my face and witnessed my actions knew just how badly I wanted him. Some figured something ominous would happen should I find my quarry and even knew that I wouldn't stop looking for my prey. It was what I hoped.

As the word went around, I knew that somebody somewhere wouldn't like it one bit, but there wasn't a thing he or she or anybody could do about it all.

Except one thing.

Someone could make damn certain I was less of a problem, by having me killed.

Time. Everything took time. Time was all I had. Time was what it was going to take. However, I was well aware you couldn't go after people with brass ones overnight. To do that and make up time, there was one last stop I needed to make.

I headed to Queens and to the former territory of the Black Panther Brigade – The Kingston Knights – The Ks. Benny Kamba was the one thug, I could trust to spread the word to the right ears about my search for Dan Friedlander.

Benjamin "Bad Jam" Kamba was a special kind of person, that is immediately apparent obvious to anyone from the Mexican drug user wasting away at the Sparks Deli supermarket to your grandmother. From an early age, the wheeling dealing drug- distributor whose young life was been marred with not only police but also rival gang problems, was a solemn soul. Before his eighteenth birthday, he had served five years for various drug related offences and was a regular guest with police authorities, whenever issues with gangland warfare sprung up. Five years ago, he was caught up in a drug sting but managed to escape. In the course of his getaway, a friend and ally of his who was more ambitious than him and was seeking to climb up the leadership rung of the K's, put five bullets into his back and left him bleeding to die in an alley, he all but gave up on life.

I wasn't exactly involved with the police sting, I was returning from the worse date I had ever had in a while. An unusually bad Cannoli meal made me want to throw up behind a dumpster. A dumpster where I found my bleeding, dying friend. He should have died but something about him made me want to save his life. I got him to a private clinic, which Seymour and I control and had a doctor tend to his wounds that eventually saved his life. At the time, I knew nothing of his life, when I did, I took steps to reform him. Despite my unbiased opinions towards his life, I informed him that we had implanted an electronic capsule filled with a deadly poison in one of his molars and that in three months it will be ready to set off and that the first incident we hear involving him after that period of time, we'll set it off. It won't kill him but it will paralyze him for life. It was a pack oflies but he bought it. Nevertheless, it was a great incentive for him to get his shit straight. In truth, I do not know if it was the resilience of truth or the threat or the incident that brought him into my purview, whatever it was, it changed him drastically. When he was sufficiently able, he disappeared. I learned later that within three months, he had cleaned house within his organization and dealt a deadly blow of revenge against his rivals.

Though his acts where deadly and conniving, he impressed me with his silent code of honor. A morality set oflaws he derived from the Samurai code of ethics. After he had sated his resentment with his drug-dealing cohorts, he got out of the thug life, including the drug dealing business and became a youth activist. Sometime later, he sought me out and swore to be at my disposal whenever

I needed. Not only for saving his life and not turning him over to the cops but for making him turn over a new leaf.

That was the last time I saw Bad Jam, now was the time to pay him a visit and perhaps collect on a favor.

I heard he was now an upstanding member of the

community who still had links to the drug trade.

The former headquarters of the K's was now a three-story brownstone building that was encircled with Benz's with tinted windows, basketball court and a family centre courtyard.

Entering the first floor, a host of thugs, male and females populated the front room. A good number of them were black, few were white. I had the honor of being the only colored chick in the bunch. The assortment of bleached and weaved hairs, piercings, high-tops and tats were notable. I got goosebumps seein' a sweat glistering babe with six inch heels fryin' ckicken in a huge pot as a butt naked cook in one corner.

Sitting with platform chains with diamonds in em. I bet several of them owned the matching Benz's and tinted windows. These guys broke rules, street fake poor fools with their weed man. They've each paid their dues, each of them a superstar in their own right, each capable of opening several cans of whoop ass. I wouldna be surprised if they were a couple of gats, a couple of rats, real or imaginary, a couple of wives. Nearly all the guys were playing customed-made, customed-paid, custom-fitted Playstation 2 Lorenzo fitted, a couple were playing ping pong, some of the women were smoking and gossiping with each other, while others were watching the game on one of the three large plasma TVs.

Each without making it obvious eyed me, spying me. Glancing with bigger caps, peelin', chillin', willin', drillin' and killin' the feelin' they might have to kill someone.

'Yo Niggas!' I yelled over the din of noise, forcing everyone's attention.

Instantly, everyone stopped. Those with firearms drew them out. I spotted AK's, Smith & Wesson, Colts, even an

Uzi, all aimed at me. There was a clenched rage stirring in the air. A cathartic moment no one would want to face.

I saw the contorted anger in their faces and I began to feel bad.

Loud rap music blaring over the airwaves, making my ears want to melt, yellow-wallpapered walls with so much graffiti that my eyeballs hurt, guns pointed at me, making feel the need to take a piss was more than enough of a welcome I could ever need.

This violent scene, I think of later on, is what some people might describe as an omen.

'Hey Cuz Cuz ... calm down your shit ... you'all gonna make me thin' I'm not welcome here'

'WhOt you want?' said a thuggish voice from way back.

I love the thug way of speaking. At times, I could never make heads or tails of it. At other times, its rhythmically musical to me.

With guns pointed at me, the one thought I could think of was to lighten the mood. 'Do any of you guys know where I can cash my welfare cheque?' My question was to be a jib at the sporty thieves in the room, not supposed to be glib, though one or two of them did giggle at my humour. Seeing the serious of their faces, I asked again in the same vield 'Have you seen how many facial muscles some needs to make a smile?'

'WOt? questioned another voice.

'It takes forty-three' Their twenty-two serious facial muscles to make a frown'

'WHoT you fuck say?' queried another voice.

'Bad Jam about?'

'Who da fuck are you?' It was more of a statement rather than a query.

'Dax'

A hush went over some of the boys and girls staring at me. Most of the guns directed at me started dropping.

'Hey, Queen of England keep it the fuck down' said a hoarse voice from above me. Bad Jam was standing at the top of the stairs staring straight-faced down at me. 'Get your English butt up here' he ordered rather brusquely.

Just below the stairs, I spotted a chick rub hips with a guy and he in return rubbing hips, touching the lips to the top of his dick then WHOO!.

Benjamin Kamba was about six foot tall with high cheekbones and lively brown eyes. His coffee stained skin barely had a tat showing but that didn't mean he had blemish skin. No, there were old cigarette burn marks littered all up his forearm, probably the result of an abusive father and an absentee mother.

I smiled at the armed congregation before joining him up the stairs. He led me into a room with barely a lightbulb in it. A lighted desktop computer made up for the light in the room. I made my way over to the computer. Not meaning to inspect the document on it, I was able to make out that he had been typing some form of newsletter for some outreach program he was sponsoring.

His attitude changed once he was out of the sight of his hommies, 'Hey Miss Dax how're you doin'? Long time no see huh?' His gaze appeared casual but my highly cultivated instinct told me that he might be ready for the unexpected. I guess that's what happens when a friend shoots you five times in the back.

'Benjamin? You look well' I said calmly 'Thanks to you'

'Nervous much' I asked glancing at the door.

'Ah … My guys are just being over protective when it comes to my safety. Not that I trust any of them' he shrugged and added 'They don't appreciate it, if I'm alone with someone they don't trust, except for someone like you'

'They know me?'

'If they didn't before today, they do now. You've been making waves'

I chuckled 'How's tricks?' I said keeping my eyes on him not even glancing at his computer.

'For the most part, good' he said 'You want a drink, some pretzels, something to eat, maybe some Cannoli …' he nervously added

'Benny!' He stopped. 'I'm glad to hear you're doing well, because I need a favor'

His face lit up 'You want Danny Friedlander?' 'What? How the hell …'

'Hey, I might be out of the business but hey I'm not out out … you get the drift? Bessides we've all heard there's a bitch who's been knocking down doors all day' I flinched inwardly at the word "bitch", I would have preferred to go to a dentist and have him drill my teeth, instead of having him use that word. 'I was gonna hear about it sooner or later'

'I get it'

'Don't you worry Miss Dax. My homies gonna put the word out, by tomorrow you'll get a shot at this guy'

'Don't you want to know why I want him?' I asked him

I saw genuine puzzlement on his face 'Ain't none of

my business' I thanked him and left.

When I finally got home, sometime after eleven, I was tired, sore and dirty.

I glanced up at the Seymour's manor house before entering. The manor was built early in 1910, was renovated in 1998, and sat in a 12,500 sq. ft. compound. It was a three stories high building with twenty-nine rooms. With 5 pre-functioned and overflowing rooms, a spa and Jacuzzi centre located on the second floor the building boasted 6 fireplaces, (4 wood burning, 2 gas), a modern gymnasium, an indoor swimming pool, a conference hall with state of the art audio visual equipment and a horse stable next to the caretaker cottage that doubled for a five car garage.

Each floor was designed specifically to an era or cultural style. The third floor, which Seymour set aside for me, was European in origin, the second floor was contemporary Canadian, while the ground floor was classically modern. A winding limestone staircase linked all the three floors with a dumbwaiter system linking all the floors with the kitchen and living room. Parts of the house were stark white marble and modern, with minimal furniture or fixtures. Several high priced pieces of art and sculpture hung on the walls or sat on various adorned pedestals.

Without a need for explanation, Vince led me up the sweeping limestone staircase leading to the third floor, passing several rooms filled with just the right amount of European baroque furniture.

Once upon a time, Vince wanted to be nothing but a grocer by day and a chef by night. Unfortunately, circumstances beyond his control saw him being drafted into the army at twenty as a cook in the Royal Marines

12$^{th}$ battalion officer's mess hall. In Kabul, he discovered he had a talent as a sniper and was summarily drafted into the Special Forces Support Regiment. He became infamously known as the *"Dark Santa"*, because he always left a "gift" whenever he made a shot that killed his target. A gift, which in some way associates to something personal of his victims. Such was his capability. Due to his efficiency, internal politics in the marines or his detachment he was seconded to a fleet protection group called *"Witchfinders"*, a special army/ civilian operation, a duty that I understood he had qualms with. Years later, Seymour literally stumbled on him, down on his luck, drunk and pissed off his head in some ramshackle tavern, half a world away. Since then, after some minor reclamation and studies he has been Seymour's man Friday in America.

Vince drew me a bath and prepared a meal, Puccini Pasta.

After removing the bandages binding my chest, I soaked the dirt off my skin, shaved my legs without drying down, then wrapped a towel around my chest, and went outside to one of the five balconies to enjoy the meal Vince had prepared.

For a while, sitting on the third floor, I sat there eating, watching the city go by on the streets below. Though it was a quiet evening, New York was picking up its third wind of the day. I knew from statistic that there would be eight to twelve deaths by morning. Two by murders of passion, another two would be "clean" police shootings and the others could be divided up into rapes, muggings, burglaries or just plain planned. I wondered if I would be one of the planned.

From behind me, my phone bleeped. I snapped out of all the things I was thinking and hurried to pick it up.

It was Apollo and Alpha.

Some of its search parameters had made several hits. Not of big Dan but of Marion Steiner. Apollo displayed thirty-three security camera snapshots of Marion in and around LA, several also in and around Castaic, seven shots of his Datsun on a road heading towards Prine, one in Prine and two others from an unknown origin.

One was from a traffic cam and the other from an ATM. The last two where blurry and was particularly hard to make him out, especially since he was not alone. However, if Apollo had made a positive identification, who am I to argue. The problem was that I did not recognise either location, but Apollo had already identified each of them.

The traffic cam was taken two days after he landed in LA on W Avenue L-8. I had no idea where that route was nor did I know why he was there. In the ATM shot, he was further back from a bulky lady cashing in some dollars. He seemed to looking directly at the woman's back as he gestured at something to his right. There was a sign that read "*Antelope V…*" to his left.

I set the images aside, there was a time to figure them out, and now was definitely not the time.

My flip phone rang again. The voice at the other end said 'Sue? You there?'

'Steph?' I answered wearily 'Sue? You sound tired, babe' 'Been busy'

'So I hear' she remarked 'You've been tearin' up my town lookin' for Dan, haven't you?'

'Steph, what's up?'

'I may have found a clue to your guy' 'Dan?'

'Yeah but just maybe'

'What's that supposed to mean?'

'Big Dan, used to hang out with this chick called Patricia' 'Patricia?

Not the same Patricia from Silke's little black book.

'His go to girl. She works at Mrs Burdock from the Drakes House. They're linked at the hip. From what I hear, he doesn't make a move without involvin' her'

I've heard of the Drakes House. It was in the news recently, from what I've heard, it's an elite cathouse.

'So? What about her?'

Across the room from me was a mirror, and when I glanced into it, I found I was grinning. I couldn't understand why, there was no reason for me to grin at all, especially as I couldn't feel my face grinning.

'We found her'

'Where?' I asked trying to keep my excitement to a minimum. 'Tomorrows paper' she replied easily 'Page four. She was found dead in the drink. The boys from the 8th are thinkin' suicide'

The hot feeling in my chest went away, leaving tightness in its place. When I glanced back at the mirror, I was not grinning anymore 'Dead?'

'Huh huh'

'What do you think?'

'She had a passport on her identifying her as Evelyn Brandt'

Evelyn Brandt! The other passport Dan picked up from Simmons.

'That's weird'

'Yeah, something shady is definitely goin' on' 'You

going to check it out'

'Yeah but not tonight. I'm goin' home. I need sleep and so do you'

'Yeah, I guess you're right … uh … could you put a hold on the investigation for 24 hours?'

'Sorry babe not my precinct'

'I know, but could you at least try' '12 hours. How about that?'

'If that's the best you can do' 'It is'

'It will have to do. Oh have your forensics' check her forehead and hands'

'Her forehead?' 'Consider it a hunch'

'You and your hunches' she bade me farewell 'Bye Sue' I did the same 'Thanks Steph' I said and hung up.

I put a call through to Ma'chellan Industries, CEO Charlie Coppinger.

Ma'chellan Industries comprised of the parent company Galencyte Pharmacia, Saxon Chemicals that provide gastroenterology drugs and other internal medicine brands. Sawal Medics that produce Antibacterial products and Mecrix Biometric which markets specialised versions of medical brands made by the three companies to the military. Most notably was that it had major investments in three media network concerns and two publishing companies.

'Hello' came the mellow voice from the other line. 'Charlie?'

'Miss Dax. It's nice to hear from you' 'Cut the bull Charles. How're you?' 'I'm fine and you?'

'I need a story pulled from tomorrow's paper' 'What story?'

'The story of a murdered woman killed by the docks, a woman called Patricia'

'It won't be easy'

'Have it delayed for at least 12 to 24 hours' 'Will do, ma'am. It might take some doing' 'Just get it done' I said before hanging up.

# FIFTEEN

I snoozed-nap for a good hour. When I woke, I felt in some measure refreshed, partially energized and eager. I realised

I had burned minutes by sleeping this long, but I didn't care. According to Silke's black book, Patricia with the notation – *Great Boobs* - from the Drakes House was an artist and a real Stradivarius when it came to whoring. Dan was going leaving town with a girl named Patricia otherwise known as the fake passport holder of Evelyn Brandt. Could it be that Silke was stepping out on his best friend's girl?

Before taking out one of the cars in the garage, the black 2015 Escalade SUV, I researched the Drake House. There wasn't much but enough.

While I slept, the Upper East Side had been showered with rain. The cleanness had gone and in its place was a thick drizzle that seemed to hold in all the wild smells of the city that were vibrant during its absent.

It took a matter of minutes, just before one a.m. when I made my way over to the Drakes House, which sat on top of a hill. Apart from it being a brick mansion, it had a reputation for being one of the discrete cathouses in the city.

I was hoping the news of Patricia's death had not reached them as I walked up to the door and knocked on the big-oak door with a bronze knocker. From the cars parked outside, it was close to their peak hour. As expected a girl in a maid's uniform answered the door and showed me into an old-fashioned parlour where lush purple and red draperies hung. The carpet was almost an inch thick, the furniture's were old as where the fixtures. Though I suspected the commissioner's office in city hall was not as furnished as this was.

Mrs Alice Burdock, the madam for Drakes House according to rumours was an ascetic person. A trait, she extended to all her girls and was welcomed by customers even if the media didn't see it that way. I half expected, when I met Mrs Burdock that she would be a bitter forty or fifty something year old with too much make up and tired eyes. Much like Madam Nova in LA. Nothing could surprise me better than this thirty-year old woman entering, looking like an associate partner from a firm oflawyers. When she entered the room through the double doors, the maid closed them behind her, leaving us alone. I tried not to look dazzled or impressed but I was.

She moved with a sensual flow and had a certain dignity when she extended her cool, slender hand for me to shake. She looked me directly in the eye. 'You're a little late, Miss Dax. But I'm at your disposal and will aid you as best as I can'

'You were expecting me, Mrs Burdock?'

'They say you've got New York by the weenies. Seeing you now and I know you've made quite an impression' she said gesturing to a chair. Her eyes were as cool as jade green and appraising. The fact that she had heard of me, my quest and that she was willing and able to assist me informed me that she might have mob connections. And why not? Prostitution is one of the Mob's long-standing money-makers.

'What have they been saying about me?' I asked as I sat down in one of the silk covered sofas.

She crossed over to a bar counter 'That you're a cunt. Knocking and busting heads in a vain attempt to find a friend. Why and what for is not a concern of others. Drink?'

'Gin and tonic please' I requested with a grin that I hoped would be guileless 'I take it you've never heard of him either?'

'Who … this Dan Friedlander? Yes I have, where he is … well that is the question for the ages, isn't it? I truly have no idea'

'Then it should be alright if I talk to Patricia?'

Her long ash blonde hair swished and her green eyes flashed as she turned to me.

'Patricia? Which one and why her?'

'I don't know. The one most familiar with a Mr Silke or his mate Dan'

'Bluebell' She remarked, walking over to me and handing me a glass.

'Is that her professional name?'

Sitting across from me, she crossed her legs before replying 'Naturally'

'May I talk to her?'

'In that case, you'll have to wait until your next visit to

New York'

Taking a sip of the heavily mixture of tonic, I asked 'What's wrong with tonight?'

'She's not here. I'm afraid'

'Mrs Burdock, I've been up most of the day, having problems with people's memories or their amnesia. Please do a girl a favour and don't be one of those people'

'The situation I'm afraid is beyond my purview' she said 'She hasn't been around for the last day or so'

'Can I at least have a way of contacting her?' 'You know better than to ask, young lady'

'I know but this is a quite urgent request' 'So I hear'

'Where can I find her?'

'I have rules here, you know. Information like that I never give out, no matter who you are'

'I understand, but is there any way you can help me without breaking your rules?'

I didn't trust her. Since I already had an idea where Patricia was, I was wondering what kind of fast one she'll use to fob me off. If that was her intention.

'My girls do take vacations, visit relatives, get sick like anyone else you know'

I intentionally adjusted my jacket so that she could see the gun tucked in the holster. Mrs Burdock raised an eyebrow, she looked something less than surprised.

'Do you intend to use that thing?' she commented, indicating the gun.

'I don't know. I think of it as a motivator. To show that I'm serious. Very serious'

'Patricia's been absent for a while. I can't be more

specific than that'

Dealing with Mrs Burdock was like trading with someone shielded by a wall of ice. She set her glass down. 'Why do you carry that?'

'I carry this because people keep trying to put bullets into me' 'Sorry to hear that. Maybe if you sought a less hazardous profession ... maybe people will be less inclined to put bullets

in you'

'And you have a suggestion I take it?'

'If you worked for me, you'd have no use for that. You have a beautiful body and face. Give me a week to get you into shape, we loose this Jane Bond vibe you got going on and I can promise, you won't ever be lacking in regulars'

'This beautiful body ...' I remarked as I reached into my satchel. 'Is as precious to me now as it will ever be, such are the times we live in'

'I agree. Such a pity'

'We live in hazardous times ...' I pulled out a couple of hundred dollar bills 'And costly times. Will this motivate you enough to help me?'

'Patricia left here in a hurry yesterday afternoon after receiving a call from someone. She was all excited'

'Excited?'

'Like her ship had come in all of a sudden' she sighed and got to her feet and went over to the bar. I watched as she stood by the counter and scribbled on a dainty scrap of pink stationery. 'She's inexperienced, naïve and doesn't know much about people, even when they take advantage of her' She handed me the scrap of pink stationery.

'This?'

'It's her address' she remarked 'Please make sure she's alright' 'I doubt I can. The damage may already have been done'

Handing her the crisps notes, I left Mrs Alice Burdock wondering what I meant.

The house where Patricia was staying sat in a courtyard next to headland on a motorway that led to the east of Harlem. It wasn't hard to find. It was five blocks from where Big Dan's ATM capture was located.

I parked about sixty yards away from the address scribbled by Mrs Burdock. I got out of the Escalade and gently closed the door. The New York night air was cool and damp, the ground wet from the summer rain.

I immediately noticed the black Chevy Sedan with tinted windows parked on the sidewalk next to the building's front door. Approaching it cautiously, I skirted the car and crouched across from one of the poorly lighted street lamps. Inside I could hear indistinct voices but I could make out the voice of big Dan. He seemed to be very anxious possibly scared.

My Makarov in my hand, I walked on the balls of my feet as I turned the corner of the house. A tightness grew within me, my search might be coming to an end. Moving quickly through the shadows, I arrived at the back door. The voices grew louder as I moved, drawing the attention of passer-by's and one or two neighbours. Turning, I sought out a place to take cover. A man's footstep, loud and hard, were close. I darted behind a parked car and ducked behind it. Light flooded out into the night, painting a yellow beam along the ground. A man's figure breached the doorway. It was not Dan, it was Father Michel. I felt the sharp cut of gratification.

'*Chiudi la porta*' said a voice from within. A voice I recognised as Monsignor Halbert. Monsignor Michel was wearing a black short-sleeved shirt and blue jeans as he moved down the steps and across the lawn. His slim shape and choppy steps hurried towards the Chevy Sedan. He didn't even glance in the direction of my Escalade parked down the road. He opened the driver's door of the Chevy Sedan and got in. The house front door had closed and there were no more voices.

Michel turned the ignition key, the motor stirred. I could hear the sluggish movement as Michel shoved the gear into reverse. I moved away from the parked car and darted towards the passenger door and jumped inside as the car backed away.

Michel slammed on the breaks. '*Signore in cielo!* ' he exclaimed in Italian.

'I've still got my gun Monsignor, so take it nice and easy'

'*Di nuovo!* You should be dead' he barked angrily. His English accent was just as daunting and broken as Halberts 'Arnett! I know he lie. He say he burning you to ash'

'I remember the occasion. He made a good effort' I said clobbering him in the face with my pistol, just hard enough to make sure I had his undivided attention. 'Drive'

Casting me with the occasional sidelong glances in my direction with those stern eyes of his, he drove slowly down the street.

'What were you doing with Dan back there?' '*Ultimi riti* '

'You killed his lady friend, Patricia?'

*'Tito 1:10. Ci sono molti insubordinati, sia inattivi chiacchieroni e ingannatori, in particolare quelli della circoncisione, la cui bocca deve essere fermato'*

What had a bible quote from Titus about idle talkers stopping the flaps of their mouths from speaking, have to do with all this? Digesting it further, it was just as I figured. He and his compadre, Father Halbert wanted to quash all those who had contact with Marion Steiner. Anna Feldman and Bruce Windemill were the first, Francesco and Shaw were the second to go, then Edwart Silke. Dan and I were next. It didn't matter if we knew anything or not, they just wanted us silenced.

'You're bastards, you know' I ranted 'God's sixth law, Thou shalt not kill and all that, doesn't that mean anything to you?'

He shrugged 'The lords workings come in manyings different ways, take Thecla or Jesus'

Jesus and Thecla. He was playing a zealot card. Despite the fact that I wanted to kill him then and there, it was time for me to get some real answers. My first question was to ask how they got their information. How they kept being ahead of me all the time.

*'La Chiesa* havings many souls, redeemers and sinners. Sinners like to talkings about their sins and ask for forgiveness, redeemers do plenty not be sinners, like the self-baptised Thecla. All ask forgiveness they givings us information when we need'

I could not imagine it, but if what he says was true then the church had an arsenal of connections and sources of information they could pool from.

'Stop, park here' I indicated with the muzzle of the gun.

'You … tough woman to bury eh? But n-now you here …. soon our work finish' he declared turning the steering wheel into the sidewalk and parking the car.

'Your work?'

'Silencings you. You are last'

'I know nothing about Marion and his discovery, why do this?'

'It not matter. You already involvings yourself, speakings to him. This … how you say… è *fuori dalla tua portata*, we havings the lord God on our side'

'You killed my friend, Agent Shaw because he was in contact with Marion?'

'*Dio lo ha*'

I observed that he did not exactly answer my question.

'Both Silke and Dan tend to kill people, especially women. I can understand your interest but why me? I wouldn't desecrate your secrets'

I sounded like I was pleading to him and hated myself for sounding that way.

'You must die, *stesso Signore Claribel e Mister Daniel*' 'Because of our proximity with Marion Steiner?' I solicited He nodded '*Si*'

'What exactly do you think he discovered?' I asked 'What was in his possession?'

He buttoned his lips, defiantly, not saying anything.

'What is so dangerous about his discovery that you'd kill to keep it secret'

'*Tutto*' he murmured 'Best you getting out of car, right now and God willing … you disappear'

That night in LA was burning in my mind, vivid again

filling me with fury. I was remembering how easy it was for them to show up, chase me down, and almost kill me. Not to mention, the fire and the assassin. Now I knew his name and who had sent him. I was remembering Marion Steiner, Agent Shaw, Francesco, and the others, massacred.

I jammed the pistol against his throat so hard that he gasped. 'I asked you a question. What is the damned secret?'

'Kill me' he wheezed against the pressure of the gun 'I not telling you. Better, you not know. You knowing plenty already'

'Who are you guys with? Not the Catholic Church, they would not sanction this kind of conduct. What sect do you belong to? You with the Priory of Scion?'

He chuckled and snorted '*Quegli ignoranti disadattati!*' he spat. They were not with the Priory but from his demeanour, Father Michel knew of them and despised them accordingly. It could mean whatever they stood for was in direct contrast with the Priory. Then again, this maybe all conjecture on my part.

What group or sect was in direct opposition to the Priory? I thought to myself.

I put the question on hold for another time.

I had most of the answers I needed from him. For right now, I had the urge to put a bullet in his head and forget him, flopping at deaths door by the roadside, but that would be just cold hearted of me.

I voiced my thoughts. 'You know, I should blow your brains all over the seat of this car'

He glanced at me and saw in my eyes, to my regret, the fact that I wouldn't do that. No matter how much I wanted to.

All I could do now was either render him unconscious, journey back to Patricia's place or make an attempt to capture Father Halbert.

I wish I had options that included his death and cuffs. Instead, I took out my flip-phone and dialled Lieutenant O'Connor. It was late, she was sleepy but she considered my request to have someone come for the priest. She promised to send someone to a rendezvous location she chose, and put Father Michel on ice.

'By the way, just got the forensic report. Olive oil was on Patricia's forehead. What's the significance?'

'What rites do priest perform on the dead or dying?' I asked her before ending the call. Leaving her to wonder.

'Let's go' I said to Monsignor Michel.

With an Italian oath, Michel started the car, engaged the gears and steered the wheel. I put a cigarette in my mouth and punched the lighter in the dash.

'Don't you have any remorse for what you guys did at the cottage?' I asked the Father

'All is God's work'

I was done, wasting my time with this fanatic.

'No, it wasn't. This is the end for you' I said as the lighter popped out of its heater.

'I having no misgivings about this' he said speeding up and without changing the tone of his voice, Michel wrenched the steering wheel. The car was travelling along an open stretch of asphalt without a curve on it, when it swerved. I was thrown against the dash, my cigarette flying across the seats.

I did not see Michel reach into his coat, but I saw the

flash of the gunshot and heard its sound as he pulled the trigger. I had, for the second time made another rookie mistake. I had failed to pat him down when I got into the vehicle.

He was fast. He was very fast. I should have remembered that from the theatre in LA. The bullet didn't hit me, the intended target. I had already leaned forward to the floor of the car. I didn't have time to think things out. I shot back. The Makarov exploded loudly inside the enclosed car. Michel made a gurgling sound in his throat and slumped forward over the steering wheel.

Michel had unconsciously chosen the perfect spot to take me out. If things had worked out the way he had hoped, he would have killed me with one quick shot, shoved me out the car while still keeping the car moving, without it ever leaving the road. However, in this instant the driverless Chevy Sedan swerved across the clear road, careened to the right and then to the left, streaking across the road. It hit a ditch as I tried to grasp for the steering wheel, but Michel's body was thrown against me. Bucking out of the ditch, the car forged through a brushwood and hurtled suddenly into a halt.

Straightening up, I shoved Michel's body off me and felt for his pulse. He didn't have one. He was as dead as a doorpost. I felt delighted maybe even relieved at the development. I had wanted him and his compadre dead and now he was dead.

I put the Makarov away and lugged his body out of the car. For a slender person, he was mainly made of muscle and bone. Searching his pockets, I found nothing, not even a phone, just lint. I got the vehicle started again and ground backward out the brushwood. The car bounced over the ditch and onto the asphalt again. I drove back to Patricia's home.

Lights were still on inside the house. The pedestrians and neighbours were absent. I circled it and found an open window. I couldn't see anyone but I could hear faint sounds. The sound of running water. I vaulted up and through the window to find myself in a bedroom.

I moved carefully through the bedroom towards the bathroom. Someone was sitting in the shower singing softly to herself. She was not going to be on American Idol but she believed she could carry a tune. I went back into the bedroom, sat down on the far side of the bed, and waited.

When she finally stopped and got out of the shower, she had a towel wrapped around her chest and nothing else.

She stopped, when she saw me. Oddly enough, she didn't seem too surprised to see me. When you find a stranger seated in your bedroom with just your birthday suit on, you have to be at least more than a little surprised.

She was however terrified of my presence. I could tell by the clasping of her shaking fingers and the drain of blood from her cheeks. Whoever this girl was, there was nothing exceptional about her but there was a strength within her.

Her petite and lean body shone with a luxuriant skin and her cropped black hair dripping with water could do with some highlights. However, her big round eyes, high cheekbones, and desirable lips compensated for her lack of beauty. She had the appearance of one of those girls that trailed the head cheerleader in a squad, doing her every bidding. Hoping to be noticed by one of the quarterbacks best friends. She was definitely not the girl next door. She was the ugly duckling sister of the girl next door. I felt a surge of pity for her.

We eyed each other.

'H-h-how did y-you get in here?' she asked 'Through a window. Don't worry, I'm no thief '

'Y-you don't look like one' she jovially countered 'One what?'

'A thief ' 'Thank you'

'Y-you w-with the Reverend?'

I ignored her question 'You're not Patricia, who are you?' 'I'm her roommate Penny'

'Ah'

'Why are you here?' 'Where's the reverend?' 'He's gone'

'And Dan?' 'Who are you?' 'Just a nobody'

She instantly relaxed 'You must be Dax?' she remarked 'You've heard of me?'

'No. But you made my unexpected guests nervous' she declared 'How nervous?'

'Very'

'Is that all?'

'The reverend talked about you' she stated. Colour seemed to be returning to her cheeks because she seemed to be getting more confident.

'He did, did he?'

'I heard them say they tried killing you and some chick named Marion with a car bomb'

Whoa! I assumed Silke and his cronies Nicky set the car bomb in Prine. This was the first time I realised that the car bomb was primed by the priests.

'We were just lucky'

She opened a closet and took out a dressing robe.

'You didn't happen to run into the reverend's buddy, by any chance'

'Father Michel?'

'Was that his name?' she asked

'Yeah'

'What happened to him? Nothing good, I hope' 'He won't be coming back'

She took the news without flinching. 'He bragged about taking you out by him lone self, you know. I didn't imagine he would. Is it true they set fire you and your ass on fire in your hotel room?'

'More or less' I said

'You must be one tough cookie'

I wondered if I was supposed to be flattered. 'Penny? You know a lot about the reverends and me'

'Do I know? How could I not know? I have been hiding my shifter ever since they came for Danny. I heard them torture the hell out of him and squeal about you and something your Tussey friend, Marion may have found'

'So Dan Friedlander was here?' 'Yes, he has been waiting' 'Waiting?'

'For Patricia. That is until they found him' 'A man called Halbert, I suppose?'

'Yes. Never heard man so full of himself before. And talk … that man can talk though most of it was in another language'

'You're a bit of a talkative yourself'

'Am part Italian, I couldn't not but listen, I talk and listen when I'm scared or nervous' she confessed 'It doesn't help when I've been hiding for twelve hours. All my nerves are shot up'

'So you've been hiding?'

'Hmm hmm' she muttered, belting the robe around her her waist.

'They must have paid you a lot to stay hidden and quiet and listen to them brag'

She knew her gig was up. She made a little sigh combined with a shrug 'What's a girl go to do in these tight times huh?'

'Indeed, how else? She's gotta roll with the punches, right?'

'Exactly, babe. I didn't like Danny, tried whenever possible to keep my distance. No offense to him. But Patricia … ha … she was all gaga for him'

'How long was he waiting for her?'

'Both of us were waiting. He made me hide when our guests arrived. It's the one piece of good fortune I think he's ever done for anyone'

'Since when?' I raised an eyebrow to strengthen the impression of ignorance my question seemed to convey.

'Since what? Hiding? …. Er since about two this afternoon. They were supposed to meet up but she didn't show up. So Danny says, anyways'

'Know where she might be?' I asked, knowing full well where she was.

She shrugged, then turned away 'Nope'

'What about the reverend? Know where I might find him?' There was a brief silence, then she asked in a quavering voice,

'Why should I help you?'

'You have any reason not to?' 'Perhaps?'

'I need to find them'

'I need a drink. You want a drink. I think we got some wine in the living room'

'No, thanks'

She stepped round me, through the bedroom door towards the living room.

I got to my feet to follow her. I walked into the larger front room when a man bobbed out of a hallway and shot at us. I ducked as I reached into my jacket and fired from inside the holster. Penny dashed forward out of the way, as my bullet hit a vase on a short table to the man's right. He jumped back, under the table. I pushed the table out to block the entrance to the hallway, using it as a shield.

My would-be-killer was average-looking, sandy hair, wearing a charcoal grey suit. He put two bullets through the table, near my shoulder. I lay on my side and moaned. I counted to eight before he took the bait. When I heard him moving towards me, I waited until he reached the table and leaned over it. As soon as his hands and head appeared, I swung striking the gun, a Luger from his hand. He reached forward to grab me by the hair, which was the only thing handy for him. My scream was not as insincere as my moan had been. I thought he was going to wrench my hair out by their roots. Rising, I struck him under the chin with the butt of the Makarov. His jowls slammed together as he went down. However, he was not done yet. He used the table to hit me, knocking me away, sprawling, making me lose grip of my gun.

He sprang up with a knife in his hand as he jumped on me.

The blade of the knife flashed as he thrust it down onto my throat. I jerked aside, catching his wrist, just in time with my hand as he started bending his hand sideward. He fell away, pulling free from my grasp and driving a shot into my ribs. Then he slashed at me with the knife again, slashing a long rent down my pant leg as I rolled away.

Scrambling to our feet, we faced each other in the hallway. Both of us panting, the gun I had dropped lay on the floor between us. 'Pick it up, cunt' he taunted, glaring at me 'Go on I dare you

and I'll slice your hand off '

'I don't need to' I confidently replied, flexing my forearm to let Peko slide into my palm. When he saw it, he raised his arm to throw his own knife.

"Baaanngg"

Penny shot him. His head flew upward, his body following it into the air before coming to rest at my feet. She had stepped into the hallway with his Luger, still dressed in her dressing robe, raised the gun firmly in both of her hands, and blew the back of his head off. Penny stood there for a long minute looking down at the dead man before walking slowly towards me. Finally, she looked at me with an absentminded expression on her face.

'You didn't have much choice' I said to her trying to console her 'It was him or us'

'I-I know … its just …' she muttered

'I know' I replied softly before bending to take a good look at our assailant 'Who the hell is this?' I asked

'T-they called him Arnett' 'Arnett?'

My black windbreaker sporting, would-be-assassin,

here and dead at my feet.

'He and … his buddies scared the hell out of me … when they were here' she professed, dropping the heavy Luger on the floor.

'Sorry to hear that' I sympathised.

'I suppose you'll be going after the reverend and Danny?' 'I suppose so if I knew where they are'

'I might know' she remarked 'How's that?'

'Our friend here …' she indicated the dead man with the jut of her chin '…was given an address where he can be reached' I looked at her with a curious eye. 'I'm not giving it to you, unless I can come with you. I need to help find Patricia' she said satisfying my curiosity.

Without looking her in the face, I said 'Patricia maybe dead for all you know Penny'

'She better not be. But if she is, then I'll know' 'Why?'

'She was my friend' she declared 'And I need to do something' There was something about the way she said "was" that maybe think she already knew Patricia's fate. I put my mind towards thinking about her request as I slipped Peko back up my forearm,

I finally said 'I'm sorry but I can't allow that'

'Then you'll have to find some other way to find him' she indignantly replied 'Please, let me help find her. S-she's the only friend worth a damn to me. Please, I owe it to her to help find her' She pleaded with me.

'I don't th …'

'Please!' She beseeched me again.

I thought for a long moment. I couldn't risk her going with me into a dangerous situation and yet I could not go without her information. I could always offer her money or blackmail or even threaten her, but there was something else about her insistent in going with me. Her motives did not exactly ring true. Unfortunately, the distant sound of sirens made up my mind for me.

'Get dressed, I'll be in the car'

She glanced around 'I'll be two minutes' she said hurrying away.

In the car while I waited, I sent off a text message to Lieutenant O'Connor's informing her that if she does not hear from me before dawn, she should track my phone and take whatever actions she deems fit. I also placed a text message to Katanga, informing her that my next port of call might be of interest to her and her associates and advised they take whatever necessary steps they might want to take. No need for me to anger the mob when I can help it. When I was done, I deleted the messages.

# SIXTEEN

It was past three a.m., sleep was a long thought away, even if I had been up for more hours in the day than I was comfortable with. Alas, as the crow flies, the directions Penny provided did not leave much to the chance of my sleeping.

To occupy my mind I tried going over every conversation Marion and I had. Wondering if he left any clues to the parchment he supposedly recovered.

We drove by a roundabout route, without effort due north that indicated the direction of an end-point. It gave a good estimate of a crow's flight distance between. Penny's eyes were distant as she calculated.

The area Penny had directed me was once a holistic retreat, not just for Christians but also for Buddhists and other conventional religions. Up until now, I never knew such places existed in New York. She guided me to a virtually abandoned monastery on the outskirts of the sanctuary. After parking the car on a verge, under a set of overhang trees, I started studying the monastery and its surroundings, fixing every detail in my mind, visualising what could be deduced of the interior layout.

The black-bricked monastery was set on a rising valley at the east end, about a half-a-mile in from its front entrance, a few windows glimmered with sallow candlelight. There was a vibe emanating from the monastery that felt very wrong. Not wrong exactly but just bad juju, it rubbed me the wrong way. Really badly. In the distance, I could make out two figures in dark habits stroll across the green angled lawn towards the front entrance. The heavy door closed soundlessly after them. A wooden landing platform built on oak piles, extended from a spot on the west side of the monastery out over the sea. A twenty-two four single-crew launch swayed on the water two hundred yards out, well clear of the swallows.

Resisting the fleeting thought that maybe I should make a run for it, I climbed out the car. The night air had been raised an centigrade or two because it was unusually warm and a half-coin looking moon was descending behind the trees.

'You should stay here' I said to Penny as she too made a move to climb out of the car.

'But …' She began, and then closed her mouth abruptly when she saw the expression on my face.

'No questions' I instructed with a finger planted firmly on top of my lips 'This might be dangerous, I wouldn't want you getting hurt' I took out my flip-phone and handed it over to her. 'If I am not back in three hours, press redial, speak to the lieutenant …. you know what to say'

She nodded in acknowledgement.

It took almost an hour of a slow reconnoitre for me to get round and through the woods surrounding the monastery to get to the broad, rough-hewn steps that wound up the monastery. Before getting there, I sabotaged the boat by letting loose its berthing line. Just in case someone tried a last-minute dashing escape.

I noticed the stone parapet well surmounted with a capstan, pulley wheels bolted to massive beams on the sides, piles of sand, gravel and ballast for construction, bags of cement, balks of timbers and the walled in enclosure on the east side of the building.

A restoration was going on but it seemed at very slow pace.

The night was a great advantage to me. Gun in hand, I circled the building again and sneaked through the unlocked heavy doors in the rear that led to a huge empty kitchen.

When I entered, I went silently over to a corridor leading from the kitchen and up a short, winding flight of stone steps. Before passing, I sighted two large ovens set into the flagged floor. At almost seven feet, they were the largest oven I had ever seen.

The wide stone steps leading from the kitchen with right-angle turns between two flights, led to a gallery that ran along one side of what appeared to be a large chapel undergoing restoration. There was a pile of rubble, small piles of sand and ballast and a confusion of building work.

On one side of the gallery was a long section of a wooden balustrade overlooking the chapel. The chapel itself had been cleared of furniture and wooden pews.

I spotted a man clothed in a dark habit with sandals and a round face lounging in a chair, sleeping. He had all the appearance of a man basking himself, catching some rays on a Spanish beach that I regarded him as a Spaniard. My opinion of him changed when I spotted beside him, propped next to his knee, an assault rifle. A Beretta Model 502 Bolt-Action Rifle. A very serious weapon made to accommodate bullets from a Remington, .0270 - .300 Winchester Magnums and a .375 Holland Magnum. I was in two minds. Either disable him here and now or avoid his orbit. I decided against disabling him and climbed the stairs, hoping that the creaks I made would not awaken him.

By the time I got to the top, I was breathing hard from my climb and sneaking about. My eyes roved steadily without intent but photographing every step of my route.

At the end of the gallery was another sentry and a door that led to a procession of corridors that I guessed led to a sanctum. I made my way past him and went down, listening at the doors. There were no obvious or suspicious sounds. I had no way to turn but my Spidey sense was tingling. My pulse was fast and my

 adrenalin was flowing more than necessary. More to the fact that my search may be ending.

I was about to turn my head when I heard a click and the muzzle of a gun pressed against my head.

'Don't make any sudden moves, Babe' Penny's voice was unmistakable. 'Take off the holster, drop the gun and the knife' I did as instructed.

Feeling the cold air on my back and I thought of the lunacy of my gullibility that had hit me like ice-cold water. The facet of the same woman who had blown apart the head of an assassin, the same woman who appeared to be clueless to the dangers she recently faced. Damn! Reality lay in other things, not in the warmth or coldness of my mind but my hazard of being stupid. She was no amateur in this kind of work. Sneaking up on me without making a sound to catch me unawares was not an easy thing to accomplish.

Penny had efficiently performed her "damsel in distress" routine to her great advantage. I would give her an A in the art of duplicity. I caught a glimpse of her face as she prodded me forward. It seemed to have been carved in ivory. In her hand was a silver .357 Smith and Wesson model 66 revolver with a black grip. It s a small easy-to-conceal weaponof choice.

Just behind her was the sleeping Spaniard I had evaded earlier. He was now upright, alert. His Beretta rifle was now slung over his shoulder and aimed at me.

I slowly took off my jacket and unstrapped the holster. I did the same with Peko's sheath strapped to my forearm. Tossing them both on the floor.

The guard came forward, picked up my weapons without taking his eyes off me, pocketed the sheath, and slung the Makarov's holster across a shoulder. He then proceeded to frisk me, slowly, like most men who have had the pleasure of having me in this sort of pickle, lingered ever so minutely on my sensitive lady parts.

Sweat broke on my brow and I was suddenly a frightened woman. Yes, frightened for myself and pity for her. Penny had no idea what she was up against.

'Anything else?' I requested

'Move slowly' she said prodding me with the gun to my head. 'I take it the authorities won't be making an appearance?'

She ignored me, as both of them shepherded me down a short path, through a door at the back of the monastery and a set of doors with flying buttresses that led through an open piazza of sorts, then down another set of stone steps leading into a subterranean vault. All the while, I spotted the odd armed monk patrolling the environment. All in all, I spotted at least seven monks.

I discerned that Penny was unfamiliar to the place, she knew next to nothing about where to go. She took cues from the guard. Beyond the door at the back of the building, lay a passage with two doors on the right.

'The second door' directed the guard. Hearing his voice for the first time, I deduced his accent was European but not Italian or Spanish. It was probably Germanic.

I stopped, making no evident rush, I turned and asked Penny 'Why?'

The muscles in her jaw twitched slightly, her eyes cold 'It's business' she said in a metallic voice.

'Business?'

'When they came to the apartment, they asked about you, just as you asked for them' her voice was terse 'It was just my luck that when Father Michel didn't return, they knew you somehow had gotten hold of him and knew you were coming back or might be.

They wanted me to set a trap for you' Penny said 'Why not kill me instead of Arnett?'

'You were more valuable' she said in a matter of fact way. 'And Patricia?'

'Oh the bitch's dead, but I think you know that' 'I thought she was your friend?'

Penny seemed to remember something important. 'She was a whore and a prima donna one at that. I hated her fuckin' guts' she uttered with hateful vehemence.

I shook my head in regret.

'You have no idea what these people are capable of, do you?' I remarked to Penny, glancing at my Spaniard-looking monk friend behind her.

'Do you?'

'What did they offer you? What was it? Money or your life?' She stuck out a lip, sneering at me.

From her reaction, I could only assume it was money 'Money huh? How much?'

'Does it matter?'

'It might help to know how much I'm worth' I paused 'And what made you accepted the proposition'

I felt her cold smile. 'No one would turn down half a million dollars just to get you here'

'They must have found the money' I mused to myself. 'Money? What money?' she asked frowning.

I heard a door open ahead of us and Father Halbert's bearded face appeared.

The feature-less handsome priest looked pleased with what he was seeing and for some occasion, himself. His hair was slick with water and the smirk I had noticed earlier was still imprinted on his smooth face. It resembled the grin a dog makes after sleeping in the sun.

'Ah *Signorina* Dax, nice to see you again' he addressed me, leaving the door open for us. 'And *Signorina* Korth. Lovely to see you too'

Penny grunted a reply.

'I can't say the same, Halbert' I whinged.

Penny followed me closely behind with the gun still positioned close to my head. Halbert and the guard followed closely, closing the door behind us.

At that moment, halfway in the middle of us entering the room, I could have disabled Penny by using the edge of my hand to catch her forearm and carry the gun outwards. A kick to the shins and a shove to my Spaniard-looking friend would disable him and Halbert quite handily. However, the problem wasn't Penny or the monk behind her, to my mind, giving what I knew about Halbert, she was already living on borrowed time. My efforts were solely directed on Halbert, his associates and their goals. I wanted to know their motives, their purposes before I was prone to take any action.

However, the image before my eyes stopped me dead in my tracks.

'Christ!' I whispered in disgust as my eyes locked on the spectacle before me.

We had entered a cell-like chamber, complete with rock walls, a chemical bucket, and cracked sink. A water hose lead from the only barred circular opening. A single naked bulb lit up the small enclosure. There were two straight-back chairs, a stool, and a table.

Instead of a foamless bunk, there was a wooden oblong rectangular frame, slightly raised from the ground with rollers at one end. Two ropes were fixed to a bar at one end, another two attached to a movable bar at the other end. Both were controlled and tied to a rotating handle on the top. In the dead centre of it was an almost seamless fulcrum and a detachable nut-bolt, making the whole contraption be capable of folding into two, either for transportation or storage, or both. It was an easy enough mechanism, the torturer would turn the handle on the top causing the ropes to pull the victim's arms and legs that are attached to the ropes. Eventually the victims, bones, sinews, ligaments would be strained to a wrenching point whereby one or both bones would dislocate with a loud crack.

I had no doubt this was a Rack, the apparatus used in torturing

Silke. Seeing the rack now, I understood how he had been so extended. From what I knew of this device, it was mainly used in medieval barbaric times to install psychosomatic terror and/ or extract information. Why in God's name would they be using such a contrivance in this day and age?

Dan Friedlander a.k.a Joshua Brandt was at the end of the chamber with both hands strapped up towards the ceiling, his legs bound tightly to the concrete floor. His big frame taking up most of the corner. He had been stripped almost naked, the only clothing he was wearing were his socks and boxer shorts, which was severely stained. His back was to us and carved on his shaggy chubby posterior were the same words carved onto Silke's back. He appeared dead but from the quivering of his bent legs, he was alive but barely. On the floor, there was not one but several pools of blood. One or two were dried up.

Father Halbert had made quick work of his torture. I had heard Dan's voice back at Penny's place only three hours ago.

Across from Dan's quivering bulk positioned next to one of the legs of the rack was a little half-filled flask of consecrated oil for church sacraments. Next to it was an overturned rucksack. Scattered around the rucksack was a small mound of documents and a mountain of dollar bills.

I stood still, gaping at the cold-bloodedness of what I was looking at. An act I wouldn't expect a priest to instigate or be a part of.

I summarised that the reason Dan Friedlander was

spared the same method of torture as Silke was because Halbert did not want anything from him, even if Dan volunteered the information. Big Dan was a means to an end. A means to lure me in, either or both, to send another "Secrets must stay secret", message.

'*La prego, signorina DAX*' Father Halbert lifted a hand, gesturing me to the stool next to a wall.

The guard shoved me further into the cell, I lurched forward over to the stool. Glancing at Penny, I could see the sight before her was no big deal to her. However, the way she salivated over the rucksack and its spilt contents was sickening, considering the sight before us.

'I see you found Francesco's money' I observed, glancing at the rucksack.

He turned to glance at the rucksack 'Oh that? It was Francesco's huh? *Non sapevo*' He chuckled, it was a deep, rumbling sound of apparent and genuine amusement. I did not believe his ignorance in the owner of the cash before him 'Can you be believing that *Signore* Friedlander here trying buying me off with that?' He lightly lashed out a boot at the rucksack before him.

'How foolish of him. I suppose he thought money could buy anything, even his life'

'Money huh' he enunciated at me '*La radice di tutti i mali*'

I could not agree more. Money was indeed the root of all evil. 'Eh ... excuse me but I must be going now' Penny interrupted, staying by the closed door, next to the guard, eyeing the cash in the room. The words came out of her mouth almost like a petition.

There was repulsion as well as craving on her face as she ogled the pile before us.

'Ah yes! How stupidity of me, *Signorina* Korth' Father Halbert exclaimed levelly, leaning over the rucksack and collecting it and the contents about it. 'Do not being forgeting your reward huh, my dear' He made his way over to Penny and handed the whole bundle over to her. She tucked her gun into waistband of her skirt, before accepting the knapsack. She was smiling with glee as he handed her the rucksack.

She did not see the athame. Halbert ran the point of the blade through her stomach, hard. Burying it deeply into her navel, twisted it before pulling it slowly out. He retrieved her gun from her waistband and pointed it at me as he watched the glee in her eyes change to disbelief, shock and then agony.

'My God' I whispered

Penny aimlessly tried to stuff her wound with the rucksack as she slowly but surely sank to her knees. Her dimming eyes glazing with puzzlement and regret as she sprawled forward onto the ground. Her blood oozed over the contents of the rucksack and across the concrete floor. Her last act was to turn her eyes towards me in plea.

The guard grinned at the spectacle of her dying. I was not at all a fan of Penny's, but his attitude towards her passing did not sit well with me at all.

'*Ragazza sciocca*' Halbert muttered as he stepped away from her. 'Money will always being turning a woman's head, twist her thinking, but you not be thinking so?' He solicited from me as he sat down on one of the chairs across from me. 'You different'

With Penny's gun in his hands still aimed at me, I asked 'I-Is this how you treat your allies?'

He looked around at me 'Friends, relations is naught in

servicing of our lord, *Piccolo uno*'

Daniel Friedlander moaned with pain from his strained stance. My eyes, like the two men in the room, redirected to his cry of pain.

I saw my opportunity.

Averting my eyes from the hung man, I enquired 'And what exactly are you protecting the lord from?'

'The corrupting of his words, his doings'

I could almost see that this man's intention was to take away the freedom of our species through fear and ignorance. And because he feared what he didn't understand, he was willing to go to any lengths to protect his immense belief in the church and Christ. Damning anything else, that got in his way.

'You aren't a Paulician, are you?' I asked, as he got to his feet. I doubt he was. I was prolonging the conversation any way I saw fit, but mainly because I wanted him to get to the answers I needed fast and before he started his torturing devices on me, now that I had seen my opportunity to escape.

He paused in his steps and turned towards me, interest sparked in his eyes. 'You knowing of them?'

'Not well. I studied it in school. A venerated sect of St. Paul followers who believe only in the Gospels of Christ but do not honour the cross or believe in the Old Testament'

'You close, *Piccolo uno. Hai fatto un lavoro veloce di quello che Signore Steiner portato alla luce*'

'How do you mean? How did I bring Marion's work to light?' I asked, glancing at one, two muzzle holes of the weapons pointed at me.

'Professor Fotherias and *Signore* Steiner's discovering at Rennes- la-Château. You see it, read it eh? So you be telling me where now' Professor Fotherias, I was guessing was Marion's professor and organiser of their excavation site at the Rennes-la-Château 'So they discovered something, something very dangerous to whatever order you belong to. Well sorry to tell you mate, but I know nothing of it'

For a second time, we all heard the slight moan emanating from Daniel Friedlander's tortured body.

'That what these delinquenting men of crime tell me' he glanced at the bleeding hunk of Dan and tapped the rack frame 'They claiming they knowing nothing of their findings. But I not believe them'

'Even if you did believe them … was it necessary to …' I waved a hand of abhorrence at the scene before me and especially at Big Dan's prone body '… all that?'

'What you having me doing?'

'Be a man of God or at least of mercy' '*Piccolo, io sono.* More than any other'

I stared at the man before me. There was nothing base about his motives. He wasn't doing all this on behalf of duty, nor the other two base necessities, money or power. Even that feeling of the fact that he has conquered something was nowhere close to defining his motive. I had an idea what his objective was but there was a simpler term to why he and his cronies were doing this. I had no idea what the mental clinical term was for what I think they had, but if I had to speculate, it would be on the border of fanatical madness.

I had heard plenty. More than I wanted to know. It was time to make my move and get the hell out of here.

I looked about me and at the guns still fixed at my torso 'You have a crude definition of mercy Monsignor, but I suppose that is neither here or there and now you expect it to be my turn to suffer the indignity of your mercy?' I queried, resting my hands lightly on the front edge of the stool I was sitting on.

I was watching, barely listening obliquely at the man before me, but listening for that little moan of pain. Waiting for that moment when my opportunity will come, which by my calculation would arrive very soon.

I watched the movement of Halbert's lips and hands as he spoke. His gun hand barely moving. The imperceptible shuffling of feet by the guard at the door, as he stood there aiming his rifle at me. They seemed unperturbed, relaxed and unsuspecting as my fingers curled round the top edge of the stool.

A' *meno che tu non voglia dirci la verità*'

I sighed 'You killed an aspiring Veterinarian for helping a man walk, a young man who had just had a birthday for his artistry skill and now, a girl who was too greedy to know how stupid she was. All for being in propinquity of the bearer of this supposed find. His father, his associates, my friend and his partner' I heaved yet another sigh 'No matter how I say it, Monsignor you'll never believe me. I know nothing of this discovery, so let's get this over with ok?'

It was a more pious response to my imminent death than any other response I had given.

'You spending plenty of time with *Signore* Steiner. You telling us he not telling you what he be finding … where he keeping … secret no one must finding or know?'

Then the moan of pain came.

Grasping the edge of the stool tightly, I took hold of it and flung it up and away, from beneath me. It went crashing into the upper part of Halbert's torso making him lurch backward. The Spaniard looking guard's hand was rigid from my surprise act, I didn't let him stay that way for long. Before he could pull the trigger of the rifle, I twirled like a dancer, using the ball of my foot in a poised ballet move to boot the rifle from his hand. Using a roundhouse repositioning kick, my leg lashed across at Halbert. The heel of my boot struck him on the elbow of his gun hand. Penny's .357 Smith and Wesson went flying from his hand.

He flew backwards away from the gun. Landing uncomfortably across the rack he scrambled up off it, to go sprawling after the gun. I quickly enforced my tactics. The heel of my palm went up, striking the guard from up and under his nose forcefully thrusting the little bones of his nose into his brain, a strike which I had no doubt would kill an elephant. I think he was dead before he registered the pain, lucky him. Shuffling backward I saw what I expected to see. Halbert on the floor, grasping for the gun. His fingers had just made contact with the barrel when I mashed down hard on his left ankle. I heard bone crack as he screamed with pain, his fingers stretched in pain as I stepped over him and gently picked up the gun.

I glanced over at my Spaniard looking guard to see if there were any reaction from him but he was dead, slumped over Penny's legs. Father Halbert wailed as he clutched the air, his damning smirk gone from his face. I slowly retrieved my holster and Peko's sheath from the guard before making my way over to Big Dan, who did not look big anymore. I felt his pulse. He barely had any. He would be dead in minutes, unless by some miracle there was some medical aid. However, from what I could discern, even the very act of moving him could prove fatal. Though I was the type to offer any sort of aid, especially the one he sought at this moment, in this circumstance, I didn't feel obliged to do that.

He killed Marion.

With one blow to the head.

No. I was not about to waste energy on this guy.

Best I could offer him was a better way to die. I unshackled him slowly. It took a while to free his rigid heavy body from his straps. When I accomplished that, I laid him outstretched on the floor. I made him feel as comfortable as I thought he could.

However, by the time I had laid him out with a prop under his head, he was not breathing.

I turned to face Halbert.

'What shall I being doing with you, Monsignor Halbert?' I said imitating his style of speech.

'You be doing nothing, *Piccolo uno*' he stated rather lucidly. 'What do you mean?'

'Meaning, you being going, forgetting everything you see. I staying here. We forgetting you knowing anything' He was talking to me as if I was subservient to him, despite the reversal of fortune. 'You're responsible for multiple deaths, not to mention torture … you think you'd go free. You butchered a friend of mine. You think the church will save you. Protect you?'

'Protecting me from what … sinners … drug lords … my duty …?'

From the little smirk he made, I was not one hundred percent certain that he would be prosecuted for the crimes he committed on behalf on some crazed notion and he knew it.

An undetermined anonymous parchment detrimental to the church? Ha! Would the courts ever believe that?

It is unlikely the Catholic Church would want to be linked to his actions, his crimes or admit that he was acting on behalf of the church, even if he was not. No. I was betting that the whole thing would be buried, quietly. Probably make him disappear. There'd be no record for anyone to find and given his familiarity or unawareness with the mob, it is likely they would be able to accomplish any task requested of them by the church.

Even the FBI would have no leg to stand on if they tend to prosecute. A certain phone call from a specific Cardinal into the right ear in Washington and the whole mess would evaporate.

'Who would believe that?'

'*Piccolo uno*, I being man of God. You being poor little rich girl driving mad for friend'

'A murdered friend'

'A dead friend. My pity'

'Just like that?'

He nodded. His disdainful smirk had returned, to me that smirk on his face was like a smile of defiance from the devil.

A taunt at me. A dare, to contradict any version of his truth I might want to tell. '*Si* '

'Doesn't work for me' I said slowly.

I raised the Smith & Wesson and deliberately fired a bullet into his eye-socket.

This second shot would have certainly drawn attention, if the first one had not. Maybe not much but I would know soon enough. Tucking the Smith & Wesson into my hip, I picked up the guard's rifle. I was hoping the heavy-duty bolt-action rifle that had almost four times the stopping power of the .375 would be effective if or when I was challenged.

I gradually opened the door and slowly made my way out and then up. Instead of taking the direct route, I ascended via a flying buttress bordering a door. I eased myself up and up over a stone gutter. Thirty seconds later, I was on the ground crouched in the shadows within the piazza, I had circled earlier.

I heard a shout, then a shuffle of footsteps.

A loud voice suddenly resounded from somewhere below from me, through one of the doors I had just eluded. I froze for an instant. The voice was unknown to me but there was cold murder in it.

'The woman is loose, she has killed two of our people. Vargel, you and Garcia get two others to cover the exits. Rondell have three men search the building, all you others the grounds. NOW!' I grinned as I saw figures in the darkness dart through a small postern door. I turned and went the other way. The earth was slanty but supple under my feet as I headed east away from the building or the road out, where I knew they would of course concentrate their search. I was hoping the route I was taking would lead me back round to the water and the platform that anchored the single-crew launch.

I moved steadily, the length of the compound, away from the threat against me. The compound was bathed in pale moonlight, scattered patches on grass and rock threw small patches of shadow making me hard to see my feet.

The sound of a shot brought me swinging round by

automatic reflex and firing. The crack of my Beretta rifle was so close to the other shot that they sounded almost as one. The monk who had concealed himself behind a rounded crest of trees, twenty paces to my left rear stumbled out from his hideaway and crumbled slowly to the ground. A soft thud slid away from him. Going over to him, I inspected the slithering object. It turned out to be a Sig Sauer FAD sniper rifle. A monk with a Sig Sauer designated snipers rifle equipped with grenade launching capabilities. Now that is a contradiction in itself.

I lay down the Beretta and snatched up the Sig Sauer, working the bolt action once I went down on one knee and waited. The sig Sauer was superb weapon, sturdy but sometimes unreliable in its accuracy. I felt the wetness before I realised I had been hit. Not hit but nicked. The laceration I could feel was just below my left armpit.

Thirty seconds passed, there was no sound of shouting or movement. No sound at all. I turned to inspect my wound. Like I thought, a scrape. Though it looked serious, I could see it was not. I got to my feet, grabbing the Beretta, crouching low, I began to run. I was a few yards away from the platform when I noticed my run was in vain. A hundred yards away, two armed monks stood on the platform guarding against my escape via the water. They didn't seem to notice that the boat had drifted some hundred yards from its berth.

I stopped and reassessed. To my west, scattered pinpoints oflight danced in the darkness as unseen hands belonging to darkened figures moved across the earth from the monastery towards me. On my north, the river bearing the platform and boat which was now cut off. To the east, where I had just come from was the way I knew would be covered soon. That left the west, which whoever was in charge would work out as my only escape venture. A venture I could not take.

There was a blind spot of sort's in-between the east and the north. The well, that if navigated well enough it could serve as a haven for me. However, the only thing in that direction was the woods. Getting to it would not help me unless I had an ace up my sleeve. After a quick think, I had my answer.

The Escalade, Seymour's car.

If it had the bonus features, which I think it had, it would be a nice way to ensure my escape and put an end to this chase. It was on the other side of the woods but between it and me were the pinpoint lights and the well. I calculated the odds. Getting to it would be difficult but not impossible.

I made my way backwards, reached a suitable spot, then laid down, legs straddled behind a nice low ridge of grass and brought the first rifle up into position. The nice plumb of grass dipped in a shallow V, giving me sufficient traverse and cover. I moistened the sight with a wet finger to make it glint and set the sight for sixty yards. The half-coin moon was over my left shoulder, making my sight line good. I lowered the rifle and waited. My aim was to create a gap big enough for me to sneak through.

It was six minutes before the first man entered my direct field of range. He was carrying a flash lamp and a rifle tucked under his arm. I let him come. I spotted the second armed man twenty feet away from him, he too was carrying a flash lamp.

I waited, middle finger curled loosely about the trigger, forefinger extended under the bolt-handle, ready to flick it up in a rapid-fire reload. Granted it was not the conventional way to handle the rifle but it was the method but it was the one taught to me by the British army besides, I was most comfortable with this technique.

I dropped the second man with a shoulder shot before he was six paces, instantly there came a flurry of shots along the line of hunters. The first man darted towards his fallen comrade, running hard to cross the distance. Allowing for his speed, I dropped him with a body shot before he was three feet away from his colleague.

He went down sprawling and began to scream. Louder than his fallen comrade.

A third figure moving across the grass on my far right was crouched, swerving away from my direct field. It was my chance. My first shot missed, my second did not. Grabbing the Sig Sauer FAD sniper rifle, I scrabbled to my feet and began running. I heard the sudden burst of fire concentrated on my old position and the thud of bullets behind me. Suddenly the firing stopped abruptly as I dove headfirst forward down into the grass.

I had made it to the blind spot.

It took me five minutes of sly subterfuge to subvert my position round the well and the rest of my pursuers and another twelve minutes of fast hiking through the woods to get to the Escalade.

Reaching the Escalade, I thanked the stars that Seymour had gotten the automatic remote option for the vehicle.

Lifting my right boot, I carefully picked at the edge of the thin black seal covering the heel and inserting a finger I peeled off the whole rubber adhesion covering that enclosed heel.

I pushed on a tiny compartmental latch within and the middle of the sole popped opened. Inside was a coil of time fuse attached to a blasting cap. I set it next to my feet. I repeated the same action with my other heel. Inside it was a B111 Taggant composite, a next-generation explosive gel, which had an adhesive tab and screw hole on its base. The British army call it *Hodex*, I dubbed them as my *"Dons"*, because they give off no energy signature and was completely inert, until activated. The small plug-in screw hole under each don was made exclusively for the coil of wire from my right heel. The flex cord was a wick incendiary designed to detonate the Hodex gel explosive in the heel of my other boot. They were each a companion piece, of the other. Neither one works without the other.

A controlled implosion like the one I intended to assemble was

dangerous and was only used as a last resort when other methods are impractical or too damaging to try. However, in this case, I wanted to put an end to the monastery and the men pursuing me once and for all. Though I had eliminated three of my pursuers, the vibe I had going in was still fresh within me, even now.

Screwing in the incendiary fuse into the don and affixing it with the blasting cap, I placed it in the glove box of the Escalade with a two-minute delay. I hoped the high concussive force combined with the fuel of the vehicle would be exacerbating enough to engulf the whole building.

A distraction I hoped will deter anyone else from coming after me.

I started the vehicle, fiddled with the remote options, directed it down the road leading to the monastery, and engaged its cruise control before jumping out of the car. I heard the sound of sirens just as I got to my feet to watch the Escalade roll down the road for forty-five seconds then veer right down the road straight towards the monastery. Several of my pursuers let loose a hail of bullets at it before they realised the progress of the vehicle was unmanned and sprinted towards it in a bid to prevent its progress. It was only a few feet away when the Escalade blew up taking two of the monks with it. It was enough to still trundle down across the path up the broad stone steps and smash through a downstairs opening. Engulfing that part of the structure and two or three of my pursuers.

I grinned as the first cop car rolled up. I walked away when I saw its occupant's reaction to the raging fire and the remaining monk.

# SEVENTEEN

Iarrived at a metro station just in time to catch the first InterCity train headed for Central Station. I'd have to take a taxi from there to finish my journey. Even if I were late, wherever I was going, it didn't really matter anymore. It wasn't exactly carnival time when I was dropped off on 73rd street. Except for a few glimmering lights, the only signs oflife, the street was deserted. It was after five in the morning when Vince opened the door for me. He informed me that I was right on time. Seymour was on the plasma waiting to hear from me.

'How timely' I said as I stepped inside the cosy house. I asked Vince to transfer his call to my bedroom.

I got a huge grin from Seymour by way of greeting and the opportunity for him to notice my damp clothes. He was wearing a grey cardigan and a NIKE sweatshirt.

He rotated his head several times, as if testing the mobility of his neck as I briefed him about my early morning rendezvous.

'You blew up the Escalade?' I apologised.

'Never mind that now. I've been worried about you' he

declared, when I was done. He didn't really look worried, but then his basic expression – formidable and practical – had never encompassed a wide range of emotions.

'Thanks, but I can take care of myself, you made sure of that' I said as I vanished from his view to undress. He did not stir from his seat in front of the boob tube as I passed. I heard a door close downstairs.

'I realise that' he stated proudly. 'Still doesn't make me not worry'

'Oh mother hen, please' I taunted

'Well here's some news for you. I spoke to a Cardinal from the Vatican …' Seymour said emphatically into the plasma 'While we're on the subject, did you know that there are five particular sins that cannot be absolved by a priest in the confessionary?'

'Is murder one of them?' I responded fervently as I started to take off my undies.

'Nope'

'Five sins? I doubt it' I pondered

'It's true. A special secretive tribunal must be convened if these particular sins have to be absolved by the Apostolic Penitentiary of the confessionary'

'Apostolistic … what ….? Five sins huh?' I asked, my interest peaked 'Any clue as to what they are?'

'Oh … er … let me see … er … breaking the seal of the confessional, is one. The other is a priest offering a confession to his own sexual partner … er … desecrating the Eucharist …'

'The Eucharist?' I asked

'Defiling the bread and wine of the altar. You know Catholics believe that the bread and wine transubstantiates into the body and blood of C...'

'Yes, I know'

'Of course you do. Oh and anyone who has directly participated in an abortion and wants to be a priest, is a no no. Oh by the by, we have a clinic to build in Boosaaso ... my promise to Cardinal Womboshi, if he aided me'

I always admired the way Seymour, at times, could switch from one subject matter to another. However, I was used to it and supposedly like Penny went with the flow.

'Where the hell is Boosooosa ...?' 'Boosaaso'

'Whatever it's called, where the hell is it?' 'Somewhere in the northeast of Somalia' 'Well you better make it a world class clinic'

'Ha ... well he reluctantly confirmed that Bishop Halbert ...' 'Bishop?'

'Ah yes, did you ever think he was a Bishop ... in any case he belonged to a very restrictive and rumoured sect within the Vatican that monitors the guiding truths relating to Christ. He believes its called *Ordine dei Cinque tagli* '

'Order of the Five Cuts?' I translated to myself.

'Huh huh, he believes it relates to stigmatic wounds. You know number of wounds Christ received on the cross. Anyway, according to him, he thinks that the sect, guard and ensure that man's faith in a divine human God, the Almighty himself and the Catholic Church is never disputed. Any negative or inauspicious truths that are unearthed or located are precipitously disposed of. Like for example ... a parchment enlightening us to the fact that the Baptist took a dump or never really baptised Christ or a stone painting depicting he had a shampoo bath with Salome just before his head was chopped off, wouldn't be a positive aspect for the church'

'Does this sect really exist?'

'Going from what you've witnessed, do you have any doubts?' I swallowed hard. Staring at his face stamped on the plasma screen. I hadn't a doubt … not in the slightest … as to what he meant. 'There must be thousands of parchments, Dead Sea scrolls, artefacts that can demoralise man's faith in a one true God. What makes this one any different …' I struggled to get the words out

'… or important enough to condone torture and murder?'

He nodded 'Find it and you might know' he stated 'Question is, should you?'

I had a good mind to forget the whole thing, then and there. I had no more debt to fulfil. Father Halbert was dead. I had demolished what remained of the sect. Agent Shaw's death had been avenged, there was nothing else in it for me except my curiosity.

'Has it stopped raining?' he absently asked.

I glanced out the rain-pelted window 'I think so'

'Well, I'll brief Prideaux in the morning, he should clear things up with the NYPD. You go get some sleep, you have some thinking to do when you wake up' he instructed

'Do I?' I muttered

'Have a good night and sleep well, Susan'

Goodnight wouldn't really have covered the time of day and we both knew that.

His image disappeared from the screen to be replaced

by the weather channel. I switched the plasma off.

* * * * * *

I spent the morning and part of the afternoon debating whether to go along with this pirate treasure hunt and then the rest to try in vain to decipher the writing on Marion's feet. I knew that if I solved it, it would be like finally appreciating Euler's number e, the beautiful equation that connects the three constants of mathematics. However, like Hemmingway when he was writing his second book, I was frustrated.

I gave up hope and went in a search of a mind greater than Alpha's or mine. I journeyed to the nearest college I thought would have a decent linguistic department. Fordham University despite its Jesuit reputation boasting of liberal arts and sciences department composed of ten colleges in all was of little help.

I had much better aid at the fourteenth ranked university in the world, Cornell. Cornell University was a prestigious Ivy League college, which offered a variety of academic and vocational courses. It also bore the title of the first US University to teach far-eastern languages and had at least a supposed reputed linguist in the Anthropology Department. A promise of a thousand dollar emolument prompted each of the linguists I found to have an audience with me. In the Administration Offices, Professor Matheson, the supposedly top expert of his field, stared at the writing for a long while before confirming what Alpha had already verified.

'Interesting, truly ....... What a rather accomplished draftsmanship ...very smart ... clever even'

'I guess … but I was hoping you could shed more light on it, Professor'

'Uh er … yes maybe … ha … who did this …. He's a clever imp whoever they are he is'

'Clever? It doesn't look anything like Zarathustra or Enochian to me, Professor Matheson'

'It's even likely that um … er … is your offer of remuneration genuine?'

I counted out ten hundred dollar bills and set them on the desk before him.

'Not only that, but the respect of a grateful undergrad' I said in an attempt to eulogised him.

'Aah' he muttered 'Well let's see … It's rather a corrupted version of the language but definitely an obscure script'

'How do you mean? I could make no sense of it'

He clicked his tongue 'That's because you're construing it or considering it all wrong' he reversed the paper on which I had written the words from Marion's feet and handed it to me 'Have you never heard ofleonardo Da Vinci?'

Da Vinci's exhibition tour in LA that Marion paid a visit to flashed into my head.

'What sort of question is that?'

He cocked an eye at me and held the paper up to my nose 'Studied any of his writings … his works?'

I thought about Da Vinci's work. Leonardo Da Vinci notes and drawing displayed an enormous amount of activity, but not only his interests and preoccupations but the composites of whatever captivated his mind. He was ambidextrous, but wrote mostly with his left hand.

In most of his notes, his writings where a mirror- image cursive of his thoughts. All his writings were continual observations around him, maintained daily throughout his life and travels, hence the implementation of a mirror cursive language. A code he adopted to maintain the secrecy of his works. Writing backwards from right to left and then at times upside down was perhaps in his mind a practical expediency.

'It's backwards!?' I exclaimed

'Huzzah for the uninitiated' replied the tenured professor with a great deal of satisfaction. 'Not only that, it's a mirror image'

He took out a pen and started deciphering the Enochian letters.

It took him ten minutes to decipher and finish the decryption after three failed attempts.

'*Wena efil … eb ereh*. This is what it says. Here … be life … anew.

Ha! What does that mean?'

I had no idea and thankfully neither did he. 'And the other part, sir? The Zarathustra?'

'Identifying this is no picnic young miss … Lesser scholars would suffer brain haemorrhage after …'

'Professor!' I interrupted, snatching up the dollar notes off the table.

'Well lets see … here is the pin … I am not terribly versed in Zarathustra, but by the look of the variation and its companion pantheon … hmm … they look like numerals to me. Hold on, a colleague of mine in Istanbul might know, if you want to wait that is?'

'Ah Professor, no … can't you decipher …?'

'Hey no no no no. Some of us take sabbaticals for this kind of project and …'

'Look Professor, I can't wait for you to contact a friend in Istanbul for a trans …'

'Hey, not to worry, with IM'ing, it shouldn't take more than an hour'

He suggested I go have lunch or check out the campus while he consults with his friend, a Professor Hadrian Mar Elijah. My bet was he really wanted to earn that thousand bucks.

I did as he suggested.

Two hours later when I returned, Professor Matheson was leaning back in his chair, beaming gladly as he read. When he saw me, he immediately got to his feet and handed me the translated portion of the Zarathustra writing.

34.650688 N

-118.19964 W

15ft E

There were a set oflatitude and longitude numbers. The 15ft E, I assumed was a unit of distant.

It could not be that simple, could it?

When I inputted the numbers into the map app of my flip phone, it located a spot a couple of thousand miles in the LA desert and to a little Presbyterian church called "The Antelope Valley Church". Nothing about it was significant, but it did ring a bell in my head.

I gladly handed Professor Matheson the 10 hundred

dollar bills and hurried back to my car.

My buccaneer treasure hunt was about to begin or end.

Marion was clever, I had to give him that. He did hint to me, not in so many words, but he did hint that only the worthy shall find what was hidden. At the time, I thought it was the money from his mob father. Now, there was no doubt in my mind as to what he had hidden.

I must say that using two dead and obscure languages, writing it in a code that only a few would be able to decipher, on the least viewed part of his body, was nothing short of brilliant.

I was three steps from Seymour's 2016 Navigator when my phone rang.

'Hello' I answered

'You left a pile of mess for us to clean up, Sue' It was Lieutenant Stephanie O'Connor. 'Sorry for the mess, no other way'

'Why were those monks armed?'    'Religious temperament?'

'Did you kill them?'

'*Que sera que sera*' I said in a matter-of-factly way. I was not about to admit to 2$^{nd}$ degree murder on an open line, even if the call was from a friend. 'If it helps the feds will be sending you some help'

'Oh they're already here. Green horns the lotof 'em. They're messin' the already fucked up situation' she snarled 'By the way, did you really have to blow the place up?'

'Yes' It was my direct and abrupt answer. 'It gave off bad juju' 'Bad juju?'

'Huh huh'

'And Otto and his merry band of whores?' *'C'est la vie'*

'You may have to come in for questionin'' 'The feds will handle all that'

'Yes but …'

'Steph … I'm kind of busy at the moment' 'All right. I'll see you when I see you then' 'Cheers, girl' I replied before hanging up.

In the car, I flipped through the photographs Alpha had downloaded during his electronic database search. I stopped at the one image where Marion was standing in the background of an ATM captured shot. He was standing directly behind a woman gesturing at something on his right. Further in the background to his left were the letterings in bold brown colours "Antelope V…" inscribed on a signpost.

Shit! He was not as smart as I gave him credit for. He must have hidden the parchment in a church, the one place anyone would go looking if they knew where to look.

I had to get to route L-8 in Los Angeles and find out what he had hidden there.

\* \* \* \* \* \* \* \*

Wilhelmina got me back to Los Angeles nine hours from the time I learned of the GPS co-ordinates. After retrieving my Shelby from the InterContinental Hotel long-stay parking lot, I left the city via Crystal Springs and headed towards Sacramento. Taking the slip road to CA-14 North towards Palmdale I headed out on Colombia way and soon found myself off the L-8, then Avenue L6. The six-hour drive culminated in spotting the Antelope

Valley Church just of the L6, Antelope town. It was not that hard to miss. I parked the Shelby in one of the tiny town's few shopping mart parking lot, a few blocks away from the church and made my way to it on foot. It was beginning to get dark, not to mention dry. I had no realistic expectations that the church would be open for business but I still couldn't at least take a hopeful peek at the place. As churches went, Antelope Valley Church was neither unpretentious nor impressive. It was just a slab of dusty desert- coloured brick and multi-coloured glass in the cumbersome shape of a sunrise. I shouldn't have been surprised since I was actually standing in Antelope Valley town. What did I expect from a

church named after the town to look like?

I inputted the co-ordinates and found to my delight that the co-ordinates did not lead exactly to the church but to the wild briar patch extending from behind it. I didn't want to encroach on where I was not wanted so I made my way up to the large wooden doors of the church.

The two parishioners I met greeted me warmly in the compound of the church and informed me that their beloved Pastor was overseeing a secluded meeting in one of the meeting halls and would be done in a matter of minutes. They wondered if they could help me. I thanked them for their hospitality but thought I should speak to the pastor.

I was dawdling outside having a cigarette in the cold night air, taking in the view when the door opened behind me. A thong of sorry-looking men piled out chatting about this and that in low voices. When they saw me, their interest changed as they ogled me on the way out of the compound.

It was five minutes afterwards that the door opened

again.

I turned to see a stockily built, grizzle-haired man of sixty- to-sixty-five grinning down at me with a bear bottle wrapped in a brown bag in his hand. He was wearing some kind of plastic mac over generously cut chinos and the sort of shirt I'd last seen sported by Burt Reynolds in the afternoon matinee *Smokey and the Bandit*.

'Dere are many truths people seek from our church'
'I'm sorry?'

'Anyone can find his truth from our church, my child' his voice held a Vegas twang oflife's bitterness not to mention the drunken smell that was getting on, on his breath.

'Oh … huh well … I think truth is a flexible perception, based on needs'

'Can I help yuh, my child?' piped the grizzled man.

Quickly stubbing out my cigarette, I asked 'Good evening sir.

I don't really know'

He scrutinised me slowly as he took a sip from the bottle 'I haven't seen yuh before have I … miss ….'

'Susan sir'

'Pleased to meet yuh' he greeted, extending his free hand. I shook his hand. He held out the brown bag at me, inviting me to join him. I politely declined. He shrugged 'Susan … yuh're new to our neck of da woods, aren't you? Yes?'

'Yes sir … and you are …?'

'Pastor Cumberback … William Cumberback, child' he said tossing his head back as he took another long sip.

'Pastor! I'm sorry but my infraction into your town is

one of desperation'

He made a small burp before answering me 'How so, my child?'

'I'm in search of someone ... a dear friend whom I think must have visited your fine church'

'Have yuh gone to da police?' he belched again with genuine concern.

'Yes' I lied.

'W-who uh ... is this friend of yours?'

I took out my phone and showed him a snapshot of Marion. He stared at it with big eyeballs. There was no doubt he was drunk two perhaps eight bottles past.

'Ah ... Larry. Larry ... um ... I forget his last name ... Larry ...?' 'Larry Stein...'

'Larry Steinberg'

'Ah ... yes ... dat's him. He's your friend?' 'More of an acquaintance'

'Oh he was a fine boy. Did not stay long but he was a true believer'

'What did he do here?'

Pastor Cumberback took another long swig from his bottle before answering 'He made a ... um ...er a donation and helped out. N-nothing much'

'Donation?'

He maneuverer his stocky frame down the steps with surprising ease, setting down the brown bag he led me round the back of the church, then pointed at a 30-foot high white crucifix glimmering in the dark.

'He donated that. Erected it ... even dig hole for it. H-he left before we could really properly dank him'

Why would Marion donate a crucifix?

'That was nice of him. Any idea where he went?'

'No my child er ... Susan ... is it ... yes ... if only ... dere were more like him. I would wish to dank dem'

'What have you been drinking?'

He glanced at the brown bag before turning to me 'Old peppered hen, why?'

'You want another?'

He stared at me and then gave me a grin before walking away 'Great idea'

He turned, and then stopped 'Will yuh join me?' 'Sure'

He guided me into one of the back rooms of the church. A room where a meeting had recently broken up. Apart from the two tables and scattered chairs, there were cigarette butts, half- filled ashtrays, paper plates and cups and empty beer bottles littering the place.

There had been a serious meeting here, but I didn't even want to begin filling my mind as to what sort.

He disappeared for couple of seconds and returned with two Grande bottles of the Peppered Hen. He handed me one as he sat across from me. We both twisted the cap off at the same time. I took a small sip while he took a long swig and exhaled loudly when he was done.

Looking at me almost cross-eyed, he said 'Now ...er Susie ... my child ... don't imagine as a man of god ... I imbibe in de ale at my leisure. I'm ...um ... how do yuh young people put it ... chillin' out ... yes? Takin' time out ... yeah?'

'It matters to me none Pastor Williams' He grinned and chuckled 'I like yuh' 'Could I ask you something?'

'Sure go ahead'

'Larry. Tell me about him'

Pastor Cumberback nodded 'H-he … he said he was here for … um … holiday … that's it, spend almost a week here. Poor little scaredy Frenchie kid'

'How'd you know he was scared?' I asked.

He threw his head back as he slugged back a big squib. 'Girlie I could tell when the ghost cows are after someone by their lying eye teeth's tongue. Poor kid was alone and he always l-looked like a coyote was stalking him' Pastor Williams burped softly 'C can't say I blame de poor boy. Good head on his shoulders though, said he was training to be a damned architect' He pointed upwards 'I believed him because he fixed de broken damaged

roof by himself dat friend of yours, even spent his own cash on de Cross. Not dat we needed it but now we have it, it looks good out dere doesn't it?'

I couldn't just disagree.

'Must bring in churchgoers far and wide' 'You betcha'

'Do you mind if I have a closer look at it?'

'Go go go knock yourself out' he said waving his hand at me.

Before leaving, I combed the yard for any sort of landscaping gear. A spade, tiller, hoe anything. I found a digging fork.

Equipped with what I knew just might be there, I followed the co-ordinates of the Zarathustra numbers from Marion's tattooed feet signified by the red dot on my phone to the marked position just in front of the crucifix. The giant crucifix looked over a gorge and arid desert looking wilderness. Was it possible Marion used the subterfuge of the crucifix to hide the treasure he found?

Could he have had something buried underneath? I was guessing he did.

I did not worry about Pastor Cumberback. In a few minutes, he would be in a drunken stupor and would probably barely remember I was there.

I counted 15 feet east and dug at the allotted position.

Under two feet of dirt, I found a Pringles, salt and vinegar cylindrical tube buried underneath. Within it was a hardcover journal belonging to and penned by a Professor Fotherias and two old parchments, carefully wrapped in cellophane and crammed in the cylinder. Of the two parchments, one was written in Aramaic. It was tattered, durable and made of a cellulose material, not unlike papyrus and according to the scribbled French transcripts contained within the journal the carbon-dating analysis put the date of the first use of the parchment as being from the first century. The other was a parchment in Coptic that more or less verified the first parchment.

I slowly and gently unwrapped the threadbare parchment that had worn holes within it and tried reading the almost faded and indecipherable writing on it. Some of the vegetable ink used in writing the parchment had faded, but not all.

I couldn't make heads or tails of it. However, in the corner of this parchment, on the top right edge that seemed almost faded and torn off, was what looked like an imprinted signet. A seal of a kind! The seal was that of a cup and fish. I stopped. I was vaguely familiar with this seal and I think most ardent Catholics would recognise it.

The seal was a memorable one. It was the seal of a carpenter who later on in life went fishing. And not only fishing but fishing for men's souls, in the first century. Wow! I could not believe it. I had in my hands words that maybe Jesus Christ penned himself. This "insignia" must be why Marion asserted that this "parchment was proof that it spoke for itself ". This was incredible.

Now I understood why Father Theodore Halbert and his cronies were very adamant about this parchment not being in the light of day. Why the Vatican in 1895 would pay a poor improvised priest, Father Bèrenger Sauniére and his housekeeper Marie Dénarmaud loads of money to keep this secret from the public domain. Now I understood it all.

I frantically opened and read the French highlighted portion from the journal.

«... *bien que cela ne peut être vérifiée jusqu'* à ce *qu'elle subit de nombreux tests, je crois que celles-ci pourraient* être *les mots d'un certain charpentier de Galilée* à son *enfant* à naître... »

I sighed.

His verification though pending, this professor believed that this was a letter from Jesus of Galilee to his unborn child. This would certainly be a problem.

Could this be real?

I would need to decrypt it first to find out what he wrote and more especially, I would have to be careful as to whom I can trust to show this to.

# *EPILOGUE*

They say a man's inspiration is visual, for us women it is in the sequence of events.

The top two floors of the two-tier penthouse in *Hotel Particuláire* on Lenox Avenue by special request had no surveillance or security measures of any kind. That is because they are premium floors, floors that cater to an elite clientele, some of whom require to be discrete in their dealings and prefer not to be in the public eye. To the staff of the *Particuláire*, we were sacred clients. Which at this exact moment was what I required, I wasn't taking any chances even if I owned the fucking hotel.

Seymour found me lounging by the side of the pool of the Presidential lounge of our hotel. I was taking a much-needed sunbath. My pink skin apart from the bandaged part was taking in as much sun as it could get.

On the plane back, using Apollo, I had just deciphered with close approximation the words on the parchment and was waiting for Seymour so that I can read and share whatever the big palaver about this parchment was with him.

We both read the letter.

*To My Beloved Treasure, Thy child, whom in truth I love.*

*... must thou begin?*

*I have many things to tell ..., but I do not wish to write to you with pen and ink.*

*... thy wait to consume the sorrow of man, the task thy heavenly father has dealt me. Thou cannot dream of thee.*

*If I ... my heart melt for reason that thou art precious to I.*

*I wish to see ..., speak face to face with thee, but the force of the most high ... much too strong for me to defy.*

*Thou ... not behold thee, like Joseph did for thou ... and as Peter is thy rock, you are the river of my spirit, treasure of my soul.*

*You will blossom like lilies in the desert, unfurl your wings ... birds in the sky and nurture roots like trees ... the dust below your feet.*

*Yes, the wicked ... swell you up, you ... be cut, pruned as you yearn to hate, love, ... you pray ... love as you desire.*

*My Beloved, do not imitate what is evil, be a light. Endure what thy will be given or taken from. I cannot comfort thee, but I promise thee, my spirit will remain within you. It will have ... desire*
*to heal thee, love ... ... ... thou without limit.*

*Please ... understand thy love you dearly... as thy rose, my shepherdess, your mother Magdalena fully loves thee.*

*Bear witness and hold thee rose in thy Heart, I shall be within thee always as you greet your friends and loved ones in my name.*

*I shall neve... forget thee. Love to you.*

*Yeshua*

Though the gaps in the missive made it hard to read, the meaning and intention was clear. A missive of hope and love. There was a tear in Seymour's eye and mine. 'That is sweet' he said after we finished. He took the parchment from me and read it silently to himself again. 'This is endearing'

'Yes it is. What shall we do with it?' 'Let Omega have for now'

He was talking about Alpha's twin, Omega. A secure storage vault of ours used mainly for the storage of scientific development or research medium from my many business concerns that I deemed not desirable, harmful to the society and/or my sense of purpose. Omega was located underneath the basement of a local post office two buildings away from my home in London. For security reasons it was accessible by only me or Seymour through a series of tunnels, if ever the need should arise. It was a very sedate and unconceivable place to equip and store not only a state of the art biometric vault but also Alpha's £3,000,000 DU99 Freehand Cold Reconfigurable 45 teraflop architectural servers with modules capable of crypt analysis and video processing.

'You don't think we should have it published?'

'It's not our place to manipulate people's faiths, good or bad' I tended to agree with him as I handed him the parchment.

We were not prophets or saints.

'Ok then, let the church know through that Cardinal of yours that we have it and we will keep it safe in assurance for our lives. If anything unseemly should happen to either of us ... well they can get the gist on what will happen next'

'You sure they'll get the message?'

'They should, but even if they don't you're going to make arrangements just in case'

'Understood'

'By the way how is the clean-up going?' I asked after a long pause

He slowly stuffed the parchment into the plastic folder and turned to me, giving me his full attention.

'As much as humanly Possible. To date five employees of the Feds have failed to return to work and disappeared, all within the same hour. I take it these were guys loyal to the mob' he smiled benignly at me 'And this is you fixing it I take it?' I didn't answer 'It's a learning experience for the Feds, though FBI won't have trouble with leaks anymore, they're going to be hard pressed in recruiting and with their personnel.

So I think they will have to be careful from now on' he said 'Fortunately, the mob's operation was in an early stage and Prideaux thinks they didn't pass on any information of value to national security. He sends his love, by the way'

Seymour was right. They wouldn't be able to find the root of their leaks without admitting they were hacked in the first place. The longer they had to think about it, the crazier they would get. I meekly agreed 'As a whole I don't think they knew much about Halbert's deal or that the mob was involved in spying on them. Francesco was just suspicious and suspicions can be deadly

when you up against fanatics like Halbert and Michel' 'That's a sore truth'

'What about the boy, Michael Jnr?' I asked laying back on the deck chair closing my eyes.

'He's still on life support, we're picking up the expenses

as long as the parents want. The doctors at Galencyte are looking into his situation'

'Good'

'This was a costly and deadly affair, Susan' I cracked one eye open.

'Since when do you care about costs?'

'Not that kind of cost. However, every time you go barraging into trouble, stuff tend to hover in limbo. This is not our line of work. This is dirty business, reserved for those people who don't care for medals or praise'

'I know. There are not many of those around, that's why we do it instead'

He rolled his eyes 'No. You chose to do this for Agent Tyler and any of the Marion Steiner or Anna Feldman's that happens to come along'

'Whom I hope are resting peacefully now'

There was a long pause before he spoke again 'Well if that's all done, can we get back to Petronas?'

'Ah yes, but first, there's a riddle that's been bothering since Kilimanjaro'

'A riddle?' 'Huh huh'

'It must be some damn riddle if you can't solve it. Ok what is it?'

I told him about the riddle of the man whose head gets blown up and he gives the bartender a healthy tip and a thank you before leaving the bar.

Seymour giggled.

'You really don't know the answer?'

'If I did, I wouldn't be racking my brain all week for it, would I?' 'The man had the hiccups' stated Seymour so apparently.

Hallelujah, I had the answer. 'Hiccups?'

An answer that was so elementary obvious, I should have known it all along.

'I bet that put your panties in a twist huh milady?' he enquired as a knock sounded on the door.

'It did at that alright' 'So as to our next COO'

'That's right I didn't tell you that I've chosen someone' He beamed gladly 'Good. Anyone I know?'

'Yes'

'It's The Shark isn't it?' I shook my head. 'Who then?' 'I've even chosen the perfect site'

'Where?' 'Prine'

'And who will head it up?'

I sat up in my deck chair and told him.

Without a word, he turned away fuming heading for the second knock on the door.

I chuckled 'Seymour?' 'Yes'

'Just kidding. Patrick Ward it is' He smiled 'Good. That is smart'

'Does that mean I can take a vacation?'

'You just took a break' he paused for a moment 'But if you insist, where would you want go?' he asked making his way towards the door.

'I'll come up with something' 'I bet you will'

Another knock sounded on the door. Seymour opened the door and took an envelope from the concierge. He read the note within, and then turned to me with a grim expression I had rarely seen on his face.

He gave me a short bow and then handed me the note. As I took it, I noticed the laminated envelop the note came in, had been forwarded from my home in Bath by Meme. The note was dated three days ago.

---

*To: Lady Yelverton,*

*My dear Susan, It is with great sadness that I learnt of the death of your uncle, His Lordship, The Viscount of Yelverton.*

*First and foremost, Viscount McFadden was a true statesman who served his country with distinction.*

*His profound optimism for the future of the commonwealth I believe should hold fast to the optimism we all share today.*

*On behalf of Myself, Prince Phillip, and the rest of the family, I wish to convey to your family our deepest condolences and sympathy at this sad time.*

*ELIZABETH R*

---

I glanced at Seymour. 'My Uncle is dead. I guess any vacation is not on the table anymore' I said 'Get Wilhelmina ready to return home. It seems I have some duties to perform. No doubt, Emily would be questioning my tardiness' I added as a tear leaked out of my left eye.

THE END

## *Susan Dax Will Return*